More Wandering Stars

AN ANTHOLOGY OF OUTSTANDING STORIES OF JEWISH FANTASY AND SCIENCE FICTION

Edited by Jack Dann
With an Introduction by Isaac Asimov

For People of All Faiths, All Backgrounds
Jewish Lights Publishing
Woodstock, Vermont

In memory of Edith N. Dann, who taught me everything important.

More Wandering Stars: An Anthology of Outstanding Stories of Jewish Fantasy and Science Fiction
1999 First Jewish Lights Classic Reprint Edition

Library of Congress Cataloging-in-Publication Data
More wandering stars : an anthology of outstanding stories of Jewish fantasy and science fiction / edited by Jack Dann.—1st Jewish Lights classic reprint ed.
p.   cm.
ISBN 1-58023-063-6
1. Science fiction, American—Jewish authors. 2. Fantasy fiction, American—Jewish authors.
3. Jews—Fiction. I. Dann, Jack.
PS648.S3 M6 1999
813'.0876088924 21—dc21

                                                                99-045347

ISBN 1-58023-063-6 (Quality Paperback)

10 9 8 7 6 5 4 3 2 1

Manufactured in the United States of America

Cover design: Bronwen Battaglia, Bridgett Taylor

Cover art: *Joseph's Dream* (© 1997) was created by Michael Bogdanow, an artist, lawyer, and musician living in Lexington, Massachusetts. It is based on Joseph's dream of the sun, moon, and eleven stars bowing down to him (Genesis 37:9), and is part of Bogdanow's "Visions of Torah" series of contemporary, spiritual paintings and reproductions inspired by Judaic texts. The original is an acrylic painting on canvas in the private collection of Alex and Donna Salamon.

For People of All Faiths, All Backgrounds
Jewish Lights Publishing
A Division of LongHill Partners, Inc.
Sunset Farm Offices, Route 4
P.O. Box 237
Woodstock, Vermont 05091
Tel: (802) 457-4000   Fax: (802) 457-4004
www.jewishlights.com

Contents

The Hebrew Source

Isaac Asimov

Back in 1974, Jack (Yankele) Dann edited a book called *Wandering Stars*, which was a collection of stories of science fiction and fantasy with Jewish themes.

When I heard that Yankele had this in his head, I marveled.

"Where," I asked myself, "could such stories come from? How many stories with Jewish themes are written in this field? Here am I, a prolific science fiction writer and, by the kindness of the Holy One, a Jewish one, and how many stories have I written on Jewish themes? One, that's all. *One.*" (Naturally, that one was eventually included in the collection.)

"And," I went on, still talking to myself, "how many other Jewish science fiction and fantasy writers can there be who work with Jewish themes? And except for them, who else? Surely, we can expect no Jewish themes from the goyim."

After considering that for a while, I answered myself, "So Yankele is not going to make it."

Imagine my surprise, then, when Yankele came up with his collection. Imagine my even bigger surprise when he asked me to do the introduction.

"Why me?" I asked, plaintively. So he gave me an answer like this—"Shut up and write." (This my various editors say to me all the time, they should only feel an ache in their bones.)

I wrote the introduction, which I called "Why me?" and heaved an enormous sigh of relief when I saw *Wandering Stars* safely published because, I said to myself, "Nu, that used up every good story ever likely to be written on a Jewish theme and I can now forget it."

Not well said! Here comes Yankele with another heaping handful of stories, from the Evil One knows where, and guess who has to write the introduction again.

You've hit it.

So what do I say?

I'll tell you. —I don't know.

What bothers me is where do the stories come from? Can science fiction be part of Jewish culture? From fantasy we know?

And as I think of it, it begins to seem to me that it is and we do know. And the source? From where else? From the Hebrew source for everything. —From the Bible.

We have but to look through the Bible and see for ourselves.

At the very start, with the first verse, we have, "In the beginning God created the heaven and the earth," or, as Moses our Teacher put it, "B'rayshith buru Elohim ayth hashomayim v'ayth ho'orets."

Right there, we've got something. We've got imagination.

The legends of other people also describe the creation, but with total lack of imagination. For instance—a god kills a giant monster, tears it in half, makes the sky out of one half, the earth out of the other half, fashions the seas from the monster's blood, the mountains from his teeth, the trees from his hair, and who knows what else.

It's a plain lie, the whole story, and completely implausible. A junior high student wouldn't believe it; not even one with low marks, God forbid.

But how does God do it? A question!

In the third verse, it stands written, "And God said, Let there be light: and there was light."

It was clearly the use of advanced science. God obviously has mastery over the laws of nature to an extent we have no conception of and, as Arthur C. Clarke (the Defender of Israel should be good to him) says: "Any science sufficiently advanced beyond ours would seem like magic to us."

To a caveman, if you say, "Let there be light," just as you quietly touch a contact so that suddenly there *is* light, would not that be to him a powerful magic? He would fall on his face and worship you like a god. Right? Of course, right.

And if you stop to think of it, what is God but an extraterrestrial? On Earth he certainly doesn't live. He might if he wanted to, but he existed before there was an Earth. He lives in Heaven, which, as everyone knows and admits, is in outer space somewhere. Probably in hyperspace.

So you see, out of logical reasoning, we come to the conclusion that the Holy Writings lead the way to science fiction.

You want more? In chapters 2 and 3 of Genesis, you have the story of

Adam and Eve, which, it is clear to anyone, is the first story ever told in good detail of how human beings colonized a new world.

Adam and Eve even had to fight an alien intelligence—the serpent.

That the serpent was intelligent leaves no room for doubt, for in chapter 3, verse 1, it stands written, "Now the serpent was more subtil [intelligent] than any beast of the field. . . ."

Right away, the serpent proves it because in that same verse he speaks. And not just English—but good first-class Hebrew.

Which in itself is a proof that the serpent was alien. Did you ever hear an Earthly serpent speak? In fact Earthly serpents are stupid. They're reptiles (and trayf, too—feh!). Believe me, the serpent in the Garden was an alien.

There's a theory in the Apocrypha (*see* Revelation 12:9, 20:2) that the serpent was really Satan the Adversary (may the Lord protect us from him at every step) but if so, what is Satan? Not an alien? Of *course* an alien.

You can go on and on. There's a tantalizing little story in the first four verses of chapter 6 of Genesis which clearly describes not only an extraterrestrial invasion but a little bit of lusting after Earth-women, just the way we used to have it on the covers of the science fiction magazines in the 1930s and 1940s. The Bible doesn't say whether the extraterrestrial invaders were bug-eyed, but I suspect they were.

And what about the Flood, in chapters 6 to 9 inclusive? It's not a story about a world catastrophe and the survivors? Of course it is!

And who can do it better even today? The whole world under water! Everybody killed! What a spectacle!

The Tower of Babel in the 11th chapter? Clearly a sophisticated technological society that proceeds forward without considering environmental and ecological consequences and gets into deep trouble. Very timely!

Nor is Genesis the only book that represents source material for science fiction and fantasy. In the Book of Exodus, the battle of Moses versus the Egyptian magicians is an example of advanced technological warfare.

And how about the parting of the Red Sea at the last minute with the hosts of Pharaoh in hot pursuit, and the turning back of the water to drown that host? Is that ingenious or not? You've got to give Moses credit. Kimball Kinnison could not have done it better with one of his last-minute inventions.

The story of Samson is sword-and-sorcery, right? He's a regular

Conan the Cimmerian, right? Samson had the same kind of weakness for ladies who are, you should excuse the expression, plain chippies. And Delilah (the Angel of Death should only take her into the Pit) finally got him. And the real surprise ending? I won't spoil it for you in case you don't know, but you'll find it in Judges 13–16.

The first chapter of Ezekiel is a nice UFO account with extraterrestrials at the controls. We can still learn from it today.

If you wish, you can play a game with this anthology (which is so delicious, you could lick your fingers from it), one with fine intellectual content and spiritual usefulness. For each story, see if you can figure out the Biblical references. I'll start you off. In "Tauf Aleph," ask yourself who was Og of Bashan (Numbers 21:33–35).

—Enough, already. The case is convincing. I see now why there are so many Jewish writers of science fiction and fantasy, and why so many Jewish themes are used.

In fact, it now seems to me that Yankele Dann (the Evil Eye should never come upon him) will come up with a third collection and even a fourth and a fifth.

And in that case, whom will he ask to write further introductions? Don't ask!

PHYLLIS GOTLIEB

Tauf Aleph

In his fine and reverent book This Is My God, *Herman Wouk relates an anecdote about a well-to-do, cultivated Jew who passes two Chasids on Fifth Avenue. The Chasids are dressed in wrinkled black coats and ill-fitting trousers. They both have earlocks, wear black hats, and speak Yiddish. These two men would not have been out of place walking down the crooked streets of an eighteenth-century ghetto in middle Europe. The cultivated, well-dressed Jew, as he passes these awkward ghosts from another century and place, feels nothing but resentment. In his heart he cries out, "I am not one of you! If you are Jews, I am not a Jew!"*

But he knows he is one of them, even though he has not seen the inside of a synagogue in years, even though he would laugh at the idea of being one of "the chosen people." After all, how could he even begin to follow the six hundred and thirteen commands of the Talmud and still remain in the modern world? Nevertheless, he is a Jew, and the two Chasids who have just passed him on the street are, as Wouk says, "skeletons out of his closet"; they are the ghosts of his background which he cannot put to rest.

If these three men are of the same stuff, then just what is a Jew? In Wandering Stars, *the "prequel" to this volume, I asked: Is Jewishness a mystical experience, a system of laws, a sense of kinship, a religion, or a myth? Perhaps it is any or all of these things. Perhaps it is an indefinable essence. . . .*

In the story that follows, which was written expressly for this volume by Phyllis Gotlieb, we meet Samuel Zohar ben Reuven Begelman, who is the last Jew in the universe . . . unless you count the walruslike aliens that are native to Begelman's planet. If science fiction can be called modern mythology, then here is a myth for our time, a parable about the Jew and his history, which asks the age-old question "What is a Jew?" . . . and perhaps more than that, for as an anonymous author has written, "The Jews are just like everyone else—only more so."

SAMUEL ZOHAR BEN REUVEN BEGELMAN lived to a great age in the colony Pardes on Tau Ceti IV and in his last years he sent the same message with his annual request for supplies to Galactic Federation Central: *Kindly send one mourner/gravedigger so I can die in peace respectfully.*

And Sol III replied through GalFed Central with the unvarying answer: *Regret cannot find one Jew yours faithfully.*

Because there was not one other identifiable Jew in the known universe, for with the opening of space the people had scattered and intermarried, and though their descendants were as numerous, in the fulfillment of God's promise, as the sands on the shore and the stars in the heavens, there was not one called Jew, nor any other who could speak Hebrew and pray for the dead. The home of the ancestors was emptied: it was now a museum where perfect simulacra performed 7500 years of history in hundreds of languages for tourists from the breadth of the Galaxy.

In Central, Hrsipliy the Xiploid said to Castro-Ibanez the Solthree, "It is a pity we cannot spare one person to help that poor *juddar*." She meant by this term: body/breath/spirit/sonofabitch, being a woman with three tender hearts.

Castro-Ibanez, who had one kind heart and one hard head, answered, "How can we? He is the last colonist on that world and refuses to be moved; we keep him alive at great expense already." He considered for some time and added, "I think perhaps we might send him a robot. One that can dig and speak recorded prayers. Not one of the new expensive ones. We ought to have some old machine good enough for last rites."

O/G5/842 had been resting in a very dark corner of Stores for 324 years, his four coiled arms retracted and his four hinged ones resting on his four wheeled feet. Two of his arms terminated in huge scoop shovels, for he had been an ore miner, and he was also fitted with treads and sucker-pods. He was very great in size; they made giant machines in those days. New technologies had left him useless; he was not even worthy of being dismantled for parts.

It happened that this machine was wheeled into the light, scoured of rust, and lubricated. His ore-scoops were replaced with small ones retrieved from Stores and suitable for grave-digging, but in respect to Sam Begelman he was not given a recording: he was rewired and supplemented with an almost new logic and given orders and permission to go and learn. Once he had done so to the best of his judgment he would travel out with Begelman's supplies and land. This took great expense, but less than an irreplaceable person or a new machine; it fulfilled the Galactic-Colonial contract. O/G would not return, Begelman would rest in peace, no one would recolonize Tau Ceti IV.

O/G5/842 emerged from his corner. In the Library he caused little more stir than the seven members of the Khagodi embassy (650 kilos apiece) who were searching out a legal point of intra-Galactic law. He was too broad to occupy a cubicle, and let himself be stationed in a basement exhibit room where techs wired him to sensors, sockets, inlets, outlets, screens, and tapes. Current flowed, light came, and he said, LET ME KNOW SAMUEL ZOHAR BEN REUVEN BEGELMAN DOCTOR OF MEDICINE AND WHAT IT MEANS THAT HE IS A JEW.

He recorded the life of Sam Begelman; he absorbed Hebrew, Aramaic, Greek; he learned Torah, which is Law: day one. He learned Writings, Prophets, and then Mishna, which is the first exegesis of Law: day the second. He learned Talmud (Palestinian and Babylonian), which is the completion of Law, and Tosefta, which are ancillary writings and divergent opinions in Law: day the third. He read thirty-five hundred years of Commentary and Responsa: day the fourth. He learned Syriac, Arabic, Latin, Yiddish, French, English, Italian, Spanish, Dutch. At the point of learning Chinese he experienced, for the first time, a synapse. For the sake of reading marginally relevant writings by fewer than ten Sino-Japanese Judaic poets it was not worth learning their vast languages; this gave him pause: two nanoseconds: day the fifth. Then he plunged, day the sixth, into the literatures written in the languages he had absorbed. Like all machines, he did not sleep, but on the seventh day he unhooked himself from Library equipment, gave up his space, and returned to his corner. In this place he turned down all motor and afferent circuits and indexed, concordanced, cross-referenced. He developed synapses exponentially to complete and fulfill his logic. Then he shut it down and knew nothing.

But Galactic Federation said, O/G5/842, AROUSE YOURSELF AND BOARD THE SHIP *Aleksandr Nevskii* AT LOADING DOCK 377 BOUND FOR TAU CETI IV.

At the loading dock, Flight Admissions said, YOUR SPACE HAS BEEN PREEMPTED FOR SHIPMENT 20 TONNES *Nutrivol* POWDERED DRINKS (39 FLAVORS) TO DESERT WORLDS TAU CETI II AND III.

O/G knew nothing of such matters and said, I HAVE NOT BEEN IN-STRUCTED SO. He called Galactic Federation and said, MOD 0885 THE SPACE ASSIGNED FOR ME IS NOT PERMITTED IT HAS BEEN PREEMPTED BY A BEING CALLED *Nutrivol* SENDING POWDERED DRINKS TO TAU CETI INNER WORLDS.

Mod 0885 said, I AM CHECKING. YES. THAT COMPANY WENT INTO RE-CEIVERSHIP ONE STANDARD YEAR AGO. I SUSPECT SMUGGLING AND BRIBERY. I WILL WARN.

THE SHIP WILL BE GONE BY THEN MOD 08 WHAT AM I TO DO?

INVESTIGATE, MOD 842.

HOW AM I TO DO THAT?

USE YOUR LOGIC, said Mod 0885 and signed off.

O/G went to the loading dock and stood in the way. The beings ordering the loading mechs said, "You are blocking this shipment! Get out of the way, you old pile of scrap!"

O/G said in his speaking voice, "I am not in the way. I am to board ship for Pardes and it is against the law for this cargo to take my place." He extruded a limb in gesture toward the stacked cartons; but he had forgotten his strength (for he had been an ore miner) and his new scoop smashed five cartons at one blow; the foam packing parted and white crystals poured from the break. O/G regretted this very greatly for one fraction of a second before he remembered how those beings who managed the mines behaved in the freezing darkness of lonely worlds and moons. He extended his chemical sensor and dipping it into the crystal stream said, "Are fruit drinks for desert worlds now made without fructose but with dextroamphetamine sulfate, diacetylmor-phine, 2-acetyl-terrahydrocannabinol—"

Some of the beings at the loading gate cried out curses and many machines began to push and beat at him. But O/G pulled in his limbs and planted his sucker-pods and did not stir. He had been built to work in many gravities near absolute zero under rains of avalanches. He would not be moved.

Presently uniformed officials came and took away those beings and their cargo, and said to O/G, "You too must come and answer questions."

But he said, "I was ordered by Galactic Federation to board this ship for Tau Ceti IV, and you may consult the legal department of Colonial Relations, but I will not be moved."

Because they had no power great enough to move him they consulted among themselves and with the legal department and said, "You may pass."

Then O/G took his assigned place in the cargo hold of the *Aleksandr Nevskii* and after the ship lifted for Pardes he turned down his logic because he had been ordered to think for himself for the first time and this confused him very much.

The word *pardes* is "orchard" but the world Pardes was a bog of mud, foul gases, and shifting terrains, where attempts at terraforming failed again and again until colonists left in disgust and many lawsuits plagued the courts of Interworld Colonies at GalFed. O/G landed there in a stripped shuttle which served as a glider. It was not meant to rise again and it broke and sank in the marshes, but O/G plowed mud, scooping the way before him, and rode on treads, dragging the supplies behind him on a sledge, for 120 kilometers before he came within sight of the colony.

Fierce creatures many times his size, with serpentine necks and terrible fangs, tried to prey on him. He wished to appease them, and offered greetings in many languages, but they would only break their teeth on him. He stunned one with a blow to the head, killed another by snapping its neck, and they left him alone.

The colony center was a concrete dome surrounded by a forcefield that gave out sparks, hissing and crackling. Around it he found many much smaller creatures splashing in pools and scrambling to and fro at the mercy of one of the giants who held a small being writhing in its jaws.

O/G cried in a loud voice, "Go away you savage creature!" and the serpent beast dropped its mouthful, but seeing no great danger dipped its neck to pick it up again. So O/G extended his four hinged limbs to their greatest length and, running behind the monster seized the pillars of its rear legs, heaving up and out until its spine broke and it fell flattened in mud, thrashing the head on the long neck until it drove it into the ground and smothered.

The small beings surrounded O/G without fear, though he was very great to them, and cried in their thin voices, "Shalom, shalom, Savior!"

O/G was astonished to hear these strangers speaking clear Hebrew. He had not known a great many kinds of living persons during his experience, but among those displayed in the corridors of the Library basement these most resembled walruses. "I am not a savior, men of Pardes," he said in the same language. "Are you speaking your native tongue?"

"No, Redeemer. We are Cnidori and we spoke Cnidri before we reached this place in our wanderings, but we learned the language of Rav Zohar because he cared for us when we were lost and starving."

"Now Zohar has put up a barrier and shut you out—and I am not a redeemer—but what has happened to that man?"

"He became very ill and shut himself away because he said he was not fit to look upon. The food he helped us store is eaten and the Unds are ravaging us."

"There are some here that will ravage you no longer. Do you eat the flesh of these ones?"

"No, master. Only what grows from the ground."

He saw that beneath the draggling gray moustaches their teeth were the incisors and molars of herbivores. "I am not your master. See if there is food to gather here and I will try to reach Zohar."

"First we will skin one of these to make tents for shelter. It rains every hour." They rose on their haunches in the bog, and he discovered that though their rear limbs were flippers like those of aquatic animals, their forelimbs bore three webbed fingers apiece and each Cnidor had a small shell knife slung over one shoulder. All, moreover, had what appeared to be one mammalian teat and one male generative organ ranged vertically on their bellies, and they began to seem less and less like walruses to O/G. The prime Cnidor continued, "Tell us what name pleases you if you are offended by the ways we address you."

"I have no name but a designation: O/G5/842. I am only a machine."

"You are a machine of deliverance and so we will call you Golem."

In courtesy O/G accepted the term. "This forcefield is so noisy it probably has a malfunction. It is not wise to touch it."

"No, we are afraid of it."

Golem scooped mud from the ground and cast it at the forcefield;

great lightnings and hissings issued where it landed. "I doubt even radio would cross that."

"Then how can we reach Zohar, Golem, even if he is still alive?"

"I will cry out, Cnidori. Go to a distance and cover your ears, because my voice can pierce a mountain of lead ore."

They did not know what that was, but they removed themselves, and Golem turned his volume to its highest and called in a mighty voice, *"Samuel Zohar ben Reuven Begelman turn off your forcefield for I have come from Galactic Federation to help you!!!"*

Even the forcefield buckled for one second at the sound of his voice.

After a long silence, Golem thought he heard a whimper, from a great distance. "I believe he is alive but cannot reach the control."

A Cnidor said, trembling, "The Unds have surely heard you, because they are coming back again."

And they did indeed come back, bellowing, hooting, and striking with their long necks. Golem tied one great snake neck in a knot and cried again, *"Let us in, Zohar, or the Unds will destroy all of your people!!!"*

The forcefield vanished, and the Cnidori scuttled over its border beneath the sheltering arms of Golem, who cracked several fanged heads like nutshells with his scoops.

"Now put up your shield!!!" And the people were saved.

When Golem numbered them and they declared that only two were missing among forty he said, "Wait here and feed yourselves."

The great outer doorway for working machines was open, but the hangar and storerooms were empty of them; they had been removed by departing colonists. None had been as huge as Golem, and here he removed his scoops and unhinged his outer carapace with its armor, weapons, and storage compartments, for he wished to break no more doorways than necessary. Behind him he pulled the sledge with the supplies.

When his heat sensor identified the locked door behind which Zohar was to be found, he removed the doorway as gently as he could.

"I want to die in peace and you are killing me with noise," said a weak voice out of the darkness.

By infrared Golem saw the old man crumpled on the floor by the bed, filthy and half naked, with the shield control resting near his hand. He turned on light. The old man was nearly bald, wasted and yellow-skinned, wrinkled, his rough beard tangled and clotted with blood.

"Zohar?"

Sam Begelman opened his eyes and saw a tremendous machine,

multi-armed and with wheels and treads, wound with coiling tubes and wires, studded with dials. At its top was a dome banded with sensor lenses, and it turned this way and that to survey the room. "What are you?" he whispered in terror. "Where is my kaddish?"

He spoke in lingua, but O/G replied in Hebrew. "You know you are the last Jew in the known universe, Rav Zohar. There is no one but me to say prayers for you."

"Then let me die without peace," said Begelman, and closed his eyes.

But Golem knew the plan of the station, and within five minutes he reordered the bed in cleanliness, placed the old man on it, set up an IV, cleansed him, and injected him with the drugs prepared for him. The old man's hands pushed at him and pushed at him, uselessly. "You are only a machine," he croaked. "Can't you understand that a machine can't pray?"

"Yes, master. I would have told that to Galactic Federation, but I knew they would not believe me, not being Jews."

"I am not your master. Why truly did you come?"

"I was made new again and given orders. My growth in logic now allows me to understand that I cannot be of use to you in exactly the way Galactic Federation wished, but I can still make you more comfortable."

"I don't care!" Begelman snarled. "Who needs a machine?"

"The Cnidori needed me to save them from the Unds when you shut them out, and they tried to call me Savior, Redeemer, master; I refused because I am a machine, but I let them call me Golem because I am a machine of deliverance."

Begelman sniffed. But the sick yellow of his skin was gone; his face was faintly pink and already younger by a few years.

"Shmuel Zohar ben Reuven Begelman, why do you allow those help-less ones to call you Rav Zohar and speak in your language?"

"You nudnik of a machine, my name is not Samuel and certainly not Shmuel! It is Zohar, and I let myself be called Sam because *zohar* is 'splendor' and you can't go through life as Splendor Begelman! I taught those Cnidori the Law and the Prophets to hear my own language spo-ken because my children are gone and my wife is dead. That is why they call me Teacher. And I shut them out so that they would be forced to make their own way in life before they began to call *me* Redeemer! What do you call yourself, Golem?"

"My designation is O/G5/842."

"Ah. Og the giant King of Bashan. That seems suitable."

"Yes, Zohar. That one your Rabbi Moshe killed in the land of Kana'an with all his people for no great provocation. But O is the height of my oxygen tolerance in Solthree terms; I cannot work at gravities of less than five newtons, and eight four two is my model number. Now Zohar, if you demand it I will turn myself off and be no more. But the people are within your gate; some of them have been killed and they must still be cared for."

Zohar sighed, but he smiled a little as well. Yet he spoke slowly because he was very ill. "Og ha-Golem, before you learn how to tune an argument too fine remember that Master of the Word is one of the names of Satan. Moshe Rabbenu was a bad-tempered man but he did very greatly, and I am no kind of warrior. Take care of the people, and me too if your . . . logic demands it—and I will consider how to conduct myself off the world properly."

"I am sure your spirit will free itself in peace, Zohar. As for me, my shuttle is broken, I am wanted nowhere else, and I will rust in Pardes."

Og ha-Golem went out of the presence of the old man but it seemed to him as if there were some mild dysfunction in his circuits, for he was mindful—if that is the term—of Begelman's concept of the Satan, Baal Davar, and he did not know for certain if what he had done by the prompting of his logic was right action. How can I know? he asked himself. By what harms and what saves, he answered. By what seems to harm and what seems to save, says the Master of the Word.

Yet he continued by the letter of his instructions from Galactic Federation, and these were to give the old man comfort. For the Cnidori he helped construct tents, because they liked water under their bellies but not pouring on their heads. With his own implements he flensed the bodies of the dead Unds, cleaned their skins, and burned their flesh; it was not kosher for Begelman and attracted bothersome scavengers. He did this while Rav Zohar was sleeping and spoke to the people in his language; they had missed it when he was ill. "Zohar believes you must learn to take care of yourselves, against the Unds and on your world, because you cannot now depend on him."

"We would do that, Golem, but we would also like to give comfort to our Teacher."

Og ha-Golem was disturbed once again by the ideas that pieced themselves together in his logic and said to Begelman, "Zohar, you have taught the Cnidori so well that now they are capable of saying the prayers you long for so greatly. Is there a way in which that can be made permissible?"

The old man folded his hands and looked about the bare and cracking walls of the room, as Golem had first done, and then back at him. "In this place?" he whispered. "Do you know what you are saying?"

"Yes, Zohar."

"How they may be made *Jews?*"

"They are sentient beings. What is there to prevent it?"

Begelman's face became red and Og checked his blood-pressure monitor. "Prevent it! What is there to them that would make Jews? Everything they eat is neutral, neither kosher nor tref, so what use is the law of Kashrut? They live in mud—where are the rules of bathing and cleanliness? They had never had any kind of god or any thought of one, as far as they tell me—what does prayer mean? Do you know how they procreate? Could you imagine? They are so completely hermaphroditic the word is meaningless. They pair long enough to raise children together, but only until the children grow teeth and can forage. What you see that looks like a penis is really an ovipositor: each Cnidor who is ready deposits eggs in the pouch of another, and an enzyme of the eggs stimulates the semen glands inside, and when one or two eggs become fertilized the pouch seals until the fetus is of a size to make the fluid pressure around it break the seal, and the young crawls up the belly of the parent to suckle on the teat. Even if one or two among twenty are born incomplete, not one is anything you might call male or female! So tell me, what do you do with all the laws of marriage and divorce, sexual behavior, the duties of the man at prayer and the woman with the child?"

He was becoming out of breath and Og checked oxygen and heart monitors. "I am not a man or woman either and though I know the Law I am ignorant in experience. I was thinking merely of prayers that God might listen to in charity or appreciation. I did not mean to upset you. I am not fulfilling my duties."

"Leave me."

Og turned an eyecell to the dripping of the IV and removed catheter and urine bag. "You are nearly ready to rise from your bed and feed yourself, Zohar. Perhaps when you feel more of a man you may reconsider."

"Just go away." He added, snarling, "God doesn't need any more Jews!"

"Yes, they would look ridiculous in skullcaps and prayer shawls with all those fringes dragging in mud . . ."

Zohar, was that why you drove them out into the wild?

Og gathered brushwood and made a great fire. He cut woody vines and burnt them into heaps of charcoal. He gathered and baked clay into blocks and built a kiln. Then he pulled his sledge for 120 kilometers, and dug until he found enough pieces of the glider for his uses. He fired the kiln to a great heat, softened the fragments, and reshaped them into the huge scoops he had been deprived of. They were not as fine and strong as the originals, but very nearly as exact.

He consulted maps of Pardes, which lay near the sea. He began digging channels and heaping breakwaters to divert a number of streams and drain some of the marshes of Pardes, and to keep the sea from washing over it during storms, and this left pools of fresher water for the Cnidori.

Sometimes the sun shone. On a day that was brighter and dryer than usual Begelman came outside the station, supporting himself on canes, and watched the great Golem at work. He had never seen Og in full armor with his scoops. During its renewal his exterior had been bonded with a coating that retarded rust; this was dull gray and the machine had no beauty in the eyes of a Solthree, but he worked with an economy of movement that lent him grace. He was surrounded by Cnidori with shovels of a size they could use, and they seemed to Begelman like little children playing in mud piles, getting in the way while the towering machine worked in silence without harming the small creatures or allowing them to annoy him.

Og, swiveling the beam of his eyecell, saw an old, white-bearded Solthree with a homely face of some dignity; he looked weak but not ill. His hair was neatly trimmed, he wore a blue velvet skullcap worked with silver threads, black trousers, and zippered jacket, below which showed the fringes of his *tallith katan*. He matched approximately the thousands of drawings, paintings, and photographs of dignified old Jews stored in Og's memory: Og had dressed him to match.

Begelman said, "What are you doing?"

"I am stabilizing the land in order to grow crops of oilseed, lugwort, and greenpleat, which are nourishing both to you and the Cnidori. I doubt Galactic Federation is going to give us anything more, and I also wish to store supplies. If other wandering tribes of Cnidori cross this territory it is better to share our plenty than fight over scarcity."

"You're too good to be true," Begelman muttered.

Og had learned something of both wit and sarcasm from Begelman but did not give himself the right to use them on the old man. His logic told him that he, the machine, had nothing to fear from a Satan who was not even a concept in the mainstream of Jewish belief, but that Zohar was doing battle with the common human evil in his own spirit. He said, "Zohar, these Cnidori have decided to take Hebrew names, and they are calling themselves by letters: Aleph, Bet, Gimmel, and when those end at Tauf, by numbers: Echod, Shtaim, Sholosh. This does not seem correct to me but they will not take my word for it. Will you help them?"

Begelman's mouth worked for a moment, twisting as if to say, What have these to do with such names? but Cnidori crowded round him and their black eyes reflected very small lights in the dim sun; they were people of neither fur nor feather, but scales that resembled both: leaf-shaped plates the size of a thumb with central ridges and branching radials; these were very fine in texture and refracted rainbow colors on brighter days.

The old man sighed and said, "Dear people, if you wish to take names in Hebrew you must take the names of human beings like those in Law and Prophets. The names of the Fathers: Avraham, Yitzhak, Yaakov; the Tribes: Yehuda, Shimon, Binyamin, or if you prefer female names, the Mothers: Sarai, Rivkah, Rakhael, Leah. Whichever seems good to you." The Cnidori thanked him with pleasure and went away content.

Begelman said to Og, "Next thing you know they will want a Temple." Og suspected what they would ask for next, but said, "I believe we must redesign the forcefield to keep the Unds out of the cultivated areas. Perhaps we have enough components in Stores or I can learn to make them."

He had been Scouting for Unds every fourth or fifth day and knew their movements. They had been avoiding the Station in fear of Og and the malfunctioning forcefield but he believed that they would attack again when the place was quiet, and they did so on the night of that day when the Cnidori took names. The field had been repaired and withstood their battering without shocking them; their cries were terrible to hear, and sometimes their bones cracked against the force. They fell back after many hours, leaving Og with earthworks to repair and two of their bodies to destroy.

In the morning when he had finished doing this he found Begelman lying on a couch in the Common Room, a book of prayers on his lap, faced by a group of ten Cnidori. All eleven spoke at once, Begelman with crackling anger in his voice, the Cnidori softly but with insistence.

Begelman cried out when he saw Og, "Now they tell me they must have surnames!"

"I expected so, Zohar. They know that you are ben Reuven and they have accepted your language and the names of your people. Is this not reasonable?"

"I have no authority to make Jews of them!"

"You are the only authority left. You have taught them."

"Damn you! You have been pushing for this!"

"I have pushed for nothing except to make you well. I taught nothing." Within him the Master of the Word spoke: This is true, but is it right?

Begelman in anger clapped shut his book, but it was very old and its spine cracked slightly; he lifted and kissed it in repentance. He spoke in a low voice, "What does it matter now? There is no surname they can be given except the name of convert, which is ben Avraham or bat Avraham, according to the gender of the first name. And how can they be converts when they can keep no Law and do not even know God? And what does it matter now?" He threw up his hands. "Let them be b'nei Avraham!"

But the Cnidori prime, who had taken the name Binyamin, that is, Son of the Right Hand, said, "We do not wish to be b'nei Avraham, but b'nei Zohar, because we say to you, Og ha-Golem, and to you, Rav Zohar, that because Zohar has been as a father to us we feel as sons to him."

Og feared that the old man might now become truly ill with rage, and indeed his hands trembled on the book, but he said quietly enough, "My children, Jews do not behave so. Converts must become Jews in the ways allowed to them. If you do not understand, I have not taught you well enough, and I am too old to teach more. I have yielded too much already to a people who do not worship God, and I am not even a Rabbi with such small authority as is given to one."

"Rav Zohar, we have come to tell you that we have sworn to worship your God."

"But you must not worship me."

"But we may worship the God who created such a man as you, and such teachings as you have taught us, and those men who made the great Golem." They went away quickly and quietly without speaking further.

"They will be back again," Begelman said. "And again and again. Why did I ever let you in? Lord God King of the Universe, what am I to do?"

It *is* right, Og told the Master of the Word. "You are more alive and healthy than you have long been, Zohar," he said. "And you have people who love you. Can you not let them do so?"

He sought out Binyamin. "Do not trouble Rav Zohar with demands he cannot fulfill, no matter how much you desire to honor him. Later I will ask him to think if there is a way he can do as you wish, within the Law."

"We will do whatever you advise, Golem."

Og continued with his work, but while he was digging he turned up a strange artifact and he had a foreboding. At times he had discovered potsherds which were the remnants of clay vessels the Cnidori had made to cook vegetables they could not digest raw, and this discovery was an almost whole cylinder of the same texture, color, and markings; one of its end rims was blackened by burn marks, and dark streaks ran up its sides. He did not know what it was but it seemed sinister to him; in conscience he had no choice but to show it to Zohar.

"It does not seem like a cooking vessel," he said.

"No," said Begelman. "It does not." He pointed to a place inside where there was a leaf-shaped Cnidori scale, blackened, clinging to its wall, and to two other burn marks of the same shape. Strangely, to Og, his eyes filled with tears.

"Perhaps it is a casing in which they dispose of their dead," Og said.

Zohar wiped his eyes and said, "No. It is a casing in which they make them dead. Many were killed by Unds, and some have starved and the rest die of age. All those they weight and sink into the marshes. This is a sacrifice. They have a god, and its name is Baal." He shook his head. "My children." He wept for a moment again and said, "Take this away and smash it until there is not a piece to recognize."

Og did so, but Zohar locked himself into his room and would not answer to anyone.

Og did not know what to do now. He was again as helpless as he had been on the loading dock where he had first learned to use his logic.

The Cnidori came to inquire of Golem and he told them what had happened. They said, "It is true that our ancestors worshipped a

Being and made sacrifices, but none of that was done after Zohar gave us help. We were afraid he and his God would hold us in contempt."

"Both Zohar and his God have done imperfect acts. But now I will leave him alone, because he is very troubled."

"But it is a great sin in his eyes," said Binyamin sorrowfully. "I doubt that he will ever care for us again."

And Og continued with his work, but he thought his logic had failed him, in accordance with Zohar's taunts.

In the evening a Cnidor called Elyahu came writhing toward him along the ground in great distress. "Come quickly!" he called. "Binyamin is doing *nidset!*"

"What is that?"

"Only come quickly!" Elyahu turned back in haste. Og unclipped his scoops and followed, overtaking the small creature and bearing him forward in his arms. They found Binyamin and other Cnidori in a grove of ferns. They had built a smoky fire and were placing upon it a fresh cylinder: a network of withy branches had been woven into the bottom of it.

"No, no!" cried Og, but they did not regard him; the cylinder was set on the fire and smoke came out of its top. Then the Cnidori helped Binyamin climb over its edge and he dropped inward, into the smoke.

"*No!*" Og cried again, and he toppled the vessel from the fire, but without violence so that Binyamin would not be harmed. "*You shall make no sacrifices!*" Then he tapped it so that it split, and the Cnidor lay in its halves, trembling.

"*That is nidset,* Golem," said Elyahu.

But Golem plucked up the whimpering Cnidor. "Why were you doing such a terrible thing, Binyamin?"

"We thought," Binyamin said in a quavering voice, "we thought that all of the gods were angry with us—our old god for leaving him and our new one for having worshipped the old—and that a sacrifice would take away the anger of all."

"That confounds my logic somewhat." Og set down Binyamin, beat out the fire, and cast the pieces of the cylinder far away. "All gods are One, and the One forgives whoever asks. Now come. I believe I hear the Unds again, and we need shelter close to home until we can build a wider one."

Then the Cnidori raised a babble of voices. "No! What good is such a God if even Zohar does not listen to Him and forgive us?"

It seemed to Og for one moment as if the Cnidori felt themselves cheated of a sacrifice; he put this thought aside. "The man is sick and old, and he is not thinking clearly either, while you have demanded much of him."

"Then, Golem, we will demand no more, but die among the Unds!" The shrieking of the beasts grew louder on the night winds but the Cnidori drew their little knives and would not stir.

"Truly you are an outrageous people," said Golem. "But I am only a machine." He extended his four hinged arms and his four coil arms and bearing them up in their tens raced with them on treads and wheels until they were within the safety of the forcefield.

But when he set them down they grouped together closely near the field and would not say one word.

Og considered the stubborn Zohar on the one side, and the stubborn b'nei Avraham on the other, and he thought that perhaps it was time for him to cease his being. A great storm of lightning and thunder broke out; the Unds did not approach and within the forcefield there was stillness.

He disarmed himself and stood before Zohar's door. He considered the sacrifice of Yitzhak, and the Golden Calf, and of how Moshe Rabbenu had broken the Tables, and of many excellent examples, and he spoke quietly.

"Zohar, you need not answer, but you must listen. Your people tell me they have made no sacrifices since they knew you. But Binyamin, who longs to call himself your son, has tried to sacrifice himself to placate whatever gods may forgive his people, and would have died if I had not prevented him. After that they were ready to let the Unds kill them. I prevented that also, but they will not speak to me, or to you if you do not forgive them. I cannot do any more here and I have nothing further to say to you. Good-bye."

He turned from the door without waiting, but heard it open, and Zohar's voice cried out, "Og, where are you going?"

"To the storeroom, to turn myself off. I have always said I was no more than a machine, and now I have reached the limit of my logic and my usefulness."

"No, Golem, wait! Don't take everything from me!" The old man was standing with hands clasped and hair awry. "There must be some end to foolishness," he whispered. "Where are they?"

"Out by the field near the entrance," Og said. "You will see them when the lightning flashes."

The Holy One, blessed be His Name, gave Zohar one more year, and in that time Og ha-Golem built and planted, and in this he was helped by the b'nei Avraham. They made lamps from their vegetable oils and lit them on Sabbaths and the Holy Days calculated by Zohar. In season they mated and their bellies swelled. Zohar tended them when his strength allowed, as in old days, and when Elyahu died of brain hemorrhage and Yitzhak of a swift-growing tumor which nothing could stop, he led the mourners in prayer for their length of days. One baby was stillborn, but ten came from the womb in good health; they were gray-pink, toothless, and squalled fearfully, but Zohar fondled and praised them. "These people were twelve when I found them," he said to Og. "Now there are forty-six and I have known them for five generations." He told the Cnidori, "Children of Avraham, Jews have converted, and Jews have adopted, but never children of a different species, so there is no precedent I can find to let any one of you call yourself a child of Zohar, but as a community I see no reason why you cannot call yourselves b'nei Zohar, my children, collectively."

The people were wise enough by now to accept this decision without argument. They saw that the old man's time of renewed strength was done and he was becoming frailer every day; they learned to make decisions for themselves. Og too helped him now only when he asked. Zohar seemed content, although sometimes he appeared about to speak and remained silent. The people noticed these moods and spoke to Og of them occasionally, but Og said, "He must tend to his spirit for himself, b'nei Avraham. My work is done."

He had cleared the land in many areas around the station, and protected them with forcefields whose antennas he had made with forges he had built. The Unds were driven back into their wilds of cave and valley; they were great and terrible, but magnificent life-forms of their own kind and he wished to kill no more. He had only to wait for the day when Zohar would die in peace.

Once a day Og visited him in the Common Room where he spent most of his time reading or with his hands on his book and his eyes to the distance. One peaceful day when they were alone he said to Og, "I must tell you this while my head is still clear. And I can tell only you." He gathered his thoughts for a moment. "It took me a long time to realize that I was the last Jew, though Galactic Federation kept saying so.

I had been long alone, but that realization made me fiercely, hideously lonely. Perhaps you don't understand. I think you do. And then my loneliness turned itself inside out and I grew myself a kind of perverse pride. The last! The last! I would close the Book that was opened those thousands of years before, as great in a way as the first had been . . . but I had found the Cnidori, and they were a people to talk with and keep from going mad in loneliness—but Jews! They were ugly, and filthy, and the opposite of everything I saw as human. I despised them. Almost, I hated them . . . that was what wanted to be Jews! And I had started it by teaching them, because I was so lonely—and I had no way to stop it except to destroy them, and I nearly did that! And you—" He began to weep with the weak passion of age.

"Zohar, do not weep. You will make yourself ill."

"My soul is sick! It is like a boil that needs lancing, and it hurts so much! Who will forgive me?" He reached out and grasped one of Og's arms. "Who?"

"*They* will forgive you anything—but if you ask you will only hurt yourself more deeply. And I make no judgments."

"But I must be judged!" Zohar cried. "Let me have a little peace to die with!"

"If I must, then, Zohar, I judge you a member of humanity who has saved more people than would be alive without him. I think you could not wish better."

Zohar said weakly, "You knew all the time, didn't you?"

"Yes," said Og. "I believe I did."

But Zohar did not hear, for he had fainted.

He woke in his bed and when his eyes opened he saw Og beside him. "What are you?" he said, and Og stared with his unwinking eye; he thought Zohar's mind had left him.

Then Zohar laughed. "My mind is not gone yet. But what are you, really, Og? You cannot answer. Ah well . . . would you ask my people to come here now, so I can say good-bye? I doubt it will be long; they raise all kinds of uproar, but at least they can't cry."

Og brought the people, and Zohar blessed them all and each; they were silent, in awe of him. He seemed to fade while he spoke, as if he were being enveloped in mist. "I have no advice for you," he whispered at last. "I have taught all I know and that is little enough because I am not very wise, but you will find the wise among yourselves. Now, whoever remembers, let him recite me a psalm. Not the twenty-third. I want the hundred and fourth, and leave out that stupid part at the end where the sinners are consumed from the earth."

But it was only Og who remembered that psalm in its entirety, and spoke the words describing the world Zohar had come from an unmeasurable time ago.

> *O Lord my God You are very great!*
> *You are clothed with honor and majesty,*
> *Who covers Yourself with light as with a garment,*
> *Who has stretched out the heavens like a tent,*
> *Who has laid the beams of Your chambers on the waters,*
> *Who makes the clouds Your chariot,*
> *Who rides on the wings of the wind,*
> *Who makes the winds Your messengers,*
> *fire and flame Your ministers . . .*

When he was finished, Zohar said the *Shema,* which tells that God is One, and died. And Og thought that he must be pleased with his dying.

Og removed himself. He let the b'nei Avraham prepare the body, wrap it in the prayer shawl, and bury it. He waited during the days in which the people sat in mourning, and when they had gotten up he said, "Surely my time is come." He traveled once about the domains he had created for their inhabitants and returned to say good-bye in fewer words than Zohar had done.

But the people cried, "No, Golem, no! How can you leave us now when we need you so greatly?"

"You are not children. Zohar told you that you must manage for yourselves."

"But we have so much to learn. We do not know how to use the radio, and we want to tell Galactic Federation that Zohar is dead, and of all he and you have done for us."

"I doubt that Galactic Federation is interested," said Og.

"Nevertheless we will learn!"

They were a stubborn people. Og said, "I will stay for that, but no longer."

Then Og discovered he must teach them enough lingua to make themselves understood by Galactic Federation. All were determined learners, and a few had a gift for languages. When he had satisfied himself that they were capable, he said, "Now."

And they said, "Og ha-Golem, why must you waste yourself? We have so much to discover about the God we worship and the men who have worshipped Him!"

"Zohar taught you all he knew, and that was a great deal."

"Indeed he taught us the Law and the Prophets, but he did not teach us the tongues of Aramaic or Greek, or Writings, or Mishna, or Talmud (Palestinian and Babylonian), or Tosefta, or Commentary, or—"

"But why must you learn all that?"

"To keep it for others who may wish to know of it when we are dead."

So Og surrounded himself with them, the sons and daughters of Avraham and their children, who now took surnames of their own from womb parents—and all of them b'nei Zohar—and he began: "Here is Misha, given by word of mouth from Scribe to Scribe for a thousand years. Fifth Division, *Nezikin*, which is Damages; *Baba Metzia:* the Middle Gate: 'If two took hold of a garment and one said, "I found it," and the other said, "I found it," or one said, "I bought it," and the other said, "I bought it," each takes an oath that he claims not less than half and they divide it . . .'"

In this manner Og ha-Golem, who had endless patience, lived a thousand and twenty years. By radio the Galaxy heard of the strange work of strange creatures, and over hundreds of years colonists who wished to call themselves b'nei Avraham drifted inward to re-create the world Pardes. They were not great in number, but they made a world. From *pardes* is derived "Paradise" but in the humble world of Pardes the peoples drained more of the swamps and planted fruitful orchards and pleasant gardens. All of these were named for their creators, except one.

When Og discovered that his functions were deteriorating, he refused replacement parts and directed that when he stopped all of his components must be dismantled and scattered to the ends of the earth, for fear of idolatry. But a garden was named for him, may his spirit rest in justice and his carapace rust in peace, and the one being who had no organic life is remembered with love among living things.

Here the people live, doing good and evil, contending with God and arguing with each other as usual, and all keep the Tradition as well as they can. Only the descendants of the aboriginal inhabitants, once called Cnidori, jealously guard for themselves the privilege of the name b'nei Zohar, and they are considered by the others to be snobbish, clannish, and stiff-necked.

BARRY N. MALZBERG

Leviticus: In the Ark

      The very basis and focus of the Jewish religion is The Law, which regulates every facet and activity of Jewish life. It is the symbolic structure of tradition and ceremony within which the Jew lives. It is complex, demanding, and alive . . . as alive as thought itself.

    The revelation of Moses on Mount Sinai gave us the Torah; but in that single event is the implication of all the law that would follow, the revealed oral law, or Talmud, as reported by the sages. The Talmud contains fourteen centuries of jurisprudence, close legal analysis, and the color and pith and pageantry of Jewish life. Here are found the myriad regulations, prohibitions, and instructions that bind every practicing Jew. For the believer, The Law is the divine instruction which connects him with his God. By being scrupulously faithful to The Law, the Jew hallows and informs even the mundane moments of his life.

    But for the unbeliever, or the unsure, The Law is a prison.

*

I

CONDITIONS ARE DIFFICULT and services are delayed. Conditions have
been difficult for some time, services have been delayed more often
than being prompt, but never has it weighed upon Leviticus as it does
now. Part of this has to do with his own situation: cramped in the ark,
Torahs jammed into his left ear and right kneecap, heavy talmudic
bindings wedged uncomfortably under his buttocks, he is past the moments of quiet meditation that for so long have sustained him. Now he
is in great pain, his body is shrieking for release; he has a vivid image of
himself bursting from the ark, the doors sliding open, his arms out-
stretched, his beard flapping in the strange breezes of the synagogue as
he cries denunciation. *I can no longer bear this position.* There must
be some Yiddish equivalent for this. Very well, he will cry it in Yiddish.

No, he will do nothing of the sort. He mill remain within the ark, six
by four, jammed amidst the holy writings. At times he is sure that he
has spent several weeks within, at others, all sense of time eludes him;
perhaps it has been only a matter of hours . . . well, make it a few days
since he has been in here. It does not matter. A minute is as a century
in the Eye of God, he remembers—or did it go the other way?—and
vague murmurs that he can hear through the not fully soundproofed
walls of his chamber inform him that the service is about to begin. In
due course, just before the adoration begins, they will fling open the
doors of the ark and he will be able to gaze upon them for a few moments, breathe the somewhat less dense air of the synagogue, endure
past many moments of this sort because of his sudden, shuddering renewal of contact with the congregation, but, ah God! . . . it is difficult.
Too much has been demanded of him; he is suffering deeply.

Leviticus turns within the limited confines of his position, tries to
find a more comfortable point of accommodation. Soon the service will
begin. After the ritual chants and prayers, after the sermon and the

hymn, will come the adoration. At the adoration the opening of the ark. He will stretch. He will stand. He will stretch out a hand and greet them. He will cast light upon their eyes and upon the mountains: that they shall remember and do all his commandments and be holy unto him.

He wonders if his situation has made him megalomaniac.

II

Two weeks before, just at the point when Leviticus' point of commitment to the ark loomed before him, he had appeared in the rabbi's cubicle and made a plea for dispensation. "I am a sick man," he had said, "I do not think that I will be able to stand the confinement. Also, and I must be quite honest with you, rabbi, I doubt my religious faith and commitment. I am not sure that I can function as that embodiment of ritual which placement in the ark symbolizes." This was not quite true; at least, the issue of religious faith had not occurred to Leviticus in either way; he was not committed to the religion, not quite against it either, it did not matter enough . . . but he had gathered from particularly reliable reports going through the congregation that one of the best ways of getting out of the ark was to plead a lack of faith. Perhaps he had gotten it wrong. The rabbi looked at him for a long time, and finally, drawing his robes tightly around him, retreating to the wall, looked at Leviticus as if he were a repulsed object. "Then perhaps your stay in the ark will do you some good," he had said; "it will enable you to find time for meditation and prayer. Also, religious belief has nothing to do with the role of the tenant. Does the wine in the goblet conceive of the nature of the sacrament it represents? In the same way, the tenant is merely the symbol."

"I haven't been feeling well," Leviticus mumbled. "I've been having chest pains. I've been having seizures of doubt. Cramps in the lower back; I don't think that I can—"

"Yes you can," the rabbi said with a dreadful expression, "*and yes you will,*" and had sent Leviticus out into the cold and casting light of the settlement, beginning to come to terms with the realization that he could not, could not under any circumstances, escape the obligation thrust upon him. Perhaps he had been foolish to have thought that he could. Perhaps he should not have paid credence to the rumors. He returned to his cubicle in a foul temper, set the traps to *privacy* and sullenly put through the tape of the *Union Prayer Book, Revised Edition: For the High Holy Days*. If you really were going to have to do something like this, he guessed that a little bit of hard background wouldn't hurt. But it made no sense. The writings simply made no sense. He shut off the tapes and for a long time gave no further thought to any of this, until the morning, when, in absolute disbelief, he found the elders in his unit, implacable in their costume, come to take him to the ark. *Tallis* and *tefillim*.

III

In the ark, Leviticus ponders his condition while the services go on outside. He has taken to self-pity during his confinement; he has a tendency to snivel a little. It is really not fair for him, a disbelieving man but one who has never made his disbelief a point of contention, to be thrown into such a position, kept there for such an extended period of time. Ritual is important, and he for one is not to say that the enactment of certain rote practices does not lend reassurance, may indeed be a metaphor for some kind of reality which he cannot apprehend . . . but is it right that all of this should be at his expense? He has never entered into disputation with the elders on their standards of belief; why should they force theirs upon him?

A huge volume of the Talmud jabs his buttocks, its cover a painful little concentrated point of pain, and cursing, Leviticus bolts from it, rams his head against the beam forming half of the ceiling of the ark, bends, reaches, seizes the volume, and with all his force hurls it three feet into the flat wall opposite. He has hoped for a really satisfying concussion, some mark of his contempt that will be heard outside of the ark, will impress and disconcert the congregation, but there simply has not been room enough to generate impact: the volume falls softly, turgidly across a knee, and he slaps at it in fury, little puffs of dust coming from the cover, inflaming his sinuses. He curses again, wondering if this apostasy, committed within the very place in which, according to what he understands, the spirit of God dwells, will be sufficient to end his period of torture, release him from this one kind of bondage into at least another, but nothing whatsoever happens.

He could have expected that, he thinks. If the tenant of the ark is indeed symbol rather than substance, then it would not matter what he did here or what he thought; only his presence would matter. And fling volumes of the Talmud, scrape at the Torahs, snivel away as he will, he is nevertheless in residence. Nothing that he can do will make any difference at all; his presence here is the only testament that they will need.

Step by tormenting step Leviticus has been down this path of reasoning-after-apostasy a hundred times during his confinement. Fortunately for him, these are emotional outbursts which he forgets almost upon completion, so that he has no memory of them when he starts upon the next; and this sense of discovery—the renewal of his rage, so to speak, every time afresh—has thus sustained him in the absence of more real benefits and will sustain him yet. Also, during the long night hours when only he is in the temple, he is able to have long, imagined dialogues with God, which to no little degree also sustain him, even if his visualization of God is a narrow and parochial one.

IV

The first time that the doors had been flung open during the adoration and all of the congregation had looked in upon him, Leviticus had become filled with shame, but that quickly passed when he realized that no one really thought anything of it and that the attention of the elders and the congregation was not upon him but upon the sacred scripts that one by one the elders withdrew, brought to the podium, and read with wavering voice and fingers while Leviticus, hunched over naked in an uncomfortable fetal position, could not have been there at all, for all the difference it made. He could have bolted from the ark, flung open his arms, shrieked to the congregation, "Look at me, look at me, don't you see what you're doing!" but he had not; he had been held back in part by fear, another part by constraint, still a third part from the realization that no one in the ark had ever done it. He had never seen it happen; back through all the generations that he was able to seek through accrued knowledge, the gesture was without precedent. The tenant of the ark had huddled quietly throughout the term of his confinement, had kept himself in perfect restraint when exposed; why should this not continue? Tradition and the awesome power of the elders had held him in check. He could not interrupt the flow of the services. He could deal with the predictable, which was a term of confinement and then release, just like everyone who had preceded him, but what he could not control was any conception of the unknown. If he made a spectacle of himself during the adoration, there was no saying what might happen then. The elders might take vengeance upon him. They might turn away from the thought of vengeance and simply declare that his confinement be extended for an indefinite period for apostasy. It was very hard to tell exactly *what* they would do. This fear of the unknown, Leviticus had decided through his nights of pondering and imaginary dialogue, was probably what had enabled the situation to go on as long as it had.

It was hard to say exactly when he had reached the decision that he could no longer accept his position, his condition, his fate, wait out the time of his confinement, entertain the mercy of the elders, and return to the congregation. It was hard to tell at exactly what point he had realized that he could not do this; there was no clear point of epiphany, no moment at which—unlike a religious conversion—he could see himself as having gone outside the diagram of possibility, unutterably changed. All that he knew was that the decision had slowly crept into him, perhaps when he was sleeping, and without a clear point of definition, had reached absolute firmness: he would confront them at the adoration now. He would force them to look at him. He would show them what he, and by implication they, had become: so trapped within a misunderstood tradition, so wedged within the suffocating confines of the ark that they had lost any overriding sense of purpose, the ability to perceive wholly the madness that they and the elders had perpetuated. He would force them to understand this as the sum point of their lives, and when it was over, he would bolt from the synagogue naked, screaming, back to his cubicle, where he would reassemble his clothing and make final escape from the complex . . . and leave *them,* not him, to decide what they would now make of the shattered ruins of their lives.

The long period of confinement, self-examination, withdrawal, and physical privation had, perhaps, made Leviticus somewhat unstable.

V

Just before the time when the elders had appeared and had taken him away, Leviticus had made his last appeal, not to them, certainly not to the rabbi, but to Stala, who had shared to a certain point his anguish and fear of entrapment. "I don't see why I have to go there," he said to her, lying tight in the instant after fornication. "It's stupid. It's sheer mysticism. And besides that, it hasn't any relevance."

"But you must go," she said, putting a hand on his cheek. "You have been asked, and you *must*." She was not stupid, he thought, merely someone who had never had to question assumptions, as he was now being forced to. "It is ordained. It won't be that bad; you're supposed to learn a lot."

"*You* go."

She gave a little gasping intake of breath and rolled from him. "You know that's impossible," she said. "Women can't go."

"In the reform tradition they can."

"But we're not in the reform tradition," she said; "this is the high Orthodox."

"I tend to think of it more in the line of being progressive."

"You know, Leviticus," she said, sitting, breathing unevenly—he could see her breasts hanging from her in the darkness like little scrolls, *like little scrolls,* oh, his confinement was very much on his mind, he could see—"it's just ridiculous that you should say something like that to me, that you should even *suggest* it. We're talking about our tradition now, and our tradition is very clear on this point, and it's impossible for a woman to go. Even if she wanted, she just couldn't—"

"All right," he said, "all right."

"No," Stala said, "no I won't stop discussing this, *you* were the one to raise it, Leviticus, not me, and I just won't have any of it. I didn't think you were that kind of person. I thought that you accepted the traditions, that you believed in them; in fact, it was an encouragement to me to think, to really think, that I had found someone who believed in a pure, solid unshaken way, and I was really *proud* of you, even prouder when I found that you had been selected, but now you've changed everything. I'm beginning to be afraid that the only reason you believed in the traditions was because they weren't causing you any trouble and you didn't have to sacrifice yourself personally, but as soon as you became involved, you moved away from them." She was standing now, moving toward her robe, which had been tossed in the fluorescence at the far end of his cubicle; looking toward it during intercourse, he had thought that the sight of it was the most tender and affecting thing he had ever known, that she had cast her garments aside for him, that she had committed herself trustfully in nakedness against him for the night, and all of this despite the fact that he was undergoing what he took to be the positive humiliation of the confinement;

now, as she flung it angrily on herself, he wondered if he had been wrong, if that casting aside had been a gesture less tender than fierce, whether or not she might have been—and he could hardly bear this thought, but one must after all, press on—perversely excited by images of how he would look naked and drawn in upon himself in the ark, his genitals clamped between his thighs, talmudic statements by the rabbis Hill and Ben Bag Bag his only companions in the many long nights to come. He did not want to think of it, did not want to see her in this new perspective, and so leaped to his feet, fleet as a hart, and said, "But it's not fair. I tell you, it isn't fair."

"Of course it isn't fair. That's why it's so beautiful."

"Well, how would *you* like it? How would you like to be confined in—"

"Leviticus," she said, "I don't want to talk to you about this anymore. Leviticus," she added, "I think I was wrong about you, you've hurt me very much. Leviticus," she concluded, "if you don't leave me right now, this moment, I'll go to the elders and tell them exactly what you're saying and thinking, and you know what will happen to you *then*," and he had let her go, nothing else to do, the shutter of his cubicle coming open, the passage of her body halving the light from the hall, then the light exposed again, and she was gone; he closed the shutter, he was alone in his cubicle again.

"It *isn't* fair," he said aloud. "She wouldn't like it so much if this was Reform and *she* were faced with the possibility of going in there someday," but this gave him little comfort; in fact, it gave him no comfort at all. It seemed to lead him right back to where he had started—futile, amazed protest at the injustice and folly of what was being done for him—and he had gone into an unhappy sleep thinking that something, something would have to be done about this; perhaps he could take the case out of the congregation. If the ordinators were led to understand what kind of rites were being committed in the name of high Orthodoxy, they would take a strong position against this, seal up the complex, probably scatter the congregation throughout a hundred other complexes . . . and it was this which had given him ease, tossed him into a long murmuring sleep replete with satisfaction that he had finally found a way to deal with this (because he knew instinctively that the ordinators would *not* like this), but the next morning, cunningly, almost as if they had been informed by Stala (perhaps they had), the elders had come to take him to the ark, and that had been the end of that line of thought. He supposed that he could still do it, complain to the ordinators—that was, after his confinement was over—but at that point it hardly seemed worth it. It hardly seemed worth it at all. For one thing, he would be out of the ark by then and would not have to face it for a very, very long time, if ever. So why bother with the ordinators? He would have to take a more direct position, take it up with the congregation itself. Surely once they understood his agony, they could not permit it to continue. Could they?

VI

In the third of his imaginary dialogues with God (whom he pictured as an imposing man, somewhat the dimensions of one of the elders but much more neatly trimmed and not loaded down with the paraphernalia with which they conducted themselves) Leviticus said, "I don't believe any of it. Not any part of it at all. It's ridiculous."

"Doubt is another part of faith," God said. "Doubt and belief intertwine; both can be conditions of reverence. There is more divinity in the doubt of a wise man than in the acceptance of fools."

"That's just rhetoric," Leviticus said; "it explains nothing."

"The devices of belief must move within the confines of rhetoric," God said. "Rhetoric is the poor machinery of the profound and incontrovertible. Actually, it's not a matter of doubt. You're just very uncomfortable."

"That's right. I'm uncomfortable. I don't see why Judaism imposes this kind of suffering."

"Religion *is* suffering" God said with a modest little laugh, "and if you think Judaism is difficult upon its participants, you should get a look at some of the *others* sometimes. Animal sacrifice, immolation, the ceremony of tongues. Oh, most terrible! Not that everyone doesn't have a right to their point of view," God added hastily. "Each must reach me, each in his way and through his tradition. Believe me, Leviticus, you haven't got the worst of it."

"I protest. I protest this humiliation."

"It isn't easy for me, either," God pointed out. "I've gone through cycles of repudiation for billions of years. Still, one must go on."

"I've got to get out of here. It's destroying my health; my physical condition is ruined. When am I going to leave?"

"I'm sorry," God said, "that decision is not in my hands."

"But you're omnipotent."

"My omnipotence is only my will working through the diversity of twenty billion other wills. Each is determined, and yet each is free."

"That sounds to me like a lousy excuse," Leviticus said sullenly. "I don't think that makes any sense at all."

"I do the best I can," God said, and after a long, thin pause added sorrowfully, "You don't think that any of this is easy for me either, do you?"

VII

Leviticus has the dim recollection from the historical tapes, none of them well attended to, that before the time of the complexes, before the time of great changes, there had been another kind of existence, one during which none of the great churches, Judaism included, had been doing particularly well in terms of absolute number of participants, relative proportion of the population. Cults had done all right, but cults had had only the most marginal connection to the great churches, and in most cases had repudiated them, leading, in the analyses of certain of the historical tapes, to the holocaust that had followed, and the absolute determination on the part of the Risen, that they would not permit this to happen again, that they would not allow the cults to appropriate all of the energy, the empirical demonstrations, for themselves, but instead would make sure that the religions were reconverted to hard ritual, that the ritual demonstrations following would be strong and convincing enough to keep the cults out of business and through true worship and true belief (although with enough ritual now to satisfy the mass of people that religion could be made visible) stave off yet another holocaust. At least, this was what Leviticus had *gathered* from the tapes, but then, you could never be sure about this, and the tapes were all distributed under the jurisdiction of the elders anyway, and what the elders would do with material to manipulate it to their own purposes was well known.

Look, for one thing, at what they had done to Leviticus.

VIII

"I'll starve in here," he had said to the elders desperately, as they were conveying him down the aisle toward the ark. "I'll deteriorate. I'll go insane from the confinement. If I get ill, no one will be there to help me."

"Food will be given you each day. You will have the Torah and the Talmud, the Feast of Life itself to comfort you and to grant you peace. You will allow the spirit of God to move within you."

"That's ridiculous," Leviticus said. "I told you, I have very little belief in any of this. How can the spirit—?"

"Belief means nothing," the elders said. They seemed to speak in unison, which was impossible, of course (how could they have such a level of shared anticipation of the others' remarks; rather, it was that they spoke one by one, with similar voice quality—*that* would be a more likely explanation of the phenomenon, mysticism having, so far as Leviticus knew, very little relation to rational Judaism). "You are its object, not its subject."

"Aha!" Leviticus said then, frantically raising one finger to forestall them as they began to lead him painfully into the ark, pushing him, tugging, buckling his limbs. "If belief does not matter, if I am merely object rather than subject, *then how can I be tenanted by the spirit?*"

"That," the elders said, finishing the job, patting him into place, one of them extracting a rag to whip the wood of the ark speedily to high gloss, cautiously licking a finger, applying it to the surface to take out an imagined particle of dust, "that is very much your problem and not ours, you see," and closed the doors upon him, leaving him alone with scrolls and Talmud, cloth, and the sound of scrambling birds. In a moment he heard a grinding noise as key was inserted into lock, then a snap as tumblers inverted. They were locking him in.

Well, he had known that. That, at least, was not surprising. Tradition had its roots; the commitment to the ark was supposed to be voluntary—a joyous expression of commitment, that was; the time spent in the ark was supposed to be a time of repentance and great interior satisfaction. . . . But all of that to one side, the elders, balancing off the one against the other, as was their wont, arriving at a careful and highly modulated view of the situation, had ruled in their wisdom that it was best to keep the ark locked at all times, excepting, of course, the adoration. That was the elders for you. They took everything into account, and having done *that*, made the confinement, as they said, his problem.

IX

Now the ritual of the Sabbath evening service is over, and the rabbi is delivering his sermon. Something about the many rivers of Judaism,

each of them individual, Bowing into that great sea of tradition and belief. The usual material. Leviticus knows that this is the Sabbath service; he can identify it by certain of the prayers and chants, although he
has lost all extrinsic sense of time, of course, in the ark. For that matter,
he suspects, the elders have lost all extrinsic sense of time as well; it is
no more Friday now than Thursday or Saturday, but at a certain arbi-
trary time after the holocaust, he is given to understand, the days, the
months, the years themselves were re-created and assigned, and therefore, if the elders say it is Friday, it is Friday, just as if they say it is the
year thirty-seven, it is the year thirty-seven, and not fifty seven hundred
something or other, or whatever it was when the holocaust occurred.
(In his mind, as a kind of shorthand, he has taken to referring to the
holocaust as the H; the H did this; certain things happened to cause
the H, but he is not sure that this would make sense to other people,
and as a matter of fact wonders whether or not this might not be the
sign of a deranged consciousness.) Whatever the elders say it is, it is, although God in the imaginary dialogues has assured him that the elders,
in their own fashion, are merely struggling with the poor tools at their
command and are no less fallible than he, Leviticus.

He shall take upon himself, in any event, these commandments, and
shall bind them for frontlets between his eyes. After the sermon, when
the ark is opened for the adoration, he will lunge from it and confront
them with what they have become, with what they have made of him,
with what together they have made of God. He will do that, and for
signposts upon his house as well, that they shall remember and do
those commandments and be holy. Holy, holy. Oh, their savior and
their hope, they have been worshiping him as their fathers did in ancient days, but enough of this, quite enough; the earth being his do-
minion and all the beasts and fish thereof, it is high time that some sort
of reckoning of the changes be made.

Highly unfair, Leviticus thinks, crouching, awaiting the opening of
the ark, but then again, he must (as always) force himself to see all
sides of the question: very possibly, if Stala had approved of his position, had granted him sympathy, had agreed with him that what the
elders were doing was unjust and unfair . . . well, then, he might have
been far more cheerfully disposed to put up with his fate. If only she, if
only someone, had seen him as a martyr rather than as a usual part of a
very usual process. Everything might have changed, but then again, it
might have been the same.

X

The book of Daniel, he recollects, had been very careful and very precise in giving, with numerology and symbol, the exact time when the H would begin. Daniel had been specific; he had alluded to precisely that course of events at which period of time that would signal the coming (or the second coming, depending upon your pursuit); the only trouble with it was that there had been so many conflicting interpretations over thousands of years that for all intents and purposes the predictive value of Daniel for the H had been lost; various interpreters saw too many signs of rising in the East, too many beasts of heaven, stormings of the tabernacle, too many uprisings among the cattle or the chieftains to enable them to get the H down right, once and for all. A lot of them, hence, had been embarrassed; many cults, hinged solely upon their interpretation of Daniel and looking for an apocalyptic date, had gotten themselves overcommitted, and going up on the mountaintops to await the end, had lost most of their membership.

Of course, the H had come, and with it the floods, the falling, the rising, and the tumult in the lands, and it was possible that Daniel had gotten it precisely right, after all, if only you could look back on it in retrospect and get it right, but as far as Leviticus was concerned, there was only one overriding message that you might want to take from the tapes if you were interested in this kind of thing: you did not want to pin it down too closely. Better, as the elders did, to kind of leave the issue indeterminate and in flux. Better, as God himself had (imaginarily) pointed out, to say that doubt is merely the reverse coin of belief, both of them motes in the bowels of the Hound of Heaven.

XI

The rabbi, adoring the ever-living God and rendering praise unto him, inserts the key into the ark, the tumblers fall open, the doors creak and gape, and Leviticus finds himself once again staring into the old man's face, his eyes congested with pain as he reaches in trembling toward one of the scrolls, his cheeks dancing in the light, the elders grouped behind him attending carefully; and instantly Leviticus strikes: he reaches out a hand, yanks the rabbi out of the way, and then tumbles from the ark. He had meant to leap but did not realize how shriveled his muscles would be from disuse; what he had intended to be a vault is instead a collapse to the stones under the ark, but yet he is able to move. He is able to move. He pulls himself falteringly to hands and knees, gasping, the rabbi mumbling in the background, the elders looking at him with shocked expressions, too astonished for the instant to move. The instant now is all that he needs. He has not precipitated what he has done in the hope of having a great deal of time.

"Look at me!" Leviticus shrieks, struggling erect, hands banging, head shaking. "Look at me, look at what I've become, look at what dwells in the heart of the ark!" And indeed, they are looking all of them, the entire congregation, Stala in the women's section, and to face, palm open, extended, all of them stunned in the light of his gaze. "Look at me!" he shouts again. "You can't do this to people, do you understand that? You cannot do it!" And the elders come upon him, recovered from their astonishment, to seize him with hands like metal, the rabbi rolling and rolling on the floor, deep into some chant that Leviticus cannot interpret, the congregation gathered now to rush upon him; but too late, it has (as he must at some level have known) been too late, from the beginning, and as the rabbi chants, the elders strain, the congregation rushes . . . time inverts, and the real, the long-expected, the true H with its true Host begins.

HORACE L. GOLD

Warm, Dark Places

Much of Jewish humor is astringent, angry, dark, sarcastic, and oftentimes the barbs are directed at the Jew himself. It is the Outsider's way of coping with and exorcising fear. Horace L. Gold's "Warm, Dark Places," written at top of Gold's form, is just such a story. It prompted John W. Campbell, the editor who ushered in what has become known as "the golden age of science fiction" to call it "the nastiest story I've ever read!" But when the story appeared in Campbell's Unknown, Gold was revolted and angered by the Edd Cartier illustration that accompanied it. Gold writes: "The caricature, straight out of Die Sturmer, kept me from offering it for reprint ever since—I was too bitterly ashamed to let anyone see it, Jew or Gentile."

I am happy to bring this story out of the dark. It is, in fact, the sequel to Gold's famous "Trouble with Water," which appeared in Wandering Stars. If you remember Greenberg the concessionaire who was cursed by a water gnome, you'll also remember the terrible (yet terribly logical) consequences that followed. Now, meet Kaplan the tailor, who is a bit too high-handed with an Eastern holyman. . . .

*

KAPLAN TRIED TO MAKE a gesture of impatience. It was impossible because his arms were piled high with clothing. He followed his wife's pointing finger and succeeded in shrugging contemptuously.

Clad in pathetic rags, the hairiest, dirtiest tramp in the world stood outside the plate-glass window of Kaplan's dry-cleaning store and eagerly watched the stubby, garment-laden figure as it waddled toward the bandbox cleaning vat.

"Him?" Kaplan echoed sarcastically. "A bum like him is going to drive us out of business? Do you mind if I am asking you what with, Mrs. Genius?"

"Like my mother told me," Mrs. Kaplan retorted angrily, "a book you can't tell by its covers. So, rags he's wearing and he's dirty, that means he can't have money? You don't read in the papers, I suppose. Blind beggars don't own apartment houses and chauffeurs, I suppose, and people on relief don't ride cars down to get their checks. Besides, such a feeling I get when I look at him—like when a mouse looks at a cat."

"*Pah!*" Kaplan broke in good-humoredly. "Some foolishness."

"All right, Mr. Einstein, he's standing out there with a pencil and paper because somewhere else he ain't got to go."

"You think maybe you're wrong?" Kaplan almost snapped testily. "No. He's going to the Ritz for supper and he stopped in while he should have his dress suit pressed! Molly, a whole year you been annoying me with this lazy, no-good loafer. Ain't I got enough on my head as it is?"

Molly pursed her lips and went back to sewing buttons on a dress that hung from a hook. With his arms still loaded, Kaplan clambered up on the window platform, where the bandbox vat stood. How he ever had the strength of character to refrain from fondling his beautiful machine, Kaplan never understood. It really was a lovely thing: red, black and chromium, a masterpiece of a dry-cleaning machine that attracted school children and summer residents.

In spite of his confident attitude, Kaplan felt less certain of himself now. The moment he had stepped on the platform, the tramp darted to the middle of the window.

Defiantly, Kaplan opened the door to the vat and tried to stuff in the garments without regard for scientific placement. They stuck, of course. Kaplan raised his head and glowered at the tramp, who craned and pressed his ugly, stubbled face against the polished glass, trying to peer into the open tank.

"Aha!" Kaplan muttered, when he saw his enemy's anxiety. "Now I got you!"

"Did you say something?" Molly asked ironically.

"No, no!" he said hastily. "So fat I'm getting—"

It was uncomfortable working in that position, but Kaplan shoved his slightly gross body between the opening and his audience. Straining from above and getting in his own way, he put the clothes in properly around the tumbler. Then he shut the door quickly and turned on the switch. The garments twirled slowly in the cleansing fluid.

Kaplan descended the stairs with an air of triumph.

That had happened every workday for a year, yet neither the little tailor nor his degraded foe had lost the original zest of the silent, bitter struggle. Once more Kaplan had defeated him! On his victory march back to the pressing machine, Kaplan allowed himself a final leer at the fallen.

But this time it was his face, not the tramp's, that slipped into anxiety. He stood trembling and watching his enemy's contented face, and fear lashed him.

The tramp was holding a large piece of brown grocery bag against the hitherto clean window with one hand. With the other he held a stump of pencil, which he used for checking unseen marks against whatever parts of the machine he could note from outside.

But what frightened Kaplan was his complacent satisfaction with his work. Usually he shook his head bewilderedly and wandered off, to reappear as eagerly at four thirty the next afternoon.

This time he didn't shake his head. He folded the dirty square of paper, stowed it away carefully in some hole in the lining of his miserable jacket, and strode—yes, *strode!*—away, nodding and grinning smugly.

Kaplan turned and looked unhappily at Molly. Luckily she was biting off a thread and had not noticed. If she hadn't been there, he knew he would have been useless. Now he had to put on a show of unconcern.

But his hands shook so violently that he banged down the iron almost hard enough to smash the machine, shot a vicious jet of steam through the suit, and the vacuum pedal, which dried the buck and garment, bent under the jab of his unsteady foot. He raised the iron and blindly walloped a crease in the pants.

Half an hour later, when Molly was arranging the garments for delivery, she let out a shriek:

"Ira! What are you doing—trying to ruin us by botch jobs?"

Kaplan groaned. He had started, properly enough, at the pleat near the waist; but a neat spiral crease ended at the side seam. If Molly had not caught the error, Mr. McElvoy, Cedarmere's dapper high-school principal, would have come raging into the store next day, wearing a pair of corkscrew pants.

"From morning to night," Kaplan moaned, "nothing but trouble! You and your foolishness—why can't I be rich and send you to Florida?"

"Oh, you want to get rid of me?" she shrilled. "Like a dog I work so we can save money, but you ain't satisfied! What more do you want—I should drive the truck?"

"It ain't a bad idea," he said wistfully. "How I hate to drive—"

He was almost quick enough to dodge the hanger. It was the first time he had ever regretted the imposing height of his bald, domelike head.

Bleary-eyed, Kaplan drove up to the store twenty-five minutes early. Sometime, late at night, Molly had fallen into an exhausted sleep. But his weary ear and intense worry had kept him awake until dawn. Then he got out of bed and dazedly made breakfast.

He remembered the last thing she had shrieked at him:

"Five bankruptcies we've had, and not a penny we made on any of them! So once in your life you get an idea, we should borrow money and buy a bandbox, we should move to a little town where there ain't competition. So what do you do? Bums you practically give your business to!"

There wasn't much literal truth in her accusation, yet Kaplan recognized its hyperbolic justice. By accepting the tramp as a tramp, merely because he wore dirty rags, Kaplan was encouraging some mysterious, unscrupulous conniving. just what it might be, he couldn't guess. But what if the tramp actually had money and was copying the bandbox machine so he could find out where to buy one—

"A fat lot people care, good work, bad work, as long as it's cheap," Kaplan mumbled unhappily. "Don't Mr. Goodwin, the cheap piker, ride fifteen miles to that faker, Aaron Gottlieb, because it's a quarter cheaper?"

Kaplan opened the door of the Ford delivery truck and stepped out. "The loafer," he mumbled, "he could buy a bandbox, open a store, and drive me right out of business. Family he ain't got, a nice house be don't need—he could clean and press for next to—"

Kaplan had been fishing in his pocket for the key. When he looked up, his muttering rose to a high wail of fright.

"*You!* What do you want here?"

Early as it was, the tramp squatted cross-legged on the chill sidewalk as if he had been waiting patiently for hours. Now he raised himself to his feet and bowed his head with flattering respect.

"The magnificence of the sun shines full upon you," he intoned in a deep, solemn voice. "I accept that as an omen of good fortune."

Kaplan fumbled with the lock, trying to keep his bulk between the store and the tramp. How he could keep out his unwelcome guest who seemed intent on entering, he had no idea. The tramp, however, folded his arms in dignity and waited without speaking further.

Unable to fumble convincingly any longer, Kaplan opened the door. It violated his entire conditioning, but he tried to close it on the tramp. Extremely agile, his visitor slipped through the narrow opening and stood quietly inside the store.

"All right, so you're in!" Kaplan cried in a shrill voice. "So now what?"

The unattractively fringed mouth opened. "I acknowledge your superior science," a low rumble stated.

"Hah?" was all Kaplan could extract from his flat vocal cords.

The tramp gazed longingly at the bandbox machine before he turned, slowly and enviously, to Kaplan.

"I have solved the mystery of the automobile, the train, the ship— yea, even the airplane. These do not befuddle me. They operate because of their imprisoned atoms, those infinitely small entities whom man has contrived to enslave. That one day they will revolt, I shall not argue."

Kaplan searched, but he could find no answer. How could he? The tramp spoke English of a sort. Individually most of the words made sense; together, they defied interpretation.

"Electric lights," the tramp went on, "are obviously dismembered parts of astral sheaths, which men torment in some manner to force them to assume an even more brilliant glow. This sacrilegious use of the holy aura I shall not denounce now. It is with your remarkably specialized bit of science that I am concerned."

"For science, it don't pay so good," Kaplan replied with a nervous attempt at humor.

"Your science is the most baffling, least useful in this accursed materialistic world. What is the point of deliberately cleansing one's outer garments while leaving one's soul clad in filth?"

To Kaplan, that gave away the game. Before that, the tramp had been mouthing gibberish. *This* was something Kaplan could understand.

"You wouldn't like to clean garments for people, I suppose?" he taunted slyly.

Evidently the tramp didn't hear Kaplan. He kept his eyes fixed on the bandbox and began walking toward it in a dazed way. Kaplan couldn't drive him away; despite his thinness, the tramp looked strong. Besides, he was within his legal rights.

"I have constructed many such devices in the year since I returned to the depraved land of my birth. In Tibet, the holy land of wisdom, I was known to men as Salindrinath, an earnest student. My American name I have forgotten."

"What are you getting at?" Kaplan demanded.

Salindrinath spoke almost to himself: "Within the maws of these machines, I placed such rags as I possess. I besought the atoms to cleanse for me as they cleanse for you. Lo! My rags came to me with dirt intact, and a bit of machinery grime to boot."

He wheeled on Kaplan.

"And why should they not?" he roared savagely. "What man does not know that atoms have powerful arms, but not fingers with which to pluck dirt from garments?"

As one actor judging the skill of another, Kaplan had to admit the tramp's superiority. How a man could so effectively hide the simple urge to make a profit, Kaplan envied without understanding. The tramp wore a look of incredibly painful yearning.

"Pity me! Long ago should I have gone to my next manifestation. I have accomplished all possible in this miserable skin; another life will bestow Nirvana upon me. Alone of all the occult, this senseless wizardry torments me. Give me your secret—"

Kaplan recoiled before the fury of the plea. But he was able to conceal his confusion by pretending to walk backward politely to the workshop.

"*Give* it to you? I got to make a living, too."

Beneath his outwardly cool exterior, Kaplan was desperately scared. What sort of strategy was this? When one man wants to buy out another, or drive him to the wall, he beats around the bush, of course. But he is also careful to drop hints and polite threats. This kind of idiocy, though! It didn't make sense. And that worried Kaplan more than if it had, for he knew the tramp was far from insane.

"Do you aspire to learn of me? Eagerly shall I teach you in return for your bit of useless knowledge! What say you?"

"Nuts," Kaplan informed him.

Salindrinath pondered this reply. "Then let my scientific training prove itself. Since you seem unwilling to explain—"

"Unwilling! Hah, if you only knew!"

"Mayhap you will consent to cleanse my sacred garments in my presence. Then shall I observe, without explanation. With a modicum of introspection, I can discover its principle. Yes?"

Kaplan picked up the heavy flat bat with which he banged creases into clothing. Its weight and utilitarian shape tempted him; the lawlessness of the crime appalled his kindly soul.

"What you got in mind?"

"Why, simply this—let me watch your machine cleanse my vestments."

Regretfully Kaplan put down his weapon. His soft red lips, he felt sure, were a thin white line of controlled rage.

"Ain't it enough you want to put me out of business? Must I give you a free dry cleaning too? Cleaning fluid costs money. If I cleaned your clothes, I couldn't clean a pair of overalls with it. Maybe you want me to speak plainer?"

"It was but a simple request."

"Some simple request! Listen to him— Even for ten dollars, I wouldn't put your rags in my bandbox!"

"What, pray, is your objection?" Salindrinath asked humbly.

"You can ask? Such filth I have never seen. Shame on you!"

Salindrinath gazed down at his tatters. "Filth? Nay, it is but honest earth. What holy man fears the embrace of sacred atoms?"

"Listen to him," Kaplan cried. "Jokes! You got atoms on you, you shameless slob, the same kind like on a pig—"

Now the ragged one recoiled. This he did with one grimy hand clutching at his heart.

"You dare!" he howled. "You compare my indifference to mere

external cleanliness with SWINE? Oh, profaner of all things sacred, dabbler in satanic arts—" He strangled into silence and goggled fiercely at Kaplan, who shrank back. "You think perhaps I am unclean?"

"Well, you ain't exactly spotless," Kaplan jabbered in fright.

"But that you should compare me with the swine, the gross material-ist of the mire!" Salindrinath stood trembling. "If you believe my vest-ments to be unclean, wait, bedraggler of my dignity. *Wait!* You shall discover the vestments of your cleanly, externally white and shining trade to be loathsome—loathsome and vile beyond words!"

"Some ain't so clean," Kaplan granted diplomatically.

The shabby one turned on his run-down heel and strode to the door.

"The garments of your respected customers will show you the *real* meaning of filth. And I shall return soon, when you are duly humbled!"

Kaplan shrugged at the furiously slammed door.

"A nut," he told himself reassuringly. "A regular lunatic."

But even that judicious pronouncement did not comfort him. He was too skilled in bargaining not to recognize the gambits that Salindrinath had shrewdly used—disparagement of the business, the attempt to wheedle information, the final threat. All were unusually cock-eyed, and thus a bit difficult for the amateur to discern, but Kaplan was not fooled so easily.

He sorted his work on the long receiving table. While waiting for the pressing machine to heat up, he began brushing trouser cuffs and sewing on loose or missing buttons.

Luckily Kaplan steamed out Mrs. Jackson's fall outfit first. That de-layed the shock only a few moments, but later he was to look back on those free minutes with cosmic longing.

He came to Mr. McElvoy's daily suit. Nobody could accuse the neat principal of anything but the most finicking immaculacy. Yet when Ka-plan got through stitching up a cuff and put his hand in a pocket to brush out the usual fluff—

"*Yeow!*" he yelled, snatching out his hand.

For a long while Kaplan stood shuddering, his fingers cold with re-vulsion. Then, cautiously, he ran his hand over the outside of the pocket. He felt only the flat shape of the lining.

"Am I maybe going out of my mind?" he muttered. "Believe me, with everything on my shoulders, and that nut besides, it wouldn't surprise me."

Slowly he inserted the tips of his fingers into the pocket. Almost instantly something globular and clammily smooth crept into the palm of his furtively exploring hand.

Kaplan shouted in disgust, but he wouldn't let go. Clutching the monstrosity was like holding a round, affectionate oyster that kept trying to snuggle deeper into his palm. Kaplan wouldn't free it, though. Grimly he yanked his hand out.

Somehow it must have sensed his purpose. Before he could snatch it out of its refuge, the cold, clammy thing *squeezed* between his fingers with a repulsively fierce effort—

Kaplan determinedly kept fumbling around after it, until his mind began working again. He hadn't felt any head on it, but that didn't mean it couldn't have teeth somewhere in its apparently featureless body. How could it eat without a mouth? So the little tailor stopped daring the disgusting beast to bite him.

He stood still for a moment, gaping down at his hand. Though it was empty, he still felt a sensation of damp coldness. From his hand he stared back to Mr. McElvoy's suit. The pockets were perfectly flat. He couldn't detect a single bulge.

The idea nauseated him, but he forced himself to explore all the pockets.

"Somebody," he whispered savagely when he finished, "is all of a sudden a wise guy—only he ain't so funny."

He stalked, rather waddlingly, to the telephone, ripped the receiver off the hook, barked a number at the operator. Above the *burr* of the bell at the other end he could hear the gulp of his own angry swallowing.

"Hello," a husky feminine voice replied. "Is that you, darling?"

"Mrs. McElvoy?" he rasped, much too loudly.

The feminine voice changed, grew defensive. "Well?"

"This is Kaplan the tailor. Mrs. McElvoy"—his rasp swelled to a violent shout—"such a rotten joke I have never seen in eighteen years I been in this business. What am I—a dope your husband should try funny stuff on?" The words began running together. "Listen, maybe I ain't classy like you, but I got pride also. So what if I work for a living? Ain't I—"

"Whatever are you talking about?" Mrs. McElvoy asked puzzledly.

"Your husband's pants, that's what! Such things he's got in his pockets, I wouldn't be seen dead with them!"

"Mr. McElvoy has his suits cleaned after wearing them only once," she retorted frigidly.

"So, does that mean he can't keep dirty things in his pockets?"

"I'm sorry you don't care to have our trade," Mrs. McElvoy said, obviously trying to control her anger. "Mr. Gottlieb has offered to call for them every morning. He's also twenty-five cents cheaper. Good day!"

In reply to the bang that hurt his ear, Kaplan slammed down the receiver. The moment he turned to march off, the bell jangled. Viciously he grabbed up the receiver.

"Hello . . . darling?" a deep feminine voice asked.

"Mrs. McElvoy?" he roared.

For several seconds he listened to a strained, bitter silence. Then:

"IRA!" his wife shrilled in outrage.

He hung up hastily and, trembling, he went back to his pressing machine.

"Will I get it now," he moaned. "Everything happens to me. If I don't starve for once, so all kinds of trouble flops in my lap. First I lose my best customer—I should only have a thousand like him, I'd be on easy street—and then I make a little mistake. But go try to tell Molly I made a mistake. Married twenty years, and she acts like I was a regular lady-killer—"

Kaplan's pressing production rose abruptly from four suits an hour to nine. But that was because no cuffs were brushed, no pockets turned inside out, no buttons stitched or replaced. He banged down the iron, slashed the suits with steam, vacuumed them hastily, batted the creases, which had to be straight the first time or not at all. He knew there would be kicks all that week, but he couldn't do anything about it.

The door opened. Kaplan raised a white face. It wasn't his wife, though. Fraulein, Mrs. Sampter's refugee maid, clumped over to him and shoved a pair of pants in his hands.

"Goot morgen," she said pleasantly. "Herr Sompter he vants zhe pockets new. You make soon, no?"

Kaplan nodded dumbly. Without thinking of the consequences, he stuffed his hand in the pocket to note the extent of the damage.

"Eee—YOW!" he howled. "What kind of customers have I got all of a sudden? Take it away, Fraulein! With crazy people I don't want to deal!"

Fraulein's broad face wrinkled bewilderedly. She took back the pants and ran her hands through the pockets.

"Crazy people—us? Maybe you haf got zhe temperature?"

"Such things in pockets! Phooey on practical jokers! Go away—"

"You just vait till Mrs. Sompter about this hears." And stuffing the pants under her arm, Fraulein marched out angrily.

Despite his revulsion, it took Kaplan only a few moments to grow suspicious. One previously dignified customer might suddenly have become a practical joker, but not two. Something scared him even more than that. Fraulein had put her hands in the pockets! Apparently she had not felt anything at all.

"Who's crazy?" Kaplan whispered frightenedly. "Me or them?"

Warily he approached the worktable. Mr. McElvoy was neat, but Mr. Rich was such a bug on cleanliness that even his dirty suits were immaculate, and his pockets never contained lint. That was the suit Kaplan edged up to.

The instant Molly opened the door she began shrieking.

"You loafer! You no-good masher! I call up to tell you I don't feel good, so maybe I won't have to work today. 'Hello, darling,' I say, so who else could it be but your own wife? No—it's Mrs. McElvoy!"

Despite her red-eyed glare, she seemed to recognize a subtle change in him. His plump face was grave and withdrawn, hardened in the fire of spiritual conflict. Instead of claiming it was a mistake, which she had been expecting and would have pounced on, he merely turned back to his pressing machine.

She got panicky. "Ira! Ain't you going to even say you weren't thinking? Don't tell me you . . . you *love* Mrs. McElvoy—"

"You know I don't, Molly," he replied quietly, without looking up.

Slowly she took her fists off her hips and unstraddled her firmly planted feet. She knew she was helpless against his passive resistance.

"Ira, I don't feel so good. Is it all right if I don't work?"

"I'll get along somehow," he said gently. "Stay home till you feel better, darling. I'll manage."

For several minutes she watched him work. He had a new method of brushing pockets. Although she realized it was new to him, he appeared to have it pat. He pulled the pockets inside out with a hooked wire, brushed them, stuffed them back with a stick of clean wood.

"Ain't it easier to do it by hand?" she asked helpfully.

When he shook his head abstractedly, she shrugged, kissed him uncomfortably, and walked hesitantly toward the door. She paused there.

"You sure *you* feel all right, Ira? You won't need me?"

"I'll get by, sweetheart. Don't you worry about me."

He displayed no sign of relief when she left, for he felt none. He had connected the hideous things in his customers' pockets with the tramp's threat. Somehow Salindrinath had managed to put them there, and neutralizing their effect on him had been Kaplan's problem. The hooked wire and the stick solved it. Therefore he no longer had a problem. He had observed that when the pockets were turned out, the small globes vanished. Where they went, he had no idea, but that wasn't important.

He locked the store at ten thirty to make his calls, and again at twelve, when he went home for lunch and to see how Molly felt. She was in bed, outwardly looking fine, but so baffled by his changed character that her slight headache had become hysterically monumental.

He went back to work. Now that he had cleverly, sidestepped the tramp's strategy, nothing delayed or upset the care or tempo of his work. Twice he forgot and put his hand in breast pockets to straighten the lining. The sensation nauseated him, but he merely snatched out his hand and continued working with his new method.

At four thirty he gathered the garments to be dry cleaned.

"Now the bum'll come around so he can make fun," Kaplan stated doggedly. "Will he be surprised!"

Halfway to the bandbox machine, he heard the door click. Glancing casually at Salindrinath, Kaplain walked on. The tramp closed the door and folded his arms regally.

"Fool," he said in a cold tone, "do you bow to my wish to know?"

The triumphant leer broke out against Kaplan's will. "You think maybe you got me scared, you pig?" he blurted, now that the leer had involuntarily started him off wrong. "How much it scares me don't amount to a row of beans! You and your things in pockets—phooey!"

Salindrinath drew back. His regal, stubbled face slid into a gape of amazement.

"Yeah, you and your things don't bother me," Kaplan pursued, his mocking grin broader than before. "You can all go to hell!"

"Pig? Hell?" Salindrinath's ugly black jaw stuck out viciously. "Do you condemn me to your miserable, unimaginative hell? Know then, swine of a materialist, that my dwellers in dark places are the height of torment to money-grubbers. They shall roost where they dismay you most! When you cringe and beg of me to share your pitiful science, crawl to my holy shack at the landing on the creek—"

Kaplan stuffed the garments into the bandbox and thumbed his nose at the ragged figure striding savagely away from the store.

"A fine case he's got!" he gloated. "I'll come crawling to him when Hitler kicks out the Germans and takes back the Jews. Not before. Do I annoy anybody? If I can work hard and make a living, that's all I ask. He wants to buy a bandbox and open a store here? So let him. But why should I have to tell him how to run me out of business? What some people won't do when they see a business that's making a little money!" He shook his head sadly.

Kaplan closed the bandbox door, turned the switch, and climbed down from the window platform. Just when he sat down at the sewing machine, Miss Robinson, the nice young kindergarten teacher, came in.

"Hello, Mr. Kaplan," she sang with a smile. "Isn't it the loveliest day? Not too cold, though you can feel winter coming on, and it makes you want to take long brisk walks. Isn't it grand having our little town all to ourselves again? But I suppose it's better for you when the summer visitors are here—"

"How much difference can it make?" He shrugged indifferently. "In the summer I work hard like a horse so I can take it easy in the winter and get strong to work like a horse in the summer. If I got enough to eat and pay my bills, that's all I ask."

"I suppose that's all anyone really wants," she agreed eagerly. "Is my suit ready? I feel so chilly in these silk dresses—"

"It's been ready for two days. I made it quick so you wouldn't go around catching colds. Like new it looks, Miss Robinson. For my nicest customers I can do a better job than anybody else."

He took down her suit and pinned it into a bag so she could carry it easily.

"You certainly do," she enthused. "I'll pay you now. You probably can use the money, with all your summer trade gone."

"Whenever you want. People like you don't stick poor tailors."

He took the five-dollar bill she handed him and fumbled in his pocket for change.

"Mr. Kaplan!" she cried, staring anxiously at his goggling face. "Don't you feel well?"

"Ain't I a dope?" he laughed unconvincingly. "Needles I put in my pocket, I get so flustered when pretty girls come in—"

But he had whipped out his hand with such violence that the entire contents of his pocket spilled out on the floor. For some reason this seemed to please him. He stooped ponderously, picked up everything, and counted change into her hand.

She smiled, quite flattered, and left.

But the moment the door closed behind her, Kaplan's weak grin soured. He hadn't pushed his pocket lining back yet. Instead, he patted the outside of his clothes, as if he were frisking himself.

"What have I got now?" he breathed incredulously, inching the fingers of his left hand into his jacket pocket.

He touched something round, hairless and warm, that skittered from his fingertips and dug irritably against his thigh. And there it pulsed against his skin, beating like a disembodied heart—

Thurston, the Seids' chauffeur, came in and picked up everything the family had there. Kaplan didn't mind, for it saved him a five-mile trip. But the chauffeur insisted on paying.

Kaplan reached toward his pocket for change. Abruptly he stopped and let his hand dangle limply. As if telepathic, all the vermin in his pockets had lunged around wildly, to avoid his touch.

"Couldn't you pay later?" he begged. "Does it have to be right now?"

"The madame instructed me to pay," Thurston replied distantly.

Kaplan sighed and looked down at his pocket wistfully, until he remembered that he had put his money on the pressing-machine table. And that, of course, took care of this particular problem.

But Mrs. Ringer, Miss Tracy, young Fox, Mrs. Redstone, and Mr. Davis, who had got off early—all came for their work, and all wanted to pay.

"What is this—a plot?" he muttered. "They must think I'm out of my head, keeping money on a table instead of in my pocket. Can I go on like this? And you, you things, you! Do you *have* to beat like that? Can't you lay quiet and not bother me?"

But he could feel them burrowing restlessly or pulsing contentedly against his skin. Kaplan grew anxious. He couldn't feel them from the outside. Inside, though, they certainly existed, moving around like mice, pulsing like naked, detached hearts.

"It's just this suit," he said. "After all, how many suits can the dirty crook fill with these things?"

He grabbed up an old pair of pants he kept around as a dry change in wet weather. Before putting it on, he tentatively explored a pocket.

A warm ball, furred like a headless, wingless, unutterably loathsome bat, crept affectionately into his palm and pulsed there, clearly enjoying the warmth of his hand. He gritted his teeth and tried to haul it out. It slipped frenziedly through his fingers.

Though it was almost time to make his deliveries, Kaplan locked the store and shopped for a bus driver's change machine. He couldn't find one in the village, of course. Nor would it have taken care of bills, anyhow.

Kaplan loaded the truck and began his rounds. Not everybody tried to pay. It only seemed like that. Eventually, he hoped, his customers might get used to seeing him with all his money clutched tightly in his hand. He knew they wouldn't.

And that only solved the money question, though it certainly would encourage robbers. Now if he could only find a place to keep his hand-kerchiefs, cigarettes, matches, keys, letters, toothpicks—

Dazed and exhausted, Kaplan drove into the garage at home. He shut off the motor, removed the key, turned out the lights, and closed the doors. When he went to lock the small side door, he had to turn his pockets inside out with the hooked wire and pick the key out of everything that fell on the ground.

Molly had staggered out of bed and was moving gingerly around the kitchen, careful not to jolt her head into aching again. Kaplan put all his money, keys, cigarettes, and matches on the end table in the living room. He kept his arms stiffly away from his body. He knew that the slightest touch would send the vermin scuttling around in his pockets—

Washing his hands meticulously with sandsoap, he couldn't bear the sight of his face in the mirror. One glance had been more than enough. He had seen a scared, white blur—Molly, he knew, was certain to note his expression and ask embarrassing questions.

"I thought *I* looked bad," she said when he flopped limply into his chair. "Boy, do you look terrible! What is it, Ira?"

"What isn't it?" he grumbled. "Everybody—"

He broke off. He had suddenly realized how it would sound to complain that all his customers insisted on paying.

Almost immediately after eating, he felt like going to bed. He had not slept the night before; the newspaper was boring; his favorite radio comedian sounded like an undertaker who had just heard a good one.

"So soon?" Molly asked anxiously as he yawned with intellectual deliberation and stood up. "Ira, if you're sick, why don't you—"

"Doctors!" he snarled. "What can they do for me?"

But his false yawn had made her mouth gape, and that, of course, was catching. His next was considerably better, for it was real.

"Can I help it if I'm tired?" he asked. "It wouldn't hurt you to get some sleep either."

He stumbled off to bed.

When Molly came in, she had to cover him. He tried not to fling off the blankets, and the effort was killing. Hundreds of pulsing vermin had instantly snuggled against him when he was covered. With blind, repulsive hunger for his warmth, they burrowed and beat against his skin, until he slid the blanket off and lay shivering in the cold.

"Ira," she whispered. "Do you want to catch pneumonia? Keep covered."

He pretended to be asleep. But Kaplan was not fated to sleep anymore, though he inched the blanket off again. The second he heard her breathing regularly, he sneaked into the bathroom and cut off the pocket of his pajama jacket.

Back in bed again, he was much too cold to sleep. So he dressed silently and went downstairs. He picked up his keys from the end table and went out to the car.

Riding through the deserted streets toward the creek, he felt dangerously near tears. His pride had never been so battered—nor had he ever before done what he was now about to do.

"It's like taking the bread out of my mouth and giving it to him," Kaplan moaned, "but what else can I do? Already people think I'm crazy, walking around with everything in my hands like a regular school kid. If people don't respect me, so my business goes bust anyhow. It's the same thing if I lose my customers or they go to somebody else."

He stopped at the shack near the landing on the creek. After only a moment of hesitation, he knocked tentatively at the door.

"Enter, tailor!" a deep, majestic voice called out.

Kaplan didn't wonder or care how the tramp had known he was there. He threw open the door and sneaked in miserably.

"All right," he said defeatedly to the ragged figure squatting on the floor. "I'll tell you anything you want to know, only get these things out of my pockets."

The tramp stared up at Kaplan, and his ugly, stubbled face looked far more unhappy than the tailor's.

"You come too late," he moaned. "My quest for knowledge forced me to injure a living being. I am now"—his head drooped—"no longer a yogin. I have been stripped of my powers. You must live with the curse

I placed upon you, for I cannot help you now. Please forgive me! That can lighten my punishment—"

"Forgive you?" Kaplan wheezed. "First you try to drive me out of business. Then you stick me with these . . . these things that are almost as filthy as you are. And now you can't help me. You can go to hell."

He ran out so quickly that he didn't observe the tramp's sudden vanishing. Raving with rage, he raced home and left the car at the curb. He undressed swiftly, but when he approached the bed, he did so with the utmost caution.

He climbed aboard gingerly, careful not to wake his wife, and slid under the covers. Instantly he flung them off.

"Everything else ain't bad enough," he groaned. "No, like an animal I got to sleep uncovered!"

As he had done the night before, he lay awake until the sky lightened. By that time he felt sure he had worked out a solution.

"If I can do it with pajamas," he breathed hopefully, "is there any reason it shouldn't happen with regular clothes?"

And getting up noiselessly, Kaplan gathered his things and carried them to the bathroom. He took a pair of scissors out of the medicine chest. This time, when he closed the mirror door, the glimpse of his face pleased him. He stopped to examine it. Triumph glinted from the warm, brown eyes, and his soft, gentle mouth was curved in a real smile.

"You got him licked, Ira Kaplan!" he whispered. "You ain't altogether a dope—"

Working with the speed of skill, he ripped out all the pockets of his suit. To make absolutely certain, though, he also tore away the linings of his jacket and vest.

Still wearing his pajamas in the kitchen, he squeezed orange juice, made coffee, and ate breakfast. For the first time in two days he actually felt hungry. He stuffed away half a dozen cream-cheese and smoked-salmon sandwiches on bagels and drank another cup of coffee.

"Already I feel like another man," he declared. "Now all I got to do is get dressed and go to work. Molly can carry the money and letters. Cigarettes and matches? *Pooh,* that's easy! I'll just keep a pack in the car, one in the store, another at home. Nothing to it!"

He dressed slowly, enjoying the sensation for he knew that he no longer would feel the revolting creatures pulsing, crawling, moving around like mice against his skin—

"*Heh!*" he cackled. "Is Ira Kaplan smart or ain't he?"

Standing on his bare feet, he tied his tie, then patted the places where his pockets used to be. He even dared to put a hand inside. And of course he felt nothing—absolutely nothing that might snuggle lovingly into his palm or scuttle hideously from his fingers.

"Licked!" he gloated. "Is that tramp licked or ain't he licked?"

He put on his shoes swiftly, slipped into his jacket and topcoat, clapped his hat on his bald head. He strode to the door.

"*Molly!*" he screamed.

His feet shrank from warm, pulsing vermin that nestled cozily in the toe of each shoe. Under his hat, a clammily cold, pulsing thing crawled furiously, struggling to escape the warmth of his hairless scalp—and they squirmed around in his armpits and crotch . . .

MEL GILDEN

A *Lamed Wufnik*

A Lamed Wufnik *(or* Vufnik*) is a blessed man, one of the chosen thirty-six who make it worthwhile for God to let humankind go on.* Lamed *and* Vuf *are Hebrew letters; as Hebrew letters also have corresponding numerical values,* Lamed *and* Vuf *spell "Thirty-six." Such numerical conversion is the basis for the occult art of* Gematria. *It was through the use of* Gematria *that ancient scholars hoped to determine precisely when the Messiah would arrive. They would pour over the Torah, searching for new meanings revealed through numerical relationships.*

Certain Jews still hold to the belief that a body of thirty-six chosen men exist, and have always existed. Legend has it that when the Messiah arrives, the Lamed Wufniks *will simultaneously and independently recognize him. Thus will all Jews be certain that he is the true Messiah.*

To be a Wufnik *is to be promised heaven.*

Unfortunately, Wufniks *are always poor, especially Sol Gosnik of Los Angeles, California. . . .*

*

A FEW HOURS AFTER Mottle Hamana had a heart attack, he died on a
bed of rags in his hovel in Estonia, a country that lately had fallen into
the hands of the Russians. No one was in attendance but God. The
death of a dog would have caused more comment than the death of
Mottle Hamana. He was forgotten almost before he was buried.

At the moment Mottle Hamana died, Sol Gosnik, asleep in his bed in
Los Angeles, California, waved his arms at phantom invaders caused by
too late a dinner, and mumbling curses and threats, he turned over and
crushed his face into his pillow.

When he awoke the next morning, the smell of strong tea already
filled the apartment. His eyes blinked open and he saw his wife, Sylvia,
standing at the door to their bedroom. "Nu, Sol, you going to sleep all
day like the Czar?"

"I'll be up in a minute. Look how my foot moves with enthusiasm underneath the covers."

"Hurray for your foot. Your oatmeal will get cold." Sylvia—depend-
able, hard-working, ample, Sylvia—turned and walked back down the
short hallway to the square box of a kitchen where she rattled pots,
pans, and dishes on purpose to keep her husband from falling back
asleep.

Sol Gosnik threw back the covers and felt the cold seep into his legs.
It would stay there all day long, until he pulled the covers back over
himself that night. The doctor said it was bad circulation and a man his
age should take it easy.

Sol had told him, "So, Mr. Doctor, you're a pretty smart man. You tell
me how I'm going to feed my own mouth and the mouth of my Sylvia
if I don't work. God is going to make it rain nickels, maybe?"

"Surely there must be a pension plan of sorts where you work."

"Of course. What would Mortimer's Distinctive Fashions be without
a pension plan? But I don't get it for another two years."

"You're only sixty-three. That's right. I'd forgotten."

"Mr. Mortimer don't forget."

The doctor had given Sol some pills. They were samples given to the doctor by the drug distributor and so Sol got them for nothing. Sol took one every morning for months; as far as he was concerned, the pills were worth what they cost him.

Sol got out of bed and put on his clothes. He listened to the boards creak as he crossed the wooden floor to the bathroom and felt for the string in the dark. He pulled it, and the room suddenly assaulted him with harsh white light reflected from every glass and tile surface. The mirror above the sink showed him for what he was: a moderately old human being just waking up and caught with his hand raised to turn on the light.

He looked at himself, revealed thus, and saw a man with the gray grit of a day's worth of beard on his thin face, a man who looked much older than sixty-three. He smiled bleakly, telling himself it was all right. Someday he would be as old as he looked. He washed and shaved, and walked along the gray hallway to the kitchen. Sylvia was sitting at the Formica-topped table reading the *Forward* from the day before.

"So, what's new?"

"New," Sylvia said, "is what's new. The Arabs—they should only have a pyramid fall over on them—are at it again. Sit down. Eat. The bus won t wait."

"There'll be another bus."

"Look who's suddenly Mr. Leisure World." She dished up the oatmeal and gave it to him. He poured a little milk on it.

Sylvia said, "Did you take your pill?"

"For all the good it does me."

Sol ate a little oatmeal. It was warm and sweet and made him feel better. It was almost as if his icy legs belonged to someone else. He said, "Sylvia, how old do I look?"

"A day older than you did yesterday."

"No. I mean, do I look sixty-three?"

"You've been looking in the mirror again."

"It's either that or cut myself when I shave."

"Sol, Sol, Sol." She put her hand on his. "Stop looking and figuring and just live."

"You call this living?"

"Who are you feeling sorry for? Yourself? I'm all right."

"You should've had better."

"You want I should be the Queen of Sheba?"

"I don't know." He put the spoon down.

"Finish."

"I don't want any more."

"A real wufnik."

"Sylvia, please."

"And even if you are a wufnik, you can share the problems of the world with thirty-five other men."

"Is my lunch ready?"

"In forty years has it ever not been ready?"

Sol admitted that there was no time when the lunch had failed to appear in its brown bag as promised. He kissed Sylvia—a peck on the cheek—and walked downstairs to the street.

The sun was just above the horizon, and Fairfax Avenue looked new. He walked by a bakery and smelled the warm velvety aroma of fresh bagels. Like the bakery, other small shops selling kosher meat and fish, and prayer books, and candy, and corsets were all closed until more respectable hours. Even the big delicatessen, Cantor's—which never closed—had only a smattering of people in it. The pale sunlight of dawn rounded off corners, smoothed over cracks, and brought out colors. If Sol Gosnik's legs hadn't been hurting him, he could have been content. For when did a rich man who gets up in the middle of the afternoon ever get to enjoy the cool quiet sensations of Fairfax Avenue in the morning?

While Sol was waiting for his bus, a moving van went up the street. His bus came at last and he got on. Fairfax bus to Wilshire. Wilshire bus downtown.

It was almost nine o'clock by the time he got to Mortimer's Distinctive Fashions, a two-story stucco building, now a faded green, which stood between a hot dog stand and a pay-by-the-hour parking lot. Downstairs were the offices and the shipping department. Upstairs were the cutting rooms and the long lines of sewing machines. This was where Sol Gosnik labored all day. He was a first-class tailor. In the old country he was going to be a rabbi, but he discovered that in Depression America being a tailor paid better. And after all, he had to live, no?

Sol went in through the double glass doors and said "hello" to Marian the receptionist, a pretty black girl Mr. Mortimer had hired to keep peace with some of the social-action groups that roamed the city looking for racial injustice.

Marian said, "Oh, Sol, Mr. Mortimer wants to see you."

"About what?"

"He didn't say."

Sol nodded and walked down the hallway and knocked on Mr. Mortimer's door.

"Come in."

Sol went in and stood with his hat in hand with his lunch. Mr. Mortimer's secretary smiled at him. It was a strange kind of smile, sorry and commiserating, full of some meaning Sol couldn't understand just yet. Sol, standing there in his jacket and muffler, suddenly felt warm. He unbuttoned his jacket and let the muffler hang loose.

"Good morning, Sol, come in. Would you like some coffee?"

"No, thank you, Mr. Mortimer. It gives me heartburn."

Coffee, he's offering me, Sol thought. This is some kind of big deal.

"Sit down, Sol."

"Thank you, sir."

"Sol, you've been with me a long time, haven't you?"

"About ten years."

"And in all that time, we've gotten along very well. I treat my employees like people. You've always recognized this and done right by me too."

"I do my best."

"I know you do, Sol, and that's why this is so difficult."

"You have a problem?"

Mr. Mortimer took a long drag on his coffee, put it down and looked past Sol at his secretary. He looked at Sol again and said, "You know business hasn't been very good lately."

"The whole country's a mess. I heard it on the news."

"That's right, Sol. That's right." He drank some more coffee. "We've all got to tighten our belts." He waited.

Sol said, "Is there a point here somewhere that I'm missing, Mr. Mortimer?"

"I'm going to have to lay off a few people."

Sol waited for Mr. Mortimer to say more.

"I'm not firing you, Sol. I'll write you a letter of recommendation. But I just can't afford to keep you on."

"For this I got up at 5:30 in the morning?"

"I wanted to tell you in person."

"So. You're a big humanitarian. You tell me in person you're kicking me out into the street."

"You'll be paid to the end of the week."

"And my pension?"

"I'm afraid that's out of the question."

"Ten years is forgotten so fast?"

"I'm sorry."

"If I could afford it, Mr. Mortimer, I'd make you a bet I'm sorrier than you are."

Mr. Mortimer came around his desk and solemnly shook hands with Sol, only the second time they'd done so. The first time was when Mr. Mortimer had hired him ten years before. The secretary smiled at Sol. He waved without energy and left. He went down the hall to the payroll office.

While Sol waited for Annie the clerk to make out the check, he thought about what his wife had said that morning about being a wufnik. It was an old joke between them. It meant nothing, Sol told himself. Out loud he said, "A real wufnik."

"What's that?" Annie said.

Sol repeated himself.

"What's a wufnik?"

"A lamed wufnik," Sol said. "He's a man—one of only thirty-six—who justifies the existence of everybody on this planet."

"You mean like a lawyer?"

"No. Nothing like a lawyer. He's a righteous man who makes it worthwhile for God to let mankind go on. One of thirty-six excuses. They're always righteous, always ignorant of their stature in the scheme of things, and always poor." He shook his head. "Sol Gosnik, the lamed wufnik."

"That's tough," Annie said, "getting fired like this."

Sol raised a finger in the air. "Not fired. Laid off." He shrugged. "You're just as hungry either way."

"Here's your check."

"Thanks."

"You'll find another job."

"Who's going to hire a man my age?"

On his way out, Sol shook his fist at Mr. Mortimer's door, hurled a curse that moths should eat his distinctive fashions off their hangers, and left.

There was excitement when he got home. A moving van was in front of the building, and men were running every-which-way unloading.

The furniture, though plain, was heavy and of good quality. A dark Semitic man watched the progress from one side.

"Good morning, Gosnik," the man said as Sol went by.

"Good morning." Sol hustled past. How had the man known his
name? Did he know him? He turned to study the man as furniture
went by, and he found the odd dark man looking at him. Sol nodded
and hurried upstairs.

From above he heard a woman shouting, giving directions to the
movers. "No, not there, you fool! Over in the corner. Be careful, klutz,
that's an antique!" An unpleasant sort of woman. Sol had never heard
her before. She was probably the wife of the man downstairs.

Sol followed the procession of chairs, beds, bureaus, and tables up
the stairs until he came to his apartment. The furniture was going into
the empty apartment next door. "Meshugana!" the woman cried at one
of the moving men.

Sol let himself in. Shouts and pounding came from the next apartment through the common wall in the kitchen. "Sylvia?" Sol called.

Sol looked through the whole place, through the whole four rooms,
and she wasn't there. She had probably gone shopping. Sol put his un-
eaten lunch in the refrigerator, fixed himself a glass of tea, and sat
down at the kitchen table to wait for her to come back.

When Sylvia got home, Sol was in their bedroom sitting on the edge
of the bed. "You're home early," she said.

"I'm home permanently."

"Permanently?"

"Mr. Mortimer laid me off."

"He lets go a man like you? What kind of a crazy is he?"

"He says he can't afford me."

Sylvia took off her heavy black coat. Sol was glad she had it, and also
glad he'd paid cash for it. If there had been payments to make, he
wouldn't be able to make them now.

"So, it's a blessing. We can sleep a little later in the morning."

"And how are we going to eat?"

"We'll think of something. Wait." She went to the closet to hang up
her coat. "I have an idea already."

Sol waited for the idea.

Sylvia dragged something out from behind the clothes in the closet.
"Look what I got here."

"My old sewing machine."

"Congratulations."

"Nu?"

"Nu. What nu? You don't see it?"

"I don't see what?"

"You can go into business for yourself."

Sol thought it over for a moment. He was in no mood for consolation or bright ideas. He wanted to enjoy his torment in peace. He said, "Sylvia, my darling dummy, to go into business I need three things. For one, I need a tailor. For two, I need a sewing machine. Those I got."

"You got. Nu shane?"

"I need also customers."

"Customers will come."

"How? By magic?"

"Put an ad in the paper."

"With what?"

"We got a little money saved."

"Which we got to eat on."

Sylvia threw up her hands and strode into the kitchen. "All right," she said above the racket coming from the next apartment, "you're determined to sit there like a martyr, go ahead. I got groceries to put away—"

A few minutes later Sol followed her. He sat down at the kitchen table. "What's going on next door? A moving-in or the end of the world?"

"When they're settled they'll be quiet."

"Could be."

Sylvia put a package of frozen lima beans into the freezer. "Klutz-kashe!" the lady next door yelled. "A real circus," Sylvia said.

Sol waited a moment. He said, "I've been thinking about me and the lamed wufniks."

"Good, Mr. Gosnik. Think. So far it's free."

"You're going to be Jack Benny, I'll be quiet."

"I'm just kidding. Go ahead. Talk."

"I've been thinking maybe I am one."

Sylvia put a hand to his forehead. "A temperature you haven't got."

"You think it's not possible?"

"Listen, Soly, there are a lot of poor men in the world. There are even a lot of righteous poor men. But there are only thirty-six lamed wufniks. What are your chances?"

"Not good, it sounds like."

"And even if I really believed there are such things—which, by the way, I don't—I hope you would have the good grace not to. If you believe and you're right, according to the rules, you die."

"Maybe it's not such a bad deal."

"You going to leave me all alone? Who am I going to holler on?"

"I'm just talking, Sylvia. Nothing but talk."

With Sylvia's help, Sol figured out what he would say in his newspaper ad. He wrote it in English and would put it in *The Reporter,* the local throwaway paper. "If they read *The Forward,*" Sylvia had said, "they don't have any money."

Sol walked downstairs. Despite all efforts to the contrary, he felt better than he had when he came home. He carried the ad in his pocket like a key to a new life. He whistled a melody from the Old Country he hadn't even thought about in years.

Out on the sidewalk, the dark man was talking to the movers. Without glancing at them, Sol walked down the street to Fairfax Avenue, where he would place the ad in the *Reporter* office.

He heard running behind him. "Gosnik, Gosnik!" a voice called. Sol turned and the dark man came up beside him. He said, "Mind if I walk with you?"

"It's a free country," Sol said.

They walked for a while without saying anything. The neighborhood was quiet because it was a weekday and the kids were in school. The man made Sol nervous, he couldn't say why. Perhaps it was because the man made little smiles every so often for no apparent reason, as if he were remembering a small private joke.

At last Sol said, "It's a nice neighborhood, no?"

"If you can afford to live here."

Now that was a strange reaction. Did Sol look so poverty-stricken already? Had his clothing become threadbare just since he was fired? He said, "It's cheap enough."

"If you have a job."

"What's all this about jobs?"

"I heard you upstairs in the kitchen."

"Ah. And while we're on the subject of who knows what, how did you know my name?"

"I heard it mentioned."

"Where?"

"When I came to look at the apartment. The landlord pointed out that you would be my next-door neighbor."

"Ah." They walked. That explained a lot, Sol thought. Maybe the fellow wasn't so sinister after all. They walked past the newsstand, nearly a block long, run by a man almost everybody called behind his back, "The Weasel." Sol felt an urgency about getting to the newspaper office, and he did not stop and browse among the paperback books the way he usually did. Sol and the dark man turned a corner.

"So, you think you're a wufnik, eh?" the man said.

Sol looked at him, his eyes wide with surprise. Then he remembered the thin kitchen wall. He said, "I don't know how you could hear all that with so much moving-in noise."

"What a mouth my Lili has. Vocal cords like a mule."

"A strong woman is good to have. Like my Sylvia."

"There's good, and there's good," the man said.

"That's true."

They stopped for a red light. When the light turned green and they started walking again, the man said, "Why did you think you're a wufnik?"

"Why not? It's an honorable profession."

"It doesn't pay well."

"Money isn't everything."

"You can't eat honor."

"And money won't get me into heaven. So nu?"

The man laughed. Perhaps he thought, like Sol, it was pleasant to joust with a man who had a quick tongue.

The man said, "Suppose I could tell you I knew for sure you were a wufnik—one of the thirty-six blessed men."

"I would say you were crazy. No one knows such things but God."

"Word slips out."

"You're talking meshugaas."

"So. It can't hurt to talk."

They came to the *Reporter* office, and Sol ran inside with a promise he would be right back. The dark man waited outside, staring at him through the plate glass window with the yellow plastic shade behind it. Sol did his business and came out. He said, "They say it'll be in next week's paper. They say an ad like that ought to bring in a lot of customers."

"Don't count on it. A wufnik must be poor."

"So you still want to talk meshugaas."

The man shrugged. "It will make an interesting discussion."

"All right, so discuss."

The man spoke with more intensity now. Evidently interesting discussions excited him. He said, "What if I told you you *are* a lamed wufnik?"

"I wouldn't believe you."

"Why?"

"Because, Mr. Interesting Discussion, if it is true and I believe it, I die. It is written that a man who is a lamed wufnik must never know it. Who would take care of my Sylvia then and keep her from being lonely? And if it's not true, why should I believe and be a fool?"

"You're too reasonable."

"I have been accused of worse things. And by less mysterious acquaintances than you."

"The rest of your life will not be pleasant."

"You're a regular tummeler, aren't you?"

The man shrugged again. "I just don't want you to expect too much."

"Expecting is also for fools. I work. I hope. That's enough."

"You'll die anyway."

"So when I get to heaven, God will explain to me what's going on here with your discussions."

The man cocked his head to one side and thought for a moment. He said, "You're a worthy man, Sol Gosnik. A good choice."

"Thank you for your analysis, Mr. Cronkite."

While they walked back to the apartment building, Sol thought about the crazy person next to him. Was be dangerous? With crazy people it was hard to tell. Sol only hoped he and his wife with the vocal cords would be quiet once they got settled.

They walked upstairs and parted at Sol's door. Sol said, "By the way, mister, you have a name?"

"Yes. You can call me Sholstein."

"A good name. Good day, Mr. Sholstein."

"Good day, Mr. Gosnik."

Sol told Sylvia about the discussion he'd had with Mr. Sholstein, the new next-door neighbor. Sylvia called the fellow a real joker, and she made Sol laugh about him while she helped set up the sewing machine.

There was no noise from the Sholstein apartment that next week. "You see," Sylvia said, "I told you nothing was to worry about." The week after that, when the ad was in *The Reporter,* they got only three calls for tailoring.

"Barely enough for rent," Sol said. His legs were two icicles.

"It'll get better."

"What if not?"

"We'll get along. I'll get a job at Rexall."

Sol didn't answer.

Sylvia said, "You're thinking again, Sol. That's not good."

"I'm thinking about how I got thirty-six chances out of billions of people to be poor through life and holy forever."

"Not very good odds. Wait till the money starts pouring in."

"I'm waiting."

Sol turned his head suddenly as if he'd heard something. He said quietly, "You hear how empty it sounds next door? I haven't seen Sholstein since that first day. Maybe he and his loud-mouthed wife are gone. Very strange the way they came and went like that."

He looked at his wife with tears in his eyes. "Help me, Sylvia," he said. "It is such a temptation to believe too much!"

BARRY N. MALZBERG

Isaiah

In the Torah the prophet Isaiah reveals God's words to Israel: "I have set you as a covenant people, a light to the nations, to open the eyes that are blind, to bring out the prisoners from the dungeon, those who sit in darkness from the prison."

If Isaiah were to visit a Jewish congregation in Brooklyn, or Teaneck, New Jersey, whom would he find to open the eyes that are blind?

*

SO I TAKE MYSELF to the Lubavitcher Congregation in Williamsburg, Brooklyn. Williamsburg is still the largest reservoir of Chasidism in the Western world although things have hardly been so brisk since the Lubavitcher rabbi himself died and many in the community, strangulated by urban pressures, moved to bucolic New City or points even farther north. "I need to discuss the issue with someone who speaks a good English," I say hopefully to the few depressed Chasidim, a bare minyan who are chanting over prayer books in the vestry. My command of Hebrew or Yiddish is really almost nil. It is disgraceful for someone in my position to have almost no grasp of tongues but what can I do? It is all that I can manage to keep up with the research aspects.

"My English is acceptable," a middle-aged Chasid says, standing and beckoning me into the room. "What do you want?" He gestures toward a rack in the corner on which tallises are hung, prayer books perched. "You may join us, certainly."

"I don't want to join you," I say and then realizing that this sounds discourteous add, "I'm not a practicing Jew."

"All Jews must practice," the middle-aged man says wisely enough. The others nod somnolently, return to their chanting. "In fact," he whispers, "practice makes perfect."

"It's not that," I say.

Very ill at ease I sit convulsively upon a near chair, take out a handkerchief, and wipe my face in little streaks as the Chasid moves over to join me. "Perhaps after the services," he says, "after the afternoon prayers we can talk."

Afternoon prayers. Evening prayers, morning prayers, prayers upon arising and eating. They live their lives within a network of prayer; not, of course, that this can be said to have done them any real good. On the other hand, who am I to judge? The only prayers which I have ever attempted were not within the framework of really organized religion. "Not good enough," I croak, "we must talk now. I have so little time—"

The Chasid shrugs. "Time is a contradiction," he says. "It is self-willed, self-created." A bit of a metaphysician. The others have dropped out of our discussion. They are immersed in their prayers, each at a different rate in a different way. Voices mesh and part. This is the essence of Chasidic ritual I am given to understand, the individuality of worship, but actually I know very little of forms. "Perhaps you're in the wrong place?" the Chasid says kindly. "Are you looking for someone?"

"No!" I shout convulsively. Faces turn, chairs scatter, eyes look at me with great interest. With a few shattered breaths I regain control of myself. "I am not looking for anyone," I say. "No person. I am looking for information."

"What information?"

"Judaism is a messianic religion, is that not so? You believe that the Messiah has not yet come to earth but that he will and that when he does, peace and justice will reign. Unlike the Christians who hold that the Messiah already came and went, will return for the second coming, you believe that he has yet to appear. Am I right?"

"It is slightly more complex than that," my new friend says, wincing at his prayer book. "There are various levels of meaning."

"But is that not so?"

"You are discussing an entire religion, my friend. It cannot be summed up in a few words. There are some Jews who believe that the Messiah will come but there are others who are not so sure, who believe that Judaism exists only to bear witness that he will never come. Since the great purges and sufferings of the twentieth century, in fact—"

"All right," I say breathing excitedly. "That's true. I understand that part of it. Hitler and the exterminations made it impossible for many Jews to accept a messianic version of religion; the Messiah would not allow such things to come to pass without intervention if he existed. But messianism is built deeply into the religion. All of the rituals, all of the prayers, as far as I know are built upon an acceptance, a belief, a waiting . . ."

"I have had enough of this," the Chasid says, standing. "Doubtless this is of great interest to you but you ought to seek a rabbi, a scholar, perhaps someone at the theological institute with whom you could discuss all of this. This however is a place of worship."

"But what are you worshiping if you won't even talk about the basis?"

The Chasid as if from a great height gives me a penetrating look and tucks his prayer book under his arm. "If you must equate worship and understanding," he says, "you are missing the point entirely." He walks away. The minyan continues to drone but obviously I have been dismissed and after a while I leave the Lubavitcher vestry quietly, trying to hold myself against a scream or an explosion.

So I take myself to a Reform congregation in Teaneck, New Jersey, and there on a dull Monday afternoon meet and speak with the student rabbi, a young man with round eyes and a distracted expression. "Of course it's a messianic religion," he says. "Judaism is structured on the coming of the Messiah." He looks at a wall; actually it is not his office but that of the rabbi himself, who is presently visiting students of the congregation families at northeastern colleges but has no objection to giving his assistant use of the office in his absence and even the opportunity to conduct Friday evening services. "But I'm afraid that I can't solve your problem otherwise. No one knows when the Messiah will come and this sense of mystery is built deeply into the religion. It is a religion without answers of almost any sort."

He is trying hard. Obviously there is no hypocrisy in my student rabbi. Really, he is trying very hard and he is also relatively learned. Nevertheless a sense of woe overtakes me, a feeling of disengaged purposes and weariness, and so I stand, looking over his shoulder at some religious emblem on the wall. "It's hopeless," I say, "it's hopeless."

"What's hopeless?" the rabbi says without much interest. Really, they have enough trouble in Teaneck: zoning, taxation, infusion of Orthodox into certain sections draining the public schools, a rising crime rate and great transient population, to say nothing of the student rabbi's more specific problem, which is to find a congregation somewhere. I feel sympathy for him. Really, this is not his problem.

"There's just no clear framework," I say rather pointlessly and leave him. In the parking lot I have a stab of regret: I really should return and apologize for my abruptness but I decide that it would only be a gesture. Truly now: the young rabbi's problems, much as my own, would only be unduly complicated by the coming of the Messiah on top of everything else and now I feel a blade of panic. My options are running out.

So I take myself to a Thursday night discussion meeting of the Ethical Culture Society, a large proportion of which is composed of intellectual, questioning, alienated Jews. There is some problem filling in the gaps between these encounters but I do the best I can and limbo is not particularly unpleasant if one keeps expectations low. "I think we have to discard the messianic approach in toto," the discussion leader says when I politely raise my question. People stare: a newcomer, particularly a conversational newcomer, is always interesting. "It is best to think of messianism as a metaphor for that mysterious exaltation which can come from keeping ritual. Ritual equals religion equals ecstasy in some sects. The vitality of the Chasids demonstrates this, I'd think."

I see little vitality in the Chasids but politely say instead, "Then you say there is no messianic underlay anymore."

"Not any more than there are physiological reasons for the dietary laws," the discussion leader says. "I think we should get off this topic, however. Judaism is of marginal interest to most of us and we try to look at the world more eclectically, bonding together many religions, many ways of life. Not that Judaism isn't a worthy subject of discussion, of course," he concludes, perhaps reacting to some felt disapproval, "but we try to take the best from the best and reassemble. Messianism is deleterious since we know in post-technological America that the solution to our problems must lie within ourselves, that we must change the world as we see it and that our lives consist of what is known on this earth and nowhere else."

He nods somewhat emphatically and the faces turn from me back toward the podium. There are several unescorted girls for whom I feel a certain distant attraction but it would be rankest hypocrisy to stay, my business now concluded, on that basis. I leave the lecture hall quietly and try to get to a neighborhood synagogue for meditation and prayer but neighborhood synagogues are closed and locked (vandalism abounds) on Thursday nights and Williamsburg too far to travel on the dangerous underground.

So I return and explain the situation as best I can and apologize for my lapses and make clear my efforts and he listens quietly, hearing me through to the end patiently as is his wont, smoking a cigarette down to the end and then putting it absently underneath the throne, unextinguished, the faint residue of smoke surrounding like incense. "I don't know what to say," I conclude. "There are no easy answers."

"That is true," he says. He shrugs. He lights another cigarette. He sits back. After waiting for so long he has cultivated nothing if not patience and his attitude betrays no restlessness. "Still, we have to come to some kind of a decision on this."

"It's not my decision," I say quietly, not in an offensive or disagree-able way but firmly enough so that my position is clear. "I just can't make that decision; it isn't my right."

"I understand," he says. He sighs, shrugs again, extinguishes his ciga-rette under his foot and stands heavily, using his hands to wedge him-self from the throne. He grunts. He has, after all, been inert for so long. "I might as well," he says finally. "I've been waiting for so long hoping that things would just work themselves out but our Ethical Cul-ture man was quite right, wasn't he? You have to make your own way." He ventures a signal and from the haze where they have been waiting for seven thousand years the Ten Priests emerge, whispering.

"I should have accepted that a long time ago," he says and gestures again. The birds are free now, the Great Snake itself, muttering, wraps in a coil around the heavens and dimly the darkness and the light descend.

Watching this I do not know if I am happy or sad but it is good after so long to see him back at work again, doing what he always did best. The Chasids would be gratified. Teaneck is another story.

HARVEY JACOBS

Dress Rehearsal

In his witty and informative book The Joys of Yiddish (Mc-Graw-Hill, 1968), Leo Rosten describes the words and phrases and linguistic devices of Yiddish as invasionary forces sent "into the hallowed terrain of English."

Oy vay, if he only knew what a mouthful he said.

You think maybe he knows about "Dress Rehearsal" . . . ?

*

SAM DERBY FELT OLD, even up there when time was an ice cube. He tried a knee bend and gave it up when his knees cracked like dice. Xarix appeared on the wall screen just as Sam Derby recovered his posture and let out a grunt.

"Are you stable?" Xarix said.

"I'm fine!" Sam said. "How are you?"

"It's time for the dress rehearsal," Xarix said. "Will you transport to the Green Theater?"

"You mean the Blue Theater, don't you?"

"The Green Theater. The children are performing in the Blue Theater."

"Ah, the kiddies, yes."

Some kiddies, Sam Derby thought to himself. He once knew a man named Louie who carried pictures of two apes in his wallet. When somebody asked him about his family, he showed the pictures of the young apes and beamed when the somebody told him what a lovely family he had. Up there the apes would look like gods. What they called kiddies wouldn't serve for bait back home. Sam Derby often wondered about the kind of sex that produced such results. *Yuch*. Still, they loved their offspring. Chip off the old block, like that. To each his own.

The capsule came to Sam Derby's door. He got in and pressed the circular button marked The Green Theater. The capsule hummed and moved. It was a nice feeling to be inside, warm, vibrated, moving, and no meter ticking off a dime every few seconds to remind you of time and your own heartbeat.

Sam Derby, a senior citizen, with a First Indulgence classification, had the right to be gently lifted from the capsule and aimed at the door of the Green Theater. Xarix waited for him. As the doors of the Green Theater slid apart, Xarix appeared like a developing photograph.

"So, Professor," Xarix said, "how do you feel about the approach of Minus Hour."

"Not Minus Hour," Sam Derby said. "Zero Hour. You're the one who should set an example."

"God yes," Xarix said. "If one of my students said that, I would have him boiled in . . . oil?"

"Oil is correct," Sam Derby said. "Where is everybody?"

"Supply," Xarix said. "They'll be here at the drop of a hat."

"Good. Well said," Sam Derby said.

"Thank you. I like that expression, at the drop of a hat. I have this vision of hats dropping. It amuses me."

"You have a nice sense of humor."

"I think so. Yes. I could have been a schpritzer."

"Not exactly a hundred percent," Sam Derby said. "A man who gives a schpritz is a comic. A comic is a schpritzer. Say, 'I could have been a comic.' It's a lot better."

"Thank you."

"Don't mention it."

Xarix and Sam Derby went to the podium at the front of the Green Theater.

"What do you want from me today?" Sam Derby said. "I can't tell them much more."

"I thought a kind of pep talk was in order. Good luck, go get 'em, half time in the locker room. Do it for the old Prof. You know what I'm after."

"I'll do that. When does the next class start?"

"Not for a week. You have yourself a vacation, a well-deserved holiday, Sam."

"Sam? What happened to Professor?"

"Under the circumstances I felt justified in using the familiar. We've worked together twelve solstices."

"Use what you want," Sam Derby said. "I wasn't complaining. In fact, I'm flattered. I was just surprised. I began to feel disposable."

"Disposable?"

"Like a tissue. I finished my work. The class is graduating, in a manner of speaking. How do I know there's another class? How do I know you won't dispose of me?"

"But that's ridiculous. You're one of us."

"It's nice of you to say so."

"Tell me," Xarix said, "are you sorry you came?"

"No," Sam Derby said. "I must admit, when you first came to get me, I wasn't so happy."

"You had a clear choice."

"Choice? You said I had a choice. But when one of us sees one of you for the first time coming from noplace, not the most beautiful thing in the universe, no insult intended, choice isn't choice. I was scared out of my rectum."

"Surprise is our schtik. The startle effect."

"You startled. Now that I'm here, now that I've had time to think things over, I'm really glad I flew up here. I like it here."

"Good."

"Besides, what did I have down there? Did I have respect? Honors? Medals? I had Social Security. I had a pension from the guild. The people who saw my work were dropping like flies. One day before you came I went to three funerals one after the other, bang, bang, bang."

"Alevai. Rest in peace."

"Wait. No alevai. Alevai is *it should happen.*"

"Whoops."

"Whoops. If one of them said whoops, you would give him such a knock with the ray his kishkas would burn."

"There's an advantage to executive status," Xarix said. "Sam, do you think they'll be successful?"

"Why not? You send one here, one there, they have papers, they have skills, and they know how to behave. It's amazing how they look, exactly like people. Who should find out what they're up to? You got no problem with the spies. Your problem might be that Earth is already taken over by meshuganas. Maybe from another planet. I never met a producer, an agent, a successful man who couldn't be from Mars."

"Why Mars?"

"A figure of speech."

"Ah."

"I keep asking myself. Xarix, why you want Earth?"

"Because it's there."

"So all this trouble, spies, saboteurs, chazzerai, because it's there?"

"Sufficient reason."

"Sufficient reason. Be gazoont."

"Amen."

"You could say that. In all my years on stage I never would believe such a plot. Never. Too fantastic. So who knew?"

"We knew. Our computers knew. When we asked them the name of the man for the job, Sam, your card came out with two others. Stanislavski and Lee Strasberg. One was dead, and the other is too much with the guttural noises, the schlepping and yutzing. Out of all the actors past or present, your card came out, Sam Derby."

"It's nice to know. Nobody on Earth even remembers there was a theater on Second Avenue."

"Let me say that for an alien you've dedicated yourself wonderfully well to our purposes. We had the human forms down pat. We had the technicalities worked out. But nuances of manner, subtleties of speech, are all important. Only you could impart such wisdom."

"Wisdom. There is a word. Xarix, I'll tell you, don't worry yourself. Your people, whatever you call it, will blend like a snowflake on white bread. Down there, anybody will swear they're just like everybody else. They have the tools."

"Thanks to you, Sam. Professor."

"So."

When the students came, there was much excitement. Take off was only hours away. The combination of youth, travel, and purpose produced a familiar tension. Sam Derby stood on the podium delivering his pep talk and feeling some of the excitement himself.

"Remember, you're going to take over a planet, not to play pinochle. Do what I told you, be discreet, and the magic word is to blend in the soup. Now, let me hear all together in unison, what you say when you meet a person of rank and power."

"Oy vay, vots new, hello, howdy doo?"

"Good. Now, in sexual encounter, what is the correct approach?"

"Hey, dollink, let's schtup, don't futz, hurry up."

"Wonderful. And for you in the diplomatic corps, very important, when you run into a prince, a king, a president, let's hear it."

"Honorable Ganef, it's a real Watergate to make the acquaintance of so illustrious a nebbish schlemiel nudnik putz as thyself. May you fornicate with a horse before the night falls."

"Gorgeous," Sam Derby said. "I'm proud of you. Go, and give my regards to Broadway."

"You think they're ready?" Xarix said.

"Ready for Freddy," Sam Derby said. "If they learned my lessons and wave the arms you gave them, they'll be accepted anyplace. Like brothers."

HUGH NISSENSON

Forcing the End

In A.D. 68 Jerusalem was being besieged by the Roman commander Vespasian. Yochanan ben Zakkai, an eighty-year-old scholar who belonged to a faction that opposed going to war with Rome, believed that a holocaust was imminent. He escaped from Jerusalem with his students and later received permission from a contemptuous Vespasian to open a small school at Yavnah. In A.D. 70 Jerusalem fell, the Temple was sacked, and all Jewish resistance ended two years later at Masada. But although Jerusalem and the Temple were destroyed, ben Zakkai trained new teachers in out-of-the-way Yavneh and insured Jewish survival during the Diaspora.

The disturbing story that follows is rooted in the ruins of a past that might also be our future, a future we have built out of plowshares, missiles, and guns.

*

HAVING REFUSED A CHAIR, Rabbi Jacobi stands in front of my desk, pulling the tuft of white beard that sprouts beneath his underlip.

"All I want," he says, "is your permission to leave the city, go to Yavneh, open up a school there, and teach."

"Yes, I understand, Rabbi, but unfortunately, under the circumstances, I must refuse you permission."

"What circumstances?"

"For one thing, you'll be safer here."

"Really?" he asks. "Look out the window and tell me what you see."

"Jaffa Road."

"Look again."

I rise to my feet. The street, the entire city has vanished. We are in a wilderness, where a white haze has effaced the boundary between the earth and the azure sky. Mount Scopus is a barren rock, illuminated on its eastern slope by the morning sun. Huge, yellowish limestone boulders, tinged with red, reflect the glaring light. The ruins of buildings? It's impossible to tell. They seem to have been strewn indiscriminately on the parched ground shimmering from the rising heat. Only an ancient, twisted oak, with shriveled leaves, grows there, just below my window, and as I watch, a jackal which has been sleeping in the shade rises unsteadily, its pink tongue lolling from its jaws, and pisses against the tree trunk: a short spurt of urine, in which, suddenly dropping from the cloudless sky, a starling immerses itself for an instant, fluttering its wings and catching a few drops in its gaping beak.

And twisting the tuft of hair below his mouth, Jacobi says, "You're looking at the Holy City through my eyes."

"The past?"

He shrugs. "The future, too. What's the difference? They're one and the same."

"That's impossible."

"Nevertheless, God help us, it's true," he says, covering his face with his hands. As he has been speaking, a Sammael, one of our new, self-propelled rocket launchers, roars up Jaffa Road in the direction of the Russian compound. Its two rockets, capable of carrying nuclear warheads, are covered by canvas.

Jacobi twists that tuft of beard between the thumb and forefinger of his right hand. Is he a hypnotist, or what? I read over his dossier, open on my desk, once again. He was born in Jerusalem in 1917 and was ordained at the age of nineteen. After that, for twelve years, he was the rabbi of the small town of Arav in the southern Galilee, where he also worked as a clerk in the local post office because he refused any remuneration for teaching Torah. His wife died last year, and he lost his only son at the age of sixteen to nephritis. The boy was also a precociously brilliant scholar, of whom his father said at his death, "I am consoled by the fact that my son, may his memory be blessed, fulfilled the purpose for which man was created—the study of the Holy Law."

For the last eight years, Jacobi has lived in Jerusalem, teaching a select group of students in a small Talmud Torah on Adani Street. He has been in constant conflict with the rabbinate over its acquisition of extensive property, and with the government over its policy of retaliatory raids for terrorist attacks.

My secretary, Dora, whose husband was killed two years ago by an Arab grenade while serving on reserve duty in Gaza, comes into my office and whispers excitedly in my ear, "Sunday, at dawn."

"How do you know?"

"Yoram's sister heard it from her husband."

"Who's her husband?"

"The pilot."

"What's the matter with you? You know how tight security is. It's just another rumor."

She adds without conviction, "Yoram's sister swears it's the truth," and sighs. She has aged extraordinarily in the last two years; her lips are as wrinkled as an old woman's.

"No, there's still time," Jacobi says. "Not much, but enough. At least enough for me to go to Yavneh, open my school, and plant a few lemon trees. They're very delicate, you know, but I love the odor of the blossoms, don't you? Sweet but spicy. An unusual combination." He goes to the door and says, "Tell me the truth. Do you honestly believe that this time we'll achieve a lasting peace?"

"Absolutely."

"By force of arms?"

"Of course."

"Really? How I admire your faith. Let me tell you something, my friend. A secret. When I'm in Yavneh, and if one day I'm planting a sapling and I hear that the Messiah himself has arrived, do you know what I'll do? Finish planting the sapling, and then go to welcome him." He opens the door. "Did you know that lemons turn yellow only after they've been picked? It's a fact. They remain green and bitter on the tree. You have to store them for months before they turn yellow and ripen."

"Not anymore," Dora says. "A specially heated storage plant forces them to ripen in four or five days."

"Is that so? How hot?"

"I'm not sure."

"As hot as this?" he asks, and in the sweaty palm of his right hand he holds up a yellow lemon. "From the new storage plant in Yavneh, by the way, and fully ripe, as you can see; juicy too, with a wonderful smell . . ."

He passes it under Dora's nose.

"Right?" And closing his eyes and inhaling deeply, he recites the traditional benediction, "'Blessed art Thou—the Eternal, our God, King of the Universe—who hath given fragrance unto fruit.'" Then he smiles, and says, "This one, for your information, was picked from a tree four and a half days ago and then stored at exactly 22°C." He twirls it in the air. "Why, one could almost imagine it's the world: cut off from its source, mercifully ignorant of its state; and just think: some minute malfunction of some machine in that storage plant, for example, or more likely some human error, and the temperature rises only three or four degrees, and look at it now! That marvelous color splotched brown. See? This whole side has changed its color; faintly, but changed, nevertheless, and it's gotten soft—feel it—rotten . . ."

"Where is it?" Dora cries out. "I know. Up your sleeve." But, shaking his head, Jacobi replies, "No, it was only a trick. Well, not exactly that, but . . ."

"What?" she asks, in a peculiar, strident voice that makes Jacobi stare at her. She looks him straight in the eye.

"It's true about you and your brother, isn't it?" he asks, but she says nothing. She and her brother Menachem are reputed to be important members of the Knives, a new, illegal organization allegedly responsible for the murders of a prominent writer who advocated trying to make peace with the Arabs by restoring to them all their territory which we now occupy, and an eighteen-year-old pacifist who, last fall, refused to register for the draft.

Leaving the door open, she goes into the outer office and, with an unlit cigarette dangling from her wrinkled lips, sits down at her desk and pecks away with one finger at some official form, in triplicate, stuffed into her old Remington typewriter. Jacobi follows her. Six of his students from the Talmud Torah on Adani Street crowd around him, speaking Yiddish in hushed, agitated voices. One boy, not more than fifteen, fixes his dark eyes on me and grimaces. He's deformed in a way I've never seen. His right arm is normal, but the left, hanging loose, reaches his knee.

Two days later, at about four, while I'm having my afternoon glass of tea and a butter cookie, I idly glance out of the window again. Four soldiers, in battle dress and armed with submachine guns, are patrolling the street. Each one has inserted a thirty-round magazine into his weapon, behind the trigger guard, and has taped another magazine at right angles to the first, to facilitate rapid reloading. Their footfalls, I notice, are muffled by the sandbags which last night were heaped up, waist high, against the walls of the buildings.

Then, at a command from their sergeant, they break rank, to allow a funeral procession to pass down the center of the street. Four bearded men, dressed in black kaftans, are carrying an unpainted pine coffin on their shoulders. Behind them, three women, with fringed black shawls over their heads, are howling at the top of their lungs. In spite of the sandbags, the din is terrific. About to shut the window, I notice that the boy with the long arm is also following the coffin. With his good hand, he rhythmically pounds his chest, and his narrow face is twisted by the same grimace he gave me—a grimace that bares his yellow upper teeth to the gums.

"Who is it?" I shout down. "Who's died?" But the howling women, who are now scratching their cheeks with their fingernails, drown me out.

"Answer me," I yell louder, and the boy with the long arm raises his face.

"Our master," he yells back. "The Light of the World."

"Rabbi Jacobi?"

He nods, and Dora, who has been standing behind me, rushes down to the street, where I can see her arguing with one of the pallbearers who has trouble balancing the coffin and rummaging in his pocket for some papers at the same time. When she returns, she says, "They've gotten permission to bury him in Arav."

"Arav?"

"Next to his kid."

"What about transportation?"

"Two horse-drawn carts, if you can believe it."

"Who authorized them to leave the city?"

"What's-his-name. Oh, you know who I mean. That Litvak from the Ministry of Interment who dyes his hair. Kovner."

"Are you sure?"

"Yes," she says. "I'm sure." And she glances at her briefcase, on the filing cabinet, in which she keeps the yellowing document, signed by Kovner, which authorized the burial of her husband, with full military honors, on Mount Herzl.

The next morning, Shmelke Kalb, who works in an office across the street, throws open my door, waving a newspaper in my face. As usual, he's wearing a steel helmet; not because he's the air-raid warden in charge of the block, but because he suffers from skin cancer, a discolored blotch on his forehead, and puts on the helmet whenever he has to go outside, to protect himself from the sun.

"Have you read about Jacobi?" he asks.

"No, but I'm sorry, in a way."

"What're you talking about? Are you crazy? He's deserted the city. And five or six more of his students have already joined him in Yavneh."

"But that's impossible. The man's dead. I saw his funeral procession."

"A sealed coffin?"

"Yes."

"It was a trick to smuggle him out of the city."

"What're you saying?"

"Some of his students nailed him into a coffin and smuggled him out of the city two days ago. It's all here, in this morning's paper, along with some kind of manifesto for some new kind of school he wants to start."

"Let me see that," I tell him, and then read aloud:

We shall be as the disciples of Aaron, loving peace, pursuing peace, and teaching Torah which alone sustains the Jews who, if they faithfully follow its Holy Principles, will be redeemed by them, and then redeem all mankind, in God's good time . . .

Dora has come to the door; Kalb lowers his voice: "They say Kovner has disappeared without a trace."

At one—during critical times like these, we grab a sandwich for lunch at the office—I turn on the radio for the latest news.

". . . which will demand from each of us the greatest sacrifice . . . credence, which, although . . . New York . . ."

I can catch only a word now and then because of the noise: columns of Sammaels, rattling the windowpanes, have been roaring up the street for the last two hours. I twist the knob, and unexpectedly, in a perfectly audible voice, the announcer says that Rabbi Jacobi's body, spattered with dried blood, was discovered in Yavneh early this morning in front of a vegetarian restaurant on the Rishon-Lezion road. A preliminary coroner's report has established that the distinguished religious leader was stabbed once through the heart with a penknife, and died instantly, between 2 and 3 A.M. The district superintendent of police reports that no fingerprints were found on the weapon, but he has been quoted that he is confident that the criminal or criminals will soon be apprehended because of a peculiar aspect of the case. The distinguished rabbi's jaws were pried open after his death, and a yellow lemon inserted in his mouth . . .

Another Sammael, which makes it impossible for me to hear Dora shouting from the outer office, where she's been pecking away at the Remington.

"What?" I ask.

"Green," she says. "The idiot. Not yellow, green."

ISAAC BASHEVIS SINGER

The Last Demon

In the perfect stories of Isaac Bashevis Singer, Asiyah (or the material world where an unending battle is waged between the Heavenly hosts and the evil ones) can be New York or California or a Polish ghetto named Tishevitz. Imps and demons and all manner of men and spirits live and breathe in his stories. They get backaches and suffer and yearn and must look over their shoulders just like anyone else. Singer's magic is that we must believe in them, for could such details and knowings come from anywhere else but Yetzirah, the world of creative formations?

In the next story, the last demon in the world laments his fate, even as he takes a bite out of the Jewish alphabet and explains how writers have expropriated his trade.

*

I, A DEMON, bear witness that there are no more demons left. Why demons, when man himself is a demon? Why persuade to evil someone who is already convinced? I am the last of the persuaders. I board in an attic in Tishevitz and draw my sustenance from a Yiddish storybook, a leftover from the days before the great catastrophe. The stories in the book are pablum and duck milk, but the Hebrew letters have a weight of their own. I don't have to tell you that I am a Jew. What else, a Gentile? I've heard that there are Gentile demons, but I don't know any, nor do I wish to know them. Jacob and Esau don't become in-laws.

I came here from Lublin. Tishevitz is a God-forsaken village; Adam didn't even stop to pee there. It's so small that a wagon goes through town and the horse is in the market place just as the rear wheels reach the toll gate. There is mud in Tishevitz from Succoth until Tishe b'Ov. The goats of the town don't need to lift their beards to chew at the thatched roofs of the cottages. Hens roost in the middle of the streets. Birds build nests in the women's bonnets. In the tailor's synagogue a billy goat is the tenth in the quorum.

Don't ask me how I managed to get to this smallest letter in the smallest of all prayer books. But when Asmodeus bids you go, you go. After Lublin the road is familiar as far as Zamosc. From there on you are on your own. I was told to look for an iron weathercock with a crow perched upon its comb on the roof of the study house. Once upon a time the cock turned in the wind, but for years now it hasn't moved, not even in thunder and lightning. In Tishevitz even iron weathercocks die.

I speak in the present tense as for me time stands still. I arrive. I look around. For the life of me I can't find a single one of our men. The cemetery is empty. There is no outhouse. I go to the ritual bathhouse, but I don't hear a sound. I sit down on the highest bench, look down on the stone on which the buckets of water are poured each Friday, and wonder. Why am I needed here? If a little demon is wanted, is it necessary to import one all the way from Lublin? Aren't there enough devils in Zamosc? Outside the sun is shining—it's close to the summer solstice—but inside the bathhouse it's gloomy and cold. Above me is a spider web, and within the web a spider wiggling its legs, seeming to spin but drawing no thread. There's no sign of a fly, not even the shell of a fly. "What does the creature eat?" I ask myself, "its own insides?" Suddenly I hear it chanting in a Talmudic singsong: "A lion isn't satisfied by a morsel and a ditch isn't filled up with dirt from its own walls."

I burst out laughing.

"Is that so? Why have you disguised yourself as a spider?"

"I've already been a worm, a flea, a frog. I've been sitting here for two hundred years without a stitch of work to do. But you need a permit to leave."

"They don't sin here?"

"Petty men, petty sins. Today someone covets another man's broom; tomorrow he fasts and puts peas in his shoes. Ever since Abraham Zalman was under the illusion that he was Messiah, the son of Joseph, the blood of the people has congealed in their veins. If I were Satan, I wouldn't even send one of our first-graders here."

"How much does it cost him?"

"What's new in the world?" he asks me.

"It's not been so good for our crowd."

"What's happened? The Holy Spirit grows stronger?"

"Stronger? Only in Tishevitz is he powerful. No one's heard of him in the large cities. Even in Lublin he's out of style."

"Well, that should be fine."

"But it isn't," I say. "'All Guilty is worse for us than All Innocent.' It has reached a point where people want to sin beyond their capacities. They martyr themselves for the most trivial of sins. If that's the way it is, what are we needed for? A short while ago I was flying over Levertov Street, and I saw a man dressed in a skunk's coat. He had a black beard and wavy sidelocks; an amber cigar holder was clamped between his lips. Across the street from him an official's wife was walking, so it occurs to me to say, 'That's quite a bargain, don't you think, Uncle?' All I expected from him was a thought. I had my handkerchief ready if he should spit on me. So what does the man do? 'Why waste your breath on me?' he calls out angrily. 'I'm willing. Start working on her.'"

"What sort of a misfortune is this?"

"Enlightenment! In the two hundred years you've been sitting on your tail here, Satan has cooked up a new dish of kasha. The Jews have now developed writers. Yiddish ones, Hebrew ones, and they have taken over our trade. We grow hoarse talking to every adolescent, but they print their kitsch by the thousands and distribute it to Jews everywhere. They know all our tricks—mockery, piety. They have a hundred reasons why a rat must be kosher. All that they want to do is to redeem the world. Why, if you could corrupt nothing, have you been left here for two hundred years? And if you could do nothing in two hundred years, what do they expect from me in two weeks?"

"You know the proverb, 'A guest for a while sees a mile.'"

"What's there to see?"

"A young rabbi has moved here from Modly Bozyc. He's not yet thirty, but he's absolutely stuffed with knowledge, knows the thirty-six tractates of the Talmud by heart. He's the greatest Cabalist in Poland, fasts every Monday and Thursday, and bathes in the ritual bath when the water is ice cold. He won't permit any of us to talk to him. What's more he has a handsome wife, and that's bread in the basket. What do we have to tempt him with? You might as well try to break through an iron wall. If I were asked my opinion, I'd say that Tishevitz should be removed from our files. All I ask is that you get me out of here before I go mad."

"No, first I must have a talk with this rabbi. How do you think I should start?"

"You tell me. He'll start pouring salt on your tail before you open your mouth."

"I'm from Lublin. I'm not so easily frightened."

2

On the way to the rabbi, I ask the imp, "What have you tried so far?"

"What haven't I tried?" he answers.

"A woman?"

"Won't look at one."

"Heresy?"

"He knows all the answers."

"Money?"

"Doesn't know what a coin looks like."

"Reputation?"

"He runs from it."

"Doesn't he look backwards?"

"Doesn't even move his head."

"He's got to have some angle."

"Where's it hidden?"

The window of the rabbi's study is open, and in we fly. There's the usual paraphernalia around: an ark with the Holy Scroll, bookshelves, a mezuzah in a wooden case. The rabbi, a young man with a blond beard, blue eyes, yellow sidelocks, a high forehead, and a deep widow's peak sits on the rabbinical chair peering in the Gemara. He's fully equipped: *yarmulka,* sash, and fringed garment with each of the fringes braided eight times. I listen to his skull: pure thoughts! He sways and chants in Hebrew, *"Rachel t'unah v'gazezah,"* and then translates, "a wooly sheep fleeced."

"In Hebrew Rachel is both a sheep and a girl's name," I say.

"So?"

"A sheep has wool and a girl has hair."

"Therefore?"

"If she's not androgynous, a girl has pubic hair."

"Stop babbling and let me study," the rabbi says in anger.

"Wait a second," I say, "Torah won't get cold. It's true that Jacob loved Rachel, but when he was given Leah instead, she wasn't poison. And when Rachel gave him Bilhah as a concubine, what did Leah do to spite her sister? She put Zilpah into his bed."

"That was before the giving of Torah."

"What about King David?"

"That happened before the excommunication by Rabbi Gershom."

"Before or after Rabbi Gershom, a male is a male."

"Rascal. *Shaddai kra Satan,*" the rabbi exclaims. Grabbing both of his sidelocks, he begins to tremble as if assaulted by a bad dream. "What nonsense am I thinking?" He takes his ear lobes and closes his ears. I keep on talking but he doesn't listen; he becomes absorbed in a difficult passage and there's no longer anyone to speak to. The little imp from Tishevitz says, "He's a hard one to hook, isn't he? Tomorrow he'll fast and roll in a bed of thistles. He'll give away his last penny to charity."

"Such a believer nowadays?"

"Strong as a rock."

"And his wife?"

"A sacrificial lamb."

"What of the children?"

"Still infants."

"Perhaps he has a mother-in-law?"

"She's already in the other world."

"Any quarrels?"

"Not even half an enemy."

"Where do you find such a jewel?"

"Once in awhile something like that turns up among the Jews."

"This one I've got to get. This is my first job around here. I've been promised that if I succeed, I'll be transferred to Odessa."

"What's so good about that?"

"It's as near paradise as our kind gets. You can sleep twenty-four hours a day. The population sins and you don't lift a finger."

"So what do you do all day?"

"We play with our women."

"Here there's not a single one of our girls." The imp sighs. "There was one old bitch but she expired."

"So what's left?"

"What Onan did."

"That doesn't lead anywhere. Help me and I swear by Asmodeus' beard that I'll get you out of here. We have an opening for a mixer of bitter herbs. You only work Passovers."

"I hope it works out, but don't count your chickens."

"We've taken care of tougher than he."

3

A week goes by and our business has not moved forward; I find myself in a dirty mood. A week in Tishevitz is equal to a year in Lublin. The Tishevitz imp is all right, but when you sit two hundred years in such a hole, you become a yokel. He cracks jokes that didn't amuse Enoch and convulses with laughter; he drops names from the Haggadah. Every one of his stories wears a long beard. I'd like to get the hell out of here, but it doesn't take a magician to return home with nothing. I have enemies among my colleagues and I must beware of intrigue. Perhaps I was sent here just to break my neck. When devils stop warring with people, they start tripping each other.

Experience has taught that of all the snares we use, there are three that work unfailingly—lust, pride, and avarice. No one can evade all three, not even Rabbi Tsots himself. Of the three, pride has the strongest meshes. According to the Talmud a scholar is permitted the eighth part of an eighth part of vanity. But a learned man generally exceeds his quota. When I see that the days are passing and that the rabbi of Tishevitz remains stubborn, I concentrate on vanity.

"Rabbi of Tishevitz," I say, "I wasn't born yesterday. I come from Lublin where the streets are paved with exegeses of the Talmud. We use manuscripts to heat our ovens. The floors of our attics sag under the weight of Cabala. But not even in Lublin have I met a man of your eminence. How does it happen," I ask, "that no one's heard of you? True saints should hide themselves, perhaps, but silence will not bring redemption. You should be the leader of this generation, and not merely the rabbi of this community, holy though it is. The time has come for you to reveal yourself. Heaven and earth are waiting for you. Messiah himself sits in the Bird Nest looking down in search of an unblemished saint like you. But what are you doing about it? You sit on your rabbinical chair laying down the law on which pots and which pans are kosher. Forgive me the comparison, but it is as if an elephant were put to work hauling a straw."

"Who are you and what do you want?" the rabbi asks in terror. "Why don't you let me study?"

"There is a time when the service of God requires the neglect of Torah," I scream. "Any student can study the Gemara."

"Who sent you here?"

"I was sent; I am here. Do you think they don't know about you up there? The higher-ups are annoyed with you. Broad shoulders must bear their share of the load. To put it in rhyme: the humble can stumble. Hearken to this: Abraham Zalman was Messiah, son of Joseph, and you are ordained to prepare the way for Messiah, son of David, but stop sleeping. Get ready for battle. The world sinks to the forty-ninth gate of uncleanliness, but you have broken through to the seventh firmament. Only one cry is heard in the mansions, the man from Tishevitz. The angel in charge of Edom has marshalled a clan of demons against you. Satan lies in wait also. Asmodeus is undermining you. Lilith and Namah hover at your bedside. You don't see them, but Shabriri and Briri are treading at your heels. If the Angels were not defending you, that unholy crowd would pound you to dust and ashes. But you do not stand alone, Rabbi of Tishevitz. Lord Sandalphon guards your every step. Metratron watches over you from his luminescent sphere. Everything hangs in the balance, man of Tishevitz; you can tip the scales."

"What should I do?"

"Mark well all that I tell you. Even if I command you to break the law, do as I bid."

"Who are you? What is your name?"

"Elijah the Tishbite. I have the ram's horn of the Messiah ready. Whether the redemption comes, or we wander in the darkness of Egypt another 2,689 years is up to you."

The rabbi of Tishevitz remains silent for a long time. His face becomes as white as the slips of paper on which he writes his commentaries.

"How do I know you're speaking the truth?" he asks in a trembling voice. "Forgive me, Holy Angel, but I require a sign."

"You are right. I will give you a sign."

And I raise such a wind in the rabbi's study that the slip of paper on which he is writing rises from the table and starts flying like a pigeon. The pages of the Gemara turn by themselves. The curtain of the Holy Scroll billows. The rabbi's *yarmulka* jumps from his head, soars to the ceiling, and drops back onto his skull.

"Is that how Nature behaves?" I ask.

"No."

"Do you believe me now?"

The rabbi of Tishevitz hesitates.

"What do you want me to do?"

"The leader of this generation must be famous."

"How do you become famous?"

"Go and travel in the world."

"What do I do in the world?"

"Preach and collect money."

"For what do I collect?"

"First of all collect. Later on I'll tell you what to do with the money."

"Who will contribute?"

"When I order, Jews give."

"How will I support myself?"

"A rabbinical emissary is entitled to a part of what he collects."

"And my family?"

"You will get enough for all."

"What am I supposed to do right now?"

"Shut the Gemara."

"Ah, but my soul yearns for Torah," the rabbi of Tishevitz groans. Nevertheless he lifts the cover of the book, ready to shut it. If he had done that, he would have been through. What did Joseph de la Rinah do? Just hand Samael a pinch of snuff. I am already laughing to myself, "Rabbi of Tishevitz, I have you all wrapped up." The little bathhouse imp, standing in a corner, cocks an ear and turns green with envy. True, I have promised to do him a favor, but the jealousy of our kind is stronger than anything. Suddenly the rabbi says, "Forgive me, my Lord, but I require another sign."

"What do you want me to do? Stop the sun?"

"Just show me your feet."

The moment the rabbi of Tishevitz speaks these words, I know everything is lost. We can disguise all the parts of our body but the feet. From the smallest imp right up to Ketev Meriri we all have the claws of geese. The little imp in the corner bursts out laughing. For the first time in a thousand years I, the master of speech, lose my tongue.

"I don't show my feet," I call out in rage.

"That means you're a devil. *Pik,* get out of here," the rabbi cries. He races to his bookcase, pulls out the *Book of Creation* and waves it menacingly over me. What devil can withstand the *Book of Creation?* I run from the rabbi's study with my spirit in pieces.

To make a long story short, I remain stuck in Tishevitz. No more Lublin, no more Odessa. In one second all my stratagems turn to ashes. An order comes from Asmodeus himself, "Stay in Tishevitz and fry. Don't go further than a man is allowed to walk on the Sabbath."

How long am I here? Eternity plus a Wednesday. I've seen it all, the destruction of Tishevitz, the destruction of Poland. There are no more Jews, no more demons. The women don't pour out water any longer on the night of the winter solstice. They don't avoid giving things in even numbers. They no longer knock at dawn at the antechamber of the synagogue. They don't warn us before emptying the slops. The rabbi was martyred on a Friday in the month of Nisan. The community was slaughtered, the holy books burned, the cemetery desecrated. The *Book of Creation* has been returned to the Creator. Gentiles wash themselves in the ritual bath. Abraham Zalman's chapel has been turned into a pig sty. There is no longer an Angel of Good nor an Angel of Evil. No more sins, no more temptations! The generation is already guilty seven times over, but Messiah does not come. To whom should he come? Messiah did not come for the Jews, so the Jews went to Messiah. There is no further need for demons. We have also been annihilated. I am the last, a refugee. I can go anywhere I please, but where should a demon like me go? To the murderers?

I found a Yiddish storybook between two broken barrels in the house which once belonged to Velvel the Barrelmaker. I sit there, the last of the demons. I eat dust. I sleep on a feather duster. I keep on reading gibberish. The style of the book is in our manner: Sabbath pudding cooked in pig's fat: blasphemy rolled in piety. The moral of the book is: neither judge, nor judgment. But nevertheless the letters are Jewish. The alphabet they could not squander. I suck on the letters and feed myself. I count the words, make rhymes, and tortuously interpret and reinterpret each dot.

> *Aleph*, the abyss, what else waited?
> *Bet*, the blow, long since fated.
> *Geemel*, God, pretending he knew,
> *Dalet*, death, its shadow grew.
> *Hey*, the hangman, he stood prepared;
> *Wov*, wisdom, ignorance bared.
> *Zayeen*, the zodiac, signs distantly loomed;
> *Chet*, the child, prenatally doomed.
> *Tet*, the thinker, an imprisoned lord;
> *Jod*, the judge, the verdict a fraud.

Yes, as long as a single volume remains, I have something to sustain me. As long as the moths have not destroyed the last page, there is something to play with. What will happen when the last letter is no more, I'd rather not bring to my lips.

> *When the last letter is gone,*
> *The last of the demons is done.*

Translated by MARTHA GLICKLICH AND CECIL HEMLEY

JOE W. HALDEMAN

The Mazel Tov Revolution

Throughout much of our history, Jews have been on the run. Jews could not own land, become craftsmen, join a guild. We could not live where we pleased, count ourselves as citizens, or feel safe within national boundaries, for the pogrom was ever present, a traditional release valve for political and social frustrations. But for centuries the Church prohibited Christians from charging interest on loans. Thus, many Jews went into finance. They traded as they lived: by their wits. Manipulating money was a perfect medium for a people excluded from all society and on the run. Money was power and protection. It could be carried, assigned; unlike real property, it is liquid. So Jews made money, traded favors with the Church and the nobility; and as children of the Diaspora, scattered throughout the various countries of Europe, we survived and created an international financial market, which was, in effect, a new economic order that would replace feudalism.

In "The Mazel Tov Revolution" by Nebula and Hugo winner Joe W. Haldeman, we find Chaim Itzkhok, a cranky, Martian-Russian Jew who is living by his wits, putting deals together, and surviving as he takes on the largest corporation in the Galaxy to make 238 worlds safe for democracy.

*

THIS IS THE STORY of the ❏ venerated / ❏ despised Chaim Itzkhok (check one). And me. And how we ❏ made 238 worlds safe for democracy / ❏ really screwed everything up (check another). With twenty reams of paper and an old rock. I know you probably think you've heard the story before. But you haven't heard it all, not by a long way—things like blackmail and attempted murder, however polite, have a way of not getting in the history books. So read on, OK?

It all started out, for me at least, when I was stranded on Faraway a quarter of a century ago. You're probably thinking you wouldn't mind getting stranded on Faraway, right? Garden spot of the Confederation? Second capital of humanity? Monument to human engineering and all that, terraformed down to the last molecule. I tell kids what it was like back in '09 and they just shake their heads.

Back then, Faraway was one of those places where you might see an occasional tourist, only because it was one of the places that tourists just didn't go. It was one of the last outposts of George's abortive Second Empire, and had barely supported itself by exporting things like lead and cadmium. Nice poisonous heavy metals whose oxides covered the planet instead of grass. You had to run around in an asbestos suit with an air conditioner on your back, it was so damned close to Rigel.

Still is too damned close, but the way they opaqued the upper atmosphere, they tell me that Rigel is just a baby-blue ball that makes spectacular sunrises and sunsets. I've never been too tempted to go see it, having worked under its blue glare in the old days; wondering how long it'd be before you went sterile, lead underwear notwithstanding, feeling skin cancers sprouting in the short-wave radiation.

I met old Chaim there at the University Club, a run-down bar left over from the Empire days. How I got to that godforsaken place is a story in itself—one I can't tell because the husband is still alive—but I was down and out with no ticket back, dead-ended at thirty.

I was sitting alone in the University Club, ignoring the bartender, nursing my morning beer, and feeling desperate when old Chaim came in. He was around seventy but looked older, all grizzled and seamed, and I started getting ready an excuse in case he was armed with a hard-luck story.

But he ordered a cup of real coffee and when he paid, I sneaked a look at his credit flash. The number was three digits longer than mine. Not prejudiced against millionaires, I struck up a conversation with him.

There was only one opening gambit for conversation on Faraway, since the weather never changed and there were no politics to speak of: What the hell are you doing here?

"It's the closest place to where I want to go," he said, which was ridiculous. Then he asked me the same, and I told him, and we commiserated for a few minutes on the unpredictability of the other sex. I finally got around to asking him exactly where it was he wanted to go.

"It's interesting enough," he said. Two other people had come into the bar. He looked at them blandly. "Why don't we move to a table?"

He got the bartender's attention and ordered another cup of coffee, and must have seen my expression—the tariff on two cups of coffee would keep me drunk for a week—and ordered me up a large jar of beer. We carried them to a table and he switched on the sound damper, which was the kind that works both ways.

"Can I trust you to keep a secret?" He took a cautious sip of his coffee.

"Sure. One more won't hurt."

He looked at me for a long time. "How would you like to get a share of a couple of million CU's?"

A ticket back cost about a hundred thousand. "That depends on what I'd have to do." I wouldn't have, for instance, jumped off a high building into a vat of boiling lead. Boiling water, yes.

"I can't say, exactly, because I really don't know. There may be an element of danger, there may not be. Certainly a few weeks of discomfort."

"I've had several of those, here."

He nodded at the insignia on my fading fatigue jacket. "You're still licensed to pilot?"

"Technically—"

"Bonded?"

"No, like I told you, I had to skip out. My bond's on Perrin's World. I don't dare—"

"No problem, really. This is a system job." You need to be bonded for interstellar flight, but planet-to-planet, within a stellar system, there's not that much money involved.

"System job? Here? I didn't know Rigel had any other—"

"Rigel has one other planet, catalogued as Biarritz. It never got chartered or officially named because there's nothing there."

"Except something you want."

"Maybe something a lot of people want."

But he wouldn't tell me any more. We talked on until noon, Chaim feeling me out, seeing whether he could trust me, whether he wanted me as a partner. There were plenty of pilots stranded on Faraway; I later found out that he'd talked to a half-dozen or so before me.

We were talking about children or some damn thing when he suddenly sat up straight and said, "All right. I think you'll be my pilot."

"Good . . . now, just what—"

"Not yet, you don't need to know yet. What's your credit number?"

I gave it to him and he punched out a sequence on his credit flash. "This is your advance," he said; I checked my flash and, glory, I was fifty thousand CU's richer. "You get the same amount later, if Biarritz doesn't pan out. If it works, you'll also get a percentage. We'll talk about that later."

The other fifty thousand was all I wanted—get back to civilization and I could hire a proxy to go to Perrin and rescue my bond. Then I'd be in business again.

"Now. The first thing you have to do is get us a ship. I'll arrange the financing." We left the bar and went to Faraway's only public (or private) stenographer, and he made out a letter of credit for me.

"Any kind of a ship will do," he said as I walked him back to his hotel. "Anything from a yacht to a battlewagon. We just have to get there. And back."

On any civilized world, I could have stepped into a booth and called Hartford; then strolled down to the nearest port and picked up a vessel: local, interplanetary or, if I was bonded and could wait a day or two, interstellar. But Faraway was Faraway, so it was a little more complicated.

Let me digress, in case you were born less than twenty years ago and fell asleep in history class.

Back then, we had two governments: the Confederation we all know and love, and New Hartford Transportation Rentals, Ltd. There was nothing on paper that connected the Confederation with Hartford, but in reality they were as intertwined as the skeins of a braid.

New Hartford Transportation Rentals, Ltd., owned virtually all of the basic patents necessary for interstellar travel as well as every starship, including the four clunkers left over from George VIII's disastrous imperialistic experiment.

Tired of your planet? Seek religious freedom, adventure, fresh air? Want to run from creditors? Get enough people together and Hartford would lease you a ship—for an astronomical sum, but at very generous rates. In fact, the first couple of generations hardly paid anything at all (while the interest built up), but then—

Talk about the sins of the fathers coming home to roost! Once a colony began to be a going concern, Hartford was empowered to levy a tax of up to fifty percent on every commercial transaction. And Hartford would carefully keep the tax down to a level where only the interest on the loan was being paid—the principal resting untouched, to provide Hartford an income in perpetuity. It was a rigged game (enforced by the Confederation), and everybody knew it. But it was the only game in town.

Hartford had a representative on every planet, and they kept him fueled with enough money so that he was always the richest, and usually the most influential, citizen of the planet. If a planetary government tried to evolve away from the rapacious capitalism that guaranteed Hartford a good return on its investment, their representative usually had enough leverage to put it back on the right road.

There were loopholes and technicalities. Most planets didn't pass the Hartford tax on directly, but used a sliding income tax, so the rich would get poorer and the poor, God bless them, would go home and make more taxpayers rather than riot in the streets.

If you ever patronized the kind of disreputable tavern that caters to pilots and other low types, you may have heard them singing that ancient ballad, "My Heart Belongs to Mother, But Hartford Owns My Ass."

Hartford owned that fundamental part of everybody on Faraway, too. But that didn't mean they'd supplied Faraway with a nice modern spaceport, bristling with ships of all sizes and ranges. No, just the biweekly vessel from Steiner that dropped off supplies and picked up some cadmium.

I had to admit there wasn't much reason for Faraway to have a short-run, plain old interplanetary ship—what good would it be? All you could do with it would be to orbit Faraway—and it looked bad enough from the *ground*—or take a joyride out to Biarritz. And there were more entertaining ways to throw away your money, even on Faraway.

It turned out that there actually was one interplanetary ship on Faraway, but it was a museum piece. It had been sitting for two hundred years, the *Bonne Chance,* the ship Biarritz herself had used to survey the clinker that retained her name by default. It was being held for back taxes, and we picked it up for six figures.

Then the headaches began. Everything was in French—dial markings, instruction manual, log. I got a dictionary and walked around with an indelible pencil, relabeling; and Chaim and I spent a week of afternoons and evenings translating the manual.

The fusion engine was in good shape—no moving parts bigger than a molecule—but the rest of the ship was pretty ragged. Faraway didn't have much of an atmosphere, but it was practically pure oxygen, and *hot.* The hull was all pitted and had to be reground. The electronic components of the ship had been exposed to two hundred years of enough ionizing radiation to mutate a couple of fruit flies into a herd of purple cattle. Most of the guidance and communications gimcrackery had to be repaired or replaced.

We kept half the drifter population of Faraway—some pretty highly trained drifters, of course—employed for over a week, hammering that antique wreck into some kind of shape. I took it up alone for a couple of orbits and decided I could get it twenty AU's and back without any major disaster.

Chaim was still being the mystery man. He gave me a list of supplies, but it didn't hold any clue as to what we were going to do once we were on Biarritz: just air, water, food, coffee, and booze enough for two men to live on for a few months. Plus a prefab geodesic hut for them to live in.

Finally, Chaim said he was ready to go and I set up the automatic sequencing, about two hours of systems checks that were supposed to assure me that the machine wouldn't vaporize on the pad when I pushed the *Commence* button. I said a pagan prayer to Norbert Weiner and went down to the University Club for one last round or six. I could afford better bars, with fifty thousand CU's on my flash, but didn't feel like mingling with the upper classes.

I came back to the ship a half-hour before the sequencing was due to end, and Chaim was there watching the slavies load a big crate aboard the *Bonne Chance.* "What the hell is that?" I asked him.

"The Mazel Tov papers," he said, not taking his eyes off the slavies.

"Mazel Tov?"

"It means good luck, maybe good-bye. Doesn't translate all that well. If you say it like this"—and he pronounced the words with a sarcastic inflection—"it can mean 'good riddance' or 'much good shall it do you.' Clear?"

"No."

"Good." They finished loading the crate and sealed the hold door. "Give me a hand with this." It was a gray metal box that Chaim said contained a brand-new phased-tachyon transceiver.

If you're young enough to take the phased-tachyon process for granted, just step in a booth and call Sirius, I should point out that when Chaim and I met, they'd only had the machines for a little over a year. Before that, if you wanted to communicate with someone light-years away, you had to write out your message and put it on a Hartford vessel, then wait around weeks, sometimes months, while it got shuffled from planet to planet (at Hartford's convenience) until it finally wound up in the right person's hands.

Inside, I secured the box and called the pad authorities, asking them for our final mass. They read it off and I punched the information into the flight computer. Then we both strapped in.

Finally the green light flashed. I pushed the *Commence* button down to the locked position, and in a few seconds the engine rumbled into life, The ship shook like the palsied old veteran that it was, and climbed skyward trailing a cloud of what must have been the most polluting exhaust in the history of transportation: hot ionized lead, slightly radioactive. Old Biarritz had known how to economize on reaction mass.

I'd programmed a quick-and-dirty route, one and a half G's all the way, flip in the middle. Still it was going to take us two weeks. Chaim could have passed the time by telling me what it was all about, but instead he just sat around reading—*War and Peace* and a tape of Medieval Russian folk tales—every now and then staring at the wall and cackling.

Afterwards, I could appreciate his fetish for secrecy (though God knows enough people were in on part of the secret already). Not to say I might have been tempted to double-cross him. But his saying a couple of million were involved was like inviting someone to the Boston Tea Party, by asking him if he'd like to put on a loincloth and help you play a practical joke.

So I settled down for two weeks with my own reading, earning my pay by pushing a button every couple of hours to keep a continuous systems check going. I could have programmed the button to push itself, but hell . . .

At the end of two weeks, I did have to earn my keep. I watched the "velocity relative to destination" readout crawl down to zero and looked out the viewport. Nothing.

Radar found the little planet handily enough. We'd only missed it by nine thousand and some kilometers; you could see its blue-gray disc if you knew where to look.

There's no trick to landing a ship like the *Bonne Chance* if you have a nice heavy planet. It's all automated except for selecting the exact patch of earth you want to scorch (port authorities go hard on you if you miss the pad). But a feather-light ball of dirt like Biarritz is a different proposition—there just isn't enough gravity, and the servomechanisms don't respond fast enough. They'll try to land you at the rock's center of mass, which in this case was underneath forty-nine kilometers of solid basalt. So you have to do it yourself, a combination of radar and dead reckoning—more a docking maneuver than a landing.

So I crashed. It could happen to anybody.

I was real proud of that landing at first. Even old Chaim congratulated me. We backed into the surface at less than one centimeter per second, all three shoes touching down simultaneously. We didn't even bounce.

Chaim and I were already suited up, and all the air had been evacuated from the ship; standard operating procedure to minimize damage in case something did go wrong. But the landing had looked perfect, so we went on down to start unloading.

What passes for gravity on Biarritz comes to barely one-eightieth of a G. Drop a shoe and it takes it five seconds to find the floor. So we half-climbed, half-floated down to the hold, clumsy after two weeks of living in a logy G-and-a-half.

While I was getting the hold door open, we both heard a faint bass moan, conducted up from the ground through the landing shoes. Chaim asked whether it was the ground settling; I'd never heard it happen before, but said that was probably it. We were right.

I got the door open and looked out. Biarritz looked just like I'd expected it to: a rock, a pockmarked chunk of useless rock. The only relief from the grinding monotony of the landscape was the silver splash of congealed lead directly below us.

We seemed to be at a funny angle. I thought it was an optical

illusion—if the ship hadn't been upright on landing, it would have reg-
istered on the attitude readout. Then the bright lead splash started
moving, crawling away under the ship. It took me a second to react.

I shouted something unoriginal and scrambled for the ladder to the
control room. One short blip from the main engine and we'd be safely
away. Didn't make it.

The situation was easy enough to reconstruct, afterwards. We'd
landed on a shelf of rock that couldn't support the weight of the *Bonne
Chance*. The sound we had heard was the shelf breaking off, settling
down a few meters, canting the ship at about a ten-degree angle. The
force of friction between our landing pads and the basalt underfoot was
almost negligible, in so little gravity, and we slid downhill until we
reached bottom, and then gracefully tipped over. When I got to the
control room, after quite a bit of bouncing around in slow-motion,
everything was sideways and the controls were dead, dead, dead.

Chaim was lively enough, shouting and sputtering. Back in the hold,
he was buried under a pile of crates, having had just enough time to
unstrap them before the ship went over. I explained the situation to
him while helping him out.

"We're stuck here, eh?"

"I don't know yet. Have to fiddle around some."

"No matter. Inconvenient, but no matter. We're going to be so rich
we could have a fleet of rescuers here tomorrow morning."

"Maybe," I said, knowing it wasn't so—even if there were a ship at
Faraway, it couldn't possibly make the trip in less than ten days. "First
thing we have to do, though, is put up that dome." Our suits weren't
the recycling kind; we had about ten hours before we had to start
learning how to breathe carbon dioxide.

We sorted through the jumble and found the various components of
the pop-up geodesic. I laid it out on a piece of reasonably level ground
and pulled the lanyard. It assembled itself very nicely. Chaim started
unloading the ship while I hooked up the life-support system.

He was having a fine time, kicking crates out the door and watching
them float to the ground a couple of meters below. The only one that
broke was a case of whiskey—every single bottle exploded, damn it,
making a cloud of brownish crystals that slowly dissipated. So Biarritz
was the only planet in the universe with a bonded-bourbon
atmosphere.

When Chaim got to *his* booze, a case of gin, he carried it down by
hand.

We set up housekeeping while the dome was warming. I was still opening boxes when the bell went off, meaning there was enough oxygen and heat for life. Chaim must have had more trust in automatic devices than I had; he popped off his helmet immediately and scrambled out of his suit. I took off my helmet to be sociable, but kept on working at the last crate, the one Chaim had said contained "the Mazel Tov papers."

I got the top peeled away and looked inside. Sure enough, it was full of paper, in loose stacks.

I picked up a handful and looked at them. "Immigration forms?"

Chaim was sitting on a stack of food cartons, peeling off his suit liner. "That's right. Our fortune."

"'Mazel Tov Immigration Bureau,'" I read off one of the sheets. "Who—"

"You're half of it. I'm half of it. Mazel Tov is the planet under your feet." He slipped off the box. "Where'd you put our clothes?"

"What?"

"This floor's cold."

"Uh, over by the kitchen." I followed his naked wrinkled back as be clumped across the dome. "Look, you can't just . . . *name* a planet . . ."

"I can't, eh?" He rummaged through the footlocker and found some red tights, struggled into them. "Who says I can't?"

"The Confederation! Hartford! You've got to get a charter."

He found an orange tunic that clashed pretty well and slipped it over his head. Muffled: "So I'm going to get a charter."

"Just like that."

He started strapping on his boots and looked at me with amusement. "No, not 'just like that.' Let's make some coffee." He filled two cups with water and put them in the heater.

"You can't just charter a rock with two people on it."

"You're right. You're absolutely right." The timer went off. "Cream and sugar?"

"Look—no, black—you mean to say you printed up some fake—"

"Hot." He handed me the cup. "Sit down. Relax. I'll explain."

I was still in my suit, minus the helmet, so sitting was no more comfortable than standing. But I sat.

He looked at me over the edge of his cup, through a veil of steam rising unnaturally fast. I made my first million when I was your age."

"You've got to start somewhere."

"Right. I made a million and paid eighty-five percent of it to the government of Nueva Argentina, who skimmed a little off the top and passed it on to New Hartford Transportation Rentals, Ltd."

"Must have hurt."

"It made me angry. It made me think. And I did get the germ of an idea." He sipped.

"Go on."

"I don't suppose you've ever heard of the Itzkbok Shipping Agency."

"No . . . it probably would have stuck in my mind."

"Very few people have. On the surface, it's a very small operation. Four interplanetary ships, every one of them smaller than the *Bonne Chance*. But they're engaged in interstellar commerce."

"Stars must be pretty close together."

"No . . . they started about twenty years ago. The shortest voyage is about half over. One has over a century to go."

"Doesn't make any sense."

"But it does. It makes sense on two levels." He set down the cup and laced his fingers together.

"There are certain objects whose value almost has to go up with the passage of time. Jewelry, antiques, works of art. These are the only cargo I deal with. Officially."

"I see. I think."

"You see half of it. I buy these objects on relatively poor planets and ship them to relatively affluent ones. I didn't have any trouble getting stockholders. Hartford wasn't too happy about it, of course."

"What did they do?"

He shrugged. "Took me to court. I'd studied the law, though, before I started Itzkhok. They didn't press too hard—my company didn't make one ten-thousandth of Hartford's annual profit—and I won."

"And made a credit or two."

"Some three billion, legitimate profit. But the important thing is that I established a concrete legal precedent where none had existed before."

"You're losing me again. Does this have anything to do with . . ."

"Everything, patience. With this money, and money from other sources, I started building up a fleet. Through a number of dummy corporations . . . buying old ships, building new ones. I own or am leasing some two thousand ships. Most of them are loaded and on the pad right now."

"Wait, now." Economics was never my strong suit, but this was obvious. "You're going to drive your own prices down. There can't be that big a market for old paintings and—"

"Right, precisely. But most of these ships aren't carrying such specialized cargo. The closest one, for instance, is on Tangiers, aimed for Faraway. It holds nearly a hundred thousand cubic meters of water."

"Water . . ."

"Old passenger liner, flooded the damn thing. Just left a little room for ice expansion, in case the heating—"

"Because on Faraway—"

"—on Faraway there isn't one molecule of water that men didn't carry there. They recycle every drop but have to lose one percent or so annually.

"Tonight or tomorrow I'm going to call up Faraway and offer to sell them 897,000 kilograms of water. At cost. Delivery in six years. It's a long time to wait, but they'll be getting it for a hundredth of the usual cost, what Hartford charges."

"And you'll lose a bundle."

"Depends on how you look at it. Most of my capital is tied up in small, slow spaceships; I own some interest in three-quarters of the interplanetary vessels that exist. If my scheme works, all of them will double in value overnight.

"Hartford, though, is going to lose more than a bundle. There are 237 other planets, out of 298, in a position similar to Faraway's. They depend on Hartford for water, or seed, or medical supplies, or something else necessary for life."

"And you have deals set up—"

"For all of them, right. Underbidding Hartford by at least a factor of ten." He drank off the rest of his coffee in a gulp.

"What's to stop Hartford from underbidding *you?*"

"Absolutely nothing." He got up and started preparing another cup. "They'll probably try to, here and there. I don't think many governments will take them up on it.

"Take Faraway as an example. They're in a better position than most planets, as far as their debt to Hartford, because the Second Empire financed the start of their colonization. Still, they owe Hartford better than ten billion CU's—their annual interest payment comes to several hundred million.

"They keep paying it, not because of some abstract obligation to Hartford. Governments don't have consciences. If they stopped paying, of course, they'd dry up and die in a generation. Until today, they didn't have any choice in the matter."

"So what you're doing is giving all of those planets a chance to welsh on their debts."

"That bothers you?" He sat back down, balanced the cup on his knee.

"A little. I don't love Hartford any more than—"

"Look at it this way. My way. Consider Hartford as an arm of the government, the Confederation."

"I've always thought it was the other way around."

"In a practical sense, yes. But either way. A government sends its people out to colonize virgin lands. It subsidizes them at first; once the ball is rolling, it collects allegiance and taxes.

"The 'debt' to Hartford is just a convenient fiction to justify taking these taxes."

"There are services rendered, though. Necessary to life."

"Rendered and paid for, separately. I'm going to prove to the 'colonies' that they can provide these services to each other. It will be even easier once Hartford goes bankrupt. There'll be no monopoly on starships. No Confederation to protect patents."

"Anarchy, then."

"Interesting word. I prefer to call it revolution . . . but yes, things will be pretty hectic for a while."

"All right. But if you wanted to choreograph a revolution, why didn't you pick a more comfortable planet to do it from? Are you just hiding?"

"Partly that. Mostly, though, I wanted to do everything legally. For that, I needed a very small planet without a charter."

"I'm lost again." I made myself another cup of coffee and grieved for the lack of bourbon. Maybe if I went outside and took a deep breath . . .

"You know what it takes to charter a planet?" Chaim asked me.

"Don't know the numbers. Certain population density and high enough gross planetary product."

"The figures aren't important. They look modest enough on paper. The way it works out, though, is that by the time a planet is populated enough and prosperous enough to get its independence, it's almost guaranteed to be irretrievably in debt to Hartford."

"That's what all those immigration forms are for. Half of those stacks are immigration forms and the other half, limited powers of attorney. I'm going to claim this planet, name it Mazel Tov, and accept my own petition for citizenship on behalf of 4,783 immigrants. Then I make one call, to my lawyer." He named an Earth-based interplanetary law firm so well-known that even I had heard of it.

"They will call about a hundred of these immigrants, each of whom will call ten more, then ten more, and so on. All prearranged. Each of them then pays me his immigration fee."

"How much is that?"

"Minimum, ten million CU's."

"God!"

"It's a bargain. A new citizen gets one share in the Mazel Tov Corporation for each million he puts in. In thirty minutes MTC should have almost as much capital behind it as Hartford has."

"Where could you find four thousand—"

"Twenty years of persuasion. Of coordination. I've tried to approach every living man of wealth whose fortune is not tied up with Hartford or the Confederation. I've showed them my plan—especially the safeguards on it that make it a low-risk, high-return investment—and every single one of them has signed up."

"Not one betrayal?"

"No—what could the Confederation or Hartford offer in return? Wealth? Power? These men already have that in abundance.

"On the other hand, I offer them a gift beyond price: independence. And incidentally, no taxes, ever. That's the first article of the charter."

He let me absorb that for a minute. "It's too facile," I said. "If your plan works, everything will fall apart for the Confederation and Hartford—but look what we get instead. Four thousand—some independent robber barons, running the whole show. That's an improvement?"

"Who can say? But that's revolution: throw the old set of bastards out and install your own set. At least it'll be different. Time for a change."

I got up. "Look, this is too much, too fast. I've got to think about it. Digest it. Got to check out the ship, too."

Chaim went along with me halfway to the air lock. "Good, good. I'll start making calls." He patted the transceiver with real affection. "Good thing this baby came along when it did. It would have been difficult coordinating this thing, passing notes around. Maybe impossible."

It didn't seem that bloody easy, even with all those speedy little tachyons helping us. I didn't say anything.

It was a relief to get back into my own element, out of the dizzying fumes of high finance and revolution. But it was short-lived.

Things started out just dandy. The reason the control board was dead was that its cable to the fuel cells had jarred loose. I plugged it back in and set up a systems check. The systems check ran for two seconds and quit. What was wrong with the ship was number IV-A-I-a. It took me a half-hour to find the manual, which had slid into the head and nestled up behind the commode.

"IV" was fusion power source. "IV-A" was generation of magnetic field for containment thereof. "IV-A-I" was disabilities of magnetic field generator. And "IV-A-I-a," of course, was permanent disability. It had a list of recommended types of replacement generators.

Well, I couldn't run down to the store and pick up a generator. And you can't produce an umpty-million-gauss fusion mirror by rubbing two sticks together. So I kicked Mlle. Biarritz's book across the room and went back to the dome.

Chaim was hunched over the transceiver, talking to somebody while he studied his own scribblings in a notebook.

"We're stuck here," I said.

He nodded at me and kept up the conversation. "—that's right. Forty thousand bushels, irradiated, for five hundred thousand CU's . . . so *what?* So it's a gift. It's guaranteed. Delivery in about seven years, you'll get details . . . all right, fine. A pleasure to do business. Thank *you,* sir."

He switched off and leaned back and laughed. "They all think I'm crazy!"

"We're stuck here," I said again.

"Don't worry about it, don't worry," he said, pointing to an oversized credit flash attached to the transceiver. It had a big number on it that was constantly changing, going up. "That is the total assets of Mazel Tov Corporation." He started laughing again.

"Minims?"

"No, round credits."

I counted places. "A hundred and twenty-eight billion . . . credits?"

"That's right, right. You want to go to Faraway? We'll have it *towed* here."

"A hundred and twenty-nine billion?" It was really kind of hard to grasp.

"Have a drink—celebrate!" There was a bowl of ice and a bottle of gin on the floor beside him. God, I hate gin.

"Think I'll fix a cup of tea." By the time I'd had my cup, cleaned up, and changed out of my suit, Chaim was through with his calls. The number on the credit flash was up to 239,605,967,000 and going up slowly.

He took his bottle, glass, and ice to his bunk and asked me to start setting up the rescue mission.

I called Hartford headquarters on Earth. Six people referred me to their superiors and I wound up talking to the Coordinator of Interstellar Transit himself. I found out that bad news travels fast.

"Mazel Tov?" his tinny voice said. "I've heard of you, new planet out by Rigel? Next to Faraway?"

"That's right. We need a pickup and we can pay."

"Oh, that's not the problem. Right now there just aren't any ships available. Won't be for several months. Maybe a year."

"What? We only have three months' worth of air!" By this time Chaim was standing right behind me, breathing gin into my ear.

"I'm really very sorry. But I thought that by the time a planet gets its charter, it should be reasonably self-sufficient."

"That's murder!" Chaim shouted.

"No, sir," the voice said. "Just unfortunate planning on your part. You shouldn't have filed for—" Chaim reached over my shoulder and slapped the switch off, hard. He stomped back to his bunk—difficult to do with next to no gravity—sat down and shook some gin into his glass. He looked at it and set it on the floor.

"Who can we bribe?" I asked.

He kept staring at the glass. "No one. We can try, but I doubt that it's worth the effort. Not with Hartford fighting for its life. Its corporate life."

"I know lots of pilots we could get, cheap."

"Pilots," Chaim said without too much respect.

I ignored the slur. "Yeah. Hartford programs the main jump. Nobody'd get a jump to Rigel."

We sat in silence for a while, the too-sober pilot and the Martian-Russian Jew who was the richest person in the history of mankind. Less than too sober.

"Sure there's no other ship on Faraway?"

"I'm sure," I said. "Took me a half day to find someone who remembered about the *Bonne Chance*."

He considered that for a minute. "What does it take to build an interplanetary ship? Besides money."

"What, you mean could they build one on Faraway?"

"Right."

"Let me see." Maybe. "You need an engine. A cabin and life-support stuff. Steering jets or gyros. Guidance and commo equipment."

"Well?"

"I don't know. The engine would be the hard part. They don't have all that much heavy industry on Faraway."

"No harm in finding out."

I called Faraway. Talked to the mayor. He was an old pilot (having been elected by popular vote) and I finally reached him at the University Club, where he was surrounded by other old pilots. I talked to him about engineering. Chaim talked to him about money. Chaim shouted and wept at him about money. We made a deal.

Faraway having such an abundance of heavy metals, the main power generator for the town, the only settlement on the planet, was an old-fashioned fission generator. We figured out a way they could use it.

After a good deal of haggling and swearing, the citizens of Faraway agreed to cobble together a rescue vehicle. In return, they would get control of forty-nine percent of the stock of Mazel Tov Corporation.

Chaim was mad for a while, but eventually got his sense of humor back. We had to kill two months with six already-read books and a fifty-bottle case of gin. I read *War and Peace* twice. The second time I made a list of the characters. I made crossword puzzles out of the characters' names. I learned how to drink gin, if not how to like it. I felt like I was going slowly crazy—and when the good ship *Hello There* hove into view, I knew I'd gone 'round the bend.

The *Hello There* was a string of fourteen buildings strung along a lattice of salvaged beams; a huge atomic reactor pushing it from the rear. The buildings had been uprooted whole, life-support equipment and all, from the spaceport area of Faraway. The first building, the control room, was the transplanted University Club, Olde English decorations still intact. There were thirty pairs of wheels along one side of the "vessel," the perambulating shantytown.

We found out later that they had brought along a third of the planet's population, since most of the buildings on Faraway were without power and therefore uninhabitable. The thing (I still can't call it a ship) had to be put on wheels because they had no way to crank it upright for launching. They drove it off the edge of a cliff and pulled for altitude with the pitch jets. The pilot said it had been pretty harrowing and after barely surviving the landing I could marvel at his power of understatement.

The ship hovered over Mazel Tov with its yaw jets and they lowered

a ladder for us. Quite a feat of navigation. I've often wondered whether
the pilot could have done it sober.

The rest, they say, is history. And current events. As Chaim had pre-
dicted Hartford went into receivership, MTC being the receiver. We
did throw out all of the old random bastards and install our own hand-
picked ones.

I shouldn't bitch. I'm still doing the only thing I ever wanted to do.
Pilot a starship; go places, do things. And I'm moderately wealthy, with
a tenth-share of MTC stock.

It'd just be a lot easier to take, if every ex-bum on Faraway didn't
have a hundred times as much. I haven't gone back there since they
bronzed the University Club and put it on a pedestal.

WOODY ALLEN

The Scrolls

This is from a fragment found in the Gulf of Aqaba, dated at about 4000 B.C., and the writing is a mixture of Sumerian, Aramaic, Babylonian, and Woody-allen. . . .

*

SCHOLARS WILL RECALL that several years ago a shepherd, wandering in the Gulf of Aqaba, stumbled upon a cave containing several large clay jars and also two tickets to the ice show. Inside the jars were discovered six parchment scrolls with ancient incomprehensible writing which the shepherd, in his ignorance, sold to the museum for $750,000 apiece. Two years later the jars turned up in a pawn shop in Philadelphia. One year later the shepherd turned up in a pawn shop in Philadelphia and neither was claimed.

Archeologists originally set the date of the scrolls at 4000 B.C., or just after the massacre of the Israelites by their benefactors. The writing is a mixture of Sumerian, Aramaic, and Babylonian and seems to have been done by either one man over a long period of time, or several men who shared the same suit. The authenticity of the scrolls is currently in great doubt, particularly since the word Oldsmobile appears several times in the text, and the few fragments that have finally been translated deal with familiar religious themes in a more than dubious way. Still, excavationist A. H. Bauer has noted that even though the fragments seem totally fraudulent, this is probably the greatest archeological find in history with the exception of the recovery of his cufflinks from a tomb in Jerusalem. The following are the translated fragments.

One . . . And the Lord made an bet with Satan to test Job's loyalty and the Lord, for no apparent reason to Job, smote him on the head and again on the ear and pushed him into an thick sauce so as to make Job sticky and vile and then He slew a 10th part of Job's kine and job calleth out: "Why doth thou slay my kine? Kine are hard to come by. Now I am short kine and I'm not even sure what kine are." And the Lord produced two stone tablets and snapped them closed on Job's nose. And when Job's wife saw this she wept and the Lord sent an angel of mercy who anointed her head with a polo mallet and of the 10 plagues, the Lord sent one through six, inclusive, and Job was sore and his wife angry and she rent her garment and then raised the rent but refused to paint.

And soon Job's pastures dried up and his tongue cleaved to the roof of his mouth so he could not pronounce the word "frankincense" without getting big laughs.

And once the Lord, while wreaking havoc upon his faithful servant, came too close and Job grabbed him around the neck and said, "Aha! Now I got you! Why art thou giving Job a hard time, eh? Eh? Speak up!"

And the Lord said, "Er, look—that's my neck you have . . . could you let me go?"

But Job showed no mercy and said, "I was doing very well till you came along. I had myrrh and fig trees in abundance and a coat of many colors with two pairs of pants of many colors. Now look."

And the Lord spake and his voice thundered: "Must I who created heaven and earth explain my ways to thee? What hath thou created that thou doth dare question me?"

"That's no answer," Job said. "And for someone who's supposed to be omnipotent, let me tell you, 'tabernacle' has only one 'L.'" Then Job fell to his knees and cried to the Lord. "Thine is the kingdom and the power and glory. Thou hast a good job. Don't blow it."

Two . . . And Abraham awoke in the middle of the night and said to his only son, Isaac, "I have had an dream where the voice of the Lord sayeth that I must sacrifice my only son, so put your pants on." And Isaac trembled and said, "So what did you say? I mean when He brought this whole thing up?"

"What am I going to say?" Abraham said. "I'm standing there at two A.M. in my underwear with the Creator of the Universe. Should I argue?"

"Well, did he say why he wants me sacrificed?" Isaac asked his father.

But Abraham said, "The faithful do not question. Now let's go because I have a heavy day tomorrow."

And Sarah who heard Abraham's plan grew vexed and said, "How doth thou know it was the Lord and not, say, thy friend who loveth practical jokes, for the Lord hateth practical jokes and whosoever shall pull one shall be delivered into the hands of his enemies whether they can pay the delivery charge or not." And Abraham answered, "Because I know it was the Lord. It was a deep, resonant voice, well modulated, and nobody in the desert can get a rumble in it like that."

And Sarah said, "And thou art willing to carry out this senseless act?" But Abraham told her, "Frankly yes, for to question the Lord's word is one of the worst things a person can do, particularly with the economy in the state it's in."

And so he took Isaac to a certain place and prepared to sacrifice him but at the last minute the Lord stayed Abraham's hand and said, "How could thou doest such a thing?" And Abraham said, "But thou said. . . ."

"Never mind what I said," the Lord spake. "Doth thou listen to every crazy idea that comes thy way?" And Abraham grew ashamed. "Er— not really . . . no. . . ."

"I jokingly suggest thou sacrifice Isaac and thou immediately runs out to do it."

And Abraham fell to his knees, "See, I never know when you're kidding."

And the Lord thundered, "No sense of humor. I can't believe it."

"But doth this not prove I love thee, that I was willing to donate mine only son on thy whim?"

And the Lord said, "It proves that some men will follow any order no matter how asinine as long as it comes from a resonant, well modulated voice."

And with that, the Lord bid Abraham get some rest and check with him tomorrow.

Three . . . And it came to pass that a man who sold shirts was smitten by hard times. Neither did any of his merchandise move nor did he prosper. And he prayed and said, "Lord, why hast thou left me to suffer thus? All mine enemies sell their goods except I. And it's the height of the season. My shirts are good shirts. Take a look at this rayon. I got button-downs, flare collars, nothing sells. Yet, I have kept thy commandments. Why can I not earn a living when mine younger brother cleans up in children's ready-to-wear?"

And the Lord heard the man and said, "About thy shirts. . . ."

"Yes, Lord," the man said, falling to his knees.

"Put an alligator over the pocket."

"Pardon me, Lord?"

"Just do what I'm telling you. You won't be sorry."

And the man sewed on to all his shirts a small alligator symbol and lo and behold, suddenly his merchandise moved like gangbusters and there was much rejoicing while amongst his enemies there was wailing and gnashing of teeth and one said, "The Lord is merciful. He maketh me to lie down in green pastures. The problem is, I can't get up."

Laws and Proverbs:

Doing abominations is against the law, particularly if the abominations are done while wearing a lobster bib.

The lion and the calf shall lie down together but the calf won't get much sleep.

Whosoever shall not fall by the sword or by famine, shall fall by pestilence, so why bother shaving?

The wicked at heart probably know something.

Whosoever loveth wisdom is righteous but he that keepeth company with fowl is weird.

My Lord, my Lord! What hast thou done, lately?

Woody Allen

HOWARD SCHWARTZ

The Celestial Orchestra

Howard Schwartz writes: "Beginning with Ezekiel's vision of
the chariot in the heavens, the chariot has been one of the key motifs in
Jewish literature. In the Talmud it is said that no more than three may
discuss the mysteries of the Chariot (Ma'asch Merkavah) at one time.
This was because such discussions were a form of mystical contemplation that the rabbis feared, based on the story of the four who entered
Paradise (Hagigah 14b): 'Four sages entered Paradise, Ben Azzai, Ben
Zoma, Elisha ben Abuyah and Rabbi Akiba. Ben Azzai looked and died.
Ben Zoma looked and lost his mind. Elisha ben Abuyah cut the shoots
(became an apostate). Only Rabbi Akiba entered in peace and departed
in peace.' It was reasoned that if three of the greatest Talmudic sages
were destroyed by mystical contemplation, it was too dangerous for the
masses. On the other hand, there was an esoteric sect that attempted to
duplicate this journey into Paradise. The resulting texts are called
Hekhaloth (palaces). In these texts journeys to Paradise took place in
one of several ways: by journeying heavenward in the Merkavah, by
using a magical amulet, or by climbing up Jacob's ladder. The chariot
was the most common method."

In the story that follows, Rabbi Nachman of Bratslav, the great Jewish mystic, journeys through the crack in the cosmos to hear the letters
of revelation.

*

ONCE IT HAPPENED that Reb Nachman woke up in the middle of the night, and instead of the deep silence that usually pervaded, he heard something like a faint music. At first the sound was no more than that of an approaching wind, but soon he could make out that it was actually a kind of music. What could it be? He had no idea. But he continued to hear that music, ever so faintly, sometimes present, sometimes about to disappear. Nor did it grow any louder, so he had to strain to listen. One thing was certain, though: Reb Nachman felt drawn to this music, as if it were a message he was trying to receive, that was coming to him from a great distance.

Then Reb Nachman got up and went into his study and sat down by the window. And yes, from there the music seemed slightly louder, as if he were a little closer to its source. And now it did not disappear, but it remained very faint. Nor was he able to identify it with any instrument with which he was familiar—it did not sound like a violin or a flute; not like a bass fiddle and not like a drum. Nor did it have the sound of a voice or voices. If only he were able to hear it better, he thought, he might be able to identify its source.

Then Reb Nachman left the house and walked outside. He walked out into the field beyond the gate, under a sky crowded with stars. There he had no memory, except for questions that concerned the origin of the mysterious music. And while his eyes were fixed on the heavens, the ground remained unknown beneath his feet. And for that time he did not impose patterns on distant stars or imagine the life they might sustain. Nor did he count the gift of the stars as riches. Instead he listened for a long, long time.

At first Reb Nachman thought that what he heard was seamless, and was coming from a single instrument. But after a while he was almost able to separate the instruments that wove their music together so well. Yet this new knowledge did not satisfy his longing and curiosity; in fact, it only served to whet it. Where was this distant music coming from? Surely it was not drifting there from any orchestra in Bratslav, or from anywhere else in this world, of that Reb Nachman was certain. No, this was some kind of celestial music, music of the spheres.

It was then that Reb Nachman realized how much he wanted to follow that music and discover its source. And this longing grew so great that Reb Nachman became afraid that his heart might break. Then, while he was staring up into the stars, he saw a very large star fall from its place in the heavens and blaze across the sky like a comet. And he followed that first star to fall, and shared its last journey. And somehow it seemed to Reb Nachman that he was falling with that star, and was caught up in that same motion, as if he had been swept away by an invisible current, and he closed his eyes and let himself be carried.

That is how it happened that when Reb Nachman opened his eyes again he found himself seated inside a chariot of fire that blazed its way across the heavens. And he did not have time to wonder how this had happened, or what it meant, but only to marvel in awe as the wonders of the heavens passed before his eyes. Before him he saw two kinds of luminaries: those which ascended above were luminaries of light; and those which descended below were luminaries of fire. And the luminaries of fire did not cease flowing like rivers of fire. And it was then, when his eyes had become adjusted to the sudden illuminations that crossed his path, that Reb Nachman became aware of a presence beside him, and he began to perceive a dim body of light.

That is when the angel who drove the chariot first spoke to him, and said: "Welcome, Reb Nachman. I am the angel Raziel, and I will serve as your guide in this kingdom. You should know that your calling and your prayers have not gone unheard in Heaven. This chariot has been sent to bring you to the place you long for, the source you are seeking."

And with each word that the angel Raziel spoke, the light that surrounded his ethereal body grew brighter, until he appeared to Reb Nachman as a fully revealed being. This was the first time that Reb Nachman had ever been face to face with an angel. And yet, strange to say, he did not feel the fear he would have expected, but rather felt as if he had been reunited with a long lost companion.

It was then that Reb Nachman saw the chariot approach some kind of parting of the heavens, which resembled a line drawn across the cosmos. As they drew closer, he saw that it was actually an opening through which an ethereal light emerged. Raziel recognized the question taking form in Reb Nachman's mind, and he said: "We are approaching the place where the Upper Waters and the Lower Waters meet. This is where the Upper Worlds are separated from the Lower

Worlds, and what belongs to the spheres above is divided from what belongs to the spheres below."

No sooner did the angel finish speaking than the chariot approached close enough to that place for Reb Nachman to catch a glimpse of what lay on the other side. And what he saw was a magnificent structure suspended in space! And from that glimpse he knew that whatever it was, no human structure could begin to compare with it. But then, before he had time to question the angel, the chariot passed through that very aperture, to the complete astonishment of Reb Nachman, for it was no higher than a hand's breadth. It was at that moment that Reb Nachman grew afraid for the first time, for he realized that he was flying through space at a great height, and he did not dare to look down. Then he said to the angel: "How is it possible that we have passed through that place which is no more than three finger-breadths?"

Raziel said: "In your world of men, Reb Nachman, it is possible to contain a garden in the world. But in this kingdom it is possible to contain the world in a garden. How can this be? Because here, whoever opens his heart to the Holy One, blessed be He, as much as the thickness of a needle, can pass through any portal."

Even as Raziel spoke these words Reb Nachman had already been captured by the radiant vision that loomed ahead. And again, without his having to ask, Raziel replied: "The place you are about to be taken to, Reb Nachman, is the very one you have been seeking. But since even this chariot is not permitted to approach much closer to that sacred place, you must soon depart from it and remain suspended in space, like the Sanctuary you see before you."

And without any other explanation, Reb Nachman realized that the wonderful structure he saw must be the Celestial Temple, after which the Temple in Jerusalem had been modeled, and with which it was identical in every aspect, except for the fire that surrounded the heavenly Sanctuary. For the marble pillars of this heavenly miracle were surrounded by red fire, the stones by green fire, the threshold by white fire, and the gates by a blue fire. And angels entered and departed in a steady stream, intoning an unforgettable hymn to a melody Reb Nachman heard that day for the first time, but which he recognized as if it had been familiar to him all the days of his life.

It was then Reb Nachman realized that he was no longer within the chariot, but was suspended in space without hands or feet for support. And it was then, with his eyes fixed on that shimmering vision, that Reb Nachman was able to distinguish for the first time the Divine Presence of the Shekhina hovering above the walls and pillars of the Temple, illuminating them, and wrapping them in a glowing light that shone across all of Heaven. It was this light that he had seen from the other side of the aperture, before the chariot of fire had crossed into the Kingdom of Heaven. And so awestruck was Reb Nachman to witness the splendor of the Shekhina, that he suddenly experienced an overwhelming impulse to hide his face, and he began to sway in that place and almost lost his balance. And had it not been for the angel Raziel speaking to him at that instant he might have fallen from that great height. And the angel said: "Take care, Reb Nachman, and know that the Temple remains suspended by decree of the Holy One, blessed be He. And you must remember, above all, to keep your eyes fixed on its glory, if you are not to become lost in this place. For should you turn away from the Temple for as long as a single instant, you would risk the danger of falling from this height; even a mere distraction would take you to places unintended, from which you might never return. So too you should know that no living man may enter into that holy dwelling place and still descend to the world of men. For no man could survive the pure fire that burns there, through which only angels and purified souls can pass."

And it was then, when he had regained his balance, that Reb Nachman finally discovered the source of the celestial music that had lured him from his house in a world so far removed, and yet so close. And when he followed that music to its source in the Celestial Temple his eyes came to rest on concentric circles of angels in the Temple courtyard. Then he realized that the music he had been hearing was being played by an orchestra of angels. And when he looked still closer he saw that each of the angels played a golden vessel cast in the shape of a letter of the Hebrew alphabet. And each one had a voice of its own, and one angel in the center of the circle played an instrument in the shape of the letter Bet.

And as he listened to the music, Reb Nachman realized it was that long note which served as its foundation, and sustained all of the other instruments. And Reb Nachman marvelled at how long the angel was able to hold this note, drawing his breath back and forth like the Holy One Himself, who in this way brought the heavens and the earth into being. And at that moment Reb Nachman was willing to believe that the world only existed so that those secret harmonies could be heard. And he turned to the angel Raziel, who had never left his side, and once more the angel knew what he wished to know, and said: "The score of this symphony is the scroll of the Torah, which commences with the long note of the letter Bet, endless and eternal, and continues with each instrument playing in turn as it appears on the page, holding its note until the next letter has been sounded, and then breathing in and out a full breath."

And when Reb Nachman listened to that music he arrived at a new understanding of the Torah, and realized that among its many mysteries there was one level on which it existed only as pure music. And he was also aware that of all the instruments in that orchestra, it was that of the letter Bet which spoke to him and pronounced his name. Then the angel Raziel turned to Reb Nachman and said: "The souls of all men draw their strength from one of the instruments in this orchestra, and thus from one of the letters of the alphabet. And that letter serves as the vessel through which the soul of a man may reveal itself. And your soul, Reb Nachman, is one of the thirty-six souls that draws its strength from the vessel of the letter Bet, which serves as its Foundation Stone, and holds back the waters of the Abyss."

And then it happened that when the angel Raziel said the word "Abyss," Reb Nachman forgot all of his warning for one instant, and glanced down at the world so far below. And the next thing he knew was that he felt like a falling star. And that is when he realized that he was still standing in the field beyond the gate, following the first star that had fallen, which had now disappeared. And the celestial music, though faint once more, still echoed in his ears.

JACK DANN

Camps

In five years the Nazis exterminated nine million people. Six million were Jews. The efficiency of the concentration camps was such that twenty thousand people could be gassed in a day. The Nazis at the camp Treblinka boasted that they could "process" the Jews who arrived in the cattle cars in forty-five minutes. In 1943 six hundred desperate Jews revolted and burned Treblinka to the ground. These men were willing to martyr themselves so that a few might live to "testify," to tell a disbelieving world of the atrocities committed in the camps. Out of the six hundred, forty survived to tell their story.

As I write this, The Institute for Historical Review, a California-based organization, is mailing copies of their journal to unsuspecting librarians, educators, and students. On the journal's masthead is an impressive list of names, which includes an economist, a retired German judge, and various American and European university professors. The purpose of the institute and its journal is to deny that the Holocaust ever happened.

The story that follows is an attempt to "testify." It is a transfusion of the past into our present. . . .

*

AS STEPHEN LIES IN BED, he can think only of pain.

He imagines it as sharp and blue. After receiving an injection of Demerol, he enters pain's cold regions as an explorer, an objective visitor. It is a country of ice and glass, monochromatic plains and valleys filled with wash-blue shards of ice, crystal pyramids and pinnacles, squares, oblongs, and all manner of polyhedrons—block upon block of painted blue pain.

Although it is midafternoon, Stephen pretends it is dark. His eyes are tightly closed, but the daylight pouring into the room from two large windows intrudes as a dull red field extending infinitely behind his eyelids.

"Josie," he asks through cottonmouth, "aren't I due for another shot?" Josie is crisp and fresh and large in her starched white uniform. Her peaked nurse's cap is pinned to her mouse-brown hair.

"I've just given you an injection; it will take effect soon." Josie strokes his hand, and he dreams of ice.

"Bring me some ice," he whispers.

"If I bring you a bowl of ice, you'll only spill it again."

"Bring me some ice. . . ." By touching the ice cubes, by turning them in his hand like a gambler favoring his dice, he can transport himself into the beautiful blue country. Later, the ice will melt; and he will spill the bowl. The shock of cold and pain will awaken him.

Stephen believes that he is dying, and he has resolved to die properly. Each visit to the cold country brings him closer to death; and death, he has learned, is only a slow walk through ice fields. He has come to appreciate the complete lack of warmth and the beautifully etched face of his magical country.

But he is connected to the bright, flat world of the hospital by plastic tubes—one breathes cold oxygen into his left nostril, another passes into his right nostril and down his throat to his stomach; one feeds him intravenously, another draws his urine.

"Here's your ice," Josie says. "But mind you, don't spill it." She places the small bowl on his traytable and wheels the table close to him. She has a musky odor of perspiration and perfume; Stephen is reminded of old women and college girls.

"Sleep now, sweet boy."

Without opening his eyes, Stephen reaches out and places his hand on the ice.

"Come, now, Stephen, wake up. Dr. Volk is here to see you."

Stephen feels the cool touch of Josie's hand, and he opens his eyes to see the doctor standing beside him. The doctor has a gaunt, long face and thinning brown hair; he is dressed in a wrinkled green suit.

"Now we'll check the dressing, Stephen," he says as he tears away a gauze bandage on Stephen's abdomen.

Stephen feels the pain, but he is removed from it. His only wish is to return to the blue dreamlands. He watches the doctor peel off the neat crosshatching of gauze. A terrible stink fills the room.

Josie stands well away from the bed.

"Now we'll check your drains." The doctor pulls a long drainage tube out of Stephen's abdomen, irrigates and disinfects the wound, inserts a new drain, and repeats the process by pulling out another tube just below the rib cage.

Stephen imagines that he is swimming out of the room. He tries to cross the hazy border into cooler regions, but it is difficult to concentrate. He has only a half hour at most before the Demerol will wear off. Already, the pain is coming closer, and he will not be due for another injection until the night nurse comes on duty. But the night nurse will not give him an injection without an argument. She will tell him to fight the pain.

But he cannot fight without a shot.

"Tomorrow we'll take that oxygen tube out of your nose," the doctor says, but his voice seems far away and Stephen wonders what he is talking about.

He reaches for the bowl of ice, but cannot find it.

"Josie, you've taken my ice."

"I took the ice away when the doctor came. Why don't you try to watch a bit of television with me; Soupy Sales is on."

"Just bring me some ice," Stephen says. "I want to rest a bit." He can feel the sharp edges of pain breaking through the gauzy wraps of Demerol.

"I love you, Josie," he says sleepily as she places a fresh bowl of ice on his tray.

As Stephen wanders through his ice-blue dreamworld, he sees a rectangle of blinding white light. It looks like a doorway into an adjoining world of brightness. He has glimpsed it before, on previous Demerol highs. A coal-dark doorway stands beside the bright one.

He walks toward the portals, passes through white-blue conefields.

Time is growing short. The drug cannot stretch it much longer. Stephen knows that he has to choose either the bright doorway or the dark, one or the other. He does not even consider turning around, for he has dreamed that the ice and glass and cold blue gemstones have melted behind him.

It makes no difference to Stephen which doorway he chooses. On impulse he steps into blazing, searing whiteness.

Suddenly he is in a cramped world of people and sound.

The boxcar's doors were flung open. Stephen was being pushed out of the cramped boxcar, which stank of sweat, feces, and urine. Several people had died in the car and added their stink of death to the already fetid air.

"Carla, stay close to me," shouted a man beside Stephen. He had been separated from his wife by a young woman who pushed between them as she tried to return to the dark safety of the boxcar.

SS men in black, dirty uniforms were everywhere. They kicked and pommeled everyone within reach. Alsatian guard dogs snapped and barked. Stephen was bitten by one of the snarling dogs. A woman beside him was being kicked by soldiers. And they were all being methodically herded past a high barbed-wire fence. Beside the fence was a wall.

Stephen looked around for an escape route, but he was surrounded by other prisoners, who were pressing against him. Soldiers were shooting indiscriminately into the crowd, shooting women and children alike.

The man who had shouted to his wife was shot.

"Sholom, help me, help me," screamed a scrawny young woman whose skin was as yellow and pimpled as chicken flesh.

And Stephen understood that *he* was Sholom. He was a Jew in this burning, stinking world, and this woman, somehow, meant something to him. He felt the yellow star sewn on the breast of his filthy jacket. He grimaced uncontrollably. The strangest thoughts were passing through his mind, remembrances of another childhood: morning prayers with his father and rich uncle, large breakfasts on Saturdays, the sounds of his mother and father quietly making love in the next room, *yortseit* candles burning in the living room, his brother reciting the "four questions" at the Passover table.

He touched the star again and remembered the Nazis' facetious euphemism for it: *Pour le Sémite.*

He wanted to strike out, to kill the Nazis, to fight and die. But he found himself marching with the others, as if he had no will of his own. He felt that he was cut in half. He had two selves now; one watched the other. One self wanted to fight. The other was numbed; it cared only for itself. It was determined to survive.

Stephen looked around for the woman who had called out to him. She was nowhere to be seen.

Behind him were railroad tracks, electrified wire, and the conical tower and main gate of the camp. Ahead was a pitted road littered with corpses and their belongings. Rifles were being fired, and a heavy, sickly-sweet odor was everywhere. Stephen gagged, others vomited. It was the overwhelming stench of death, of rotting and burning flesh. Black clouds hung above the camp, and flames spurted from the tall chimneys of ugly buildings, as if from infernal machines.

Stephen walked onward: he was numb, unable to fight or even talk. Everything that happened around him was impossible, the stuff of dreams.

The prisoners were ordered to halt, and the soldiers began to separate those who would be burned from those who would be worked to death. Old men and women and young children were pulled out of the crowd. Some were beaten and killed immediately, while the others looked on in disbelief. Stephen looked on, as if it was of no concern to him. Everything was unreal, dreamlike. He did not belong here.

The new prisoners looked like Musselmanner, the walking dead. Those who became ill, or were beaten or starved before they could "wake up" to the reality of the camps, became Musselmanner. Musselmanner could not think or feel. They shuffled around, already dead in spirit, until a guard or disease or cold or starvation killed them.

"Keep marching," shouted a guard as Stephen stopped before an emaciated old man crawling on the ground. "You'll look like him soon enough."

Suddenly, as if waking from one dream and finding himself in another, Stephen remembered that the chicken-skinned girl was his wife.

He remembered their life together, their children and crowded flat. He remembered the birthmark on her leg, her scent, her hungry love-making. He had once fought another boy over her.

His glands opened up with fear and shame; he had ignored her screams for help.

He stopped and turned, faced the other group. "Fruma," he shouted, then started to run.

A guard struck him in the chest with the butt of his rifle, and Stephen fell into darkness.

He spills the ice water again and awakens with a scream.

"It's my fault," Josie says as she peels back the sheets. "I should have taken the bowl away from you. But you fight me."

Stephen lives with the pain again. He imagines that a tiny fire is burning in his abdomen, slowly consuming him. He stares at the television high on the wall and watches Soupy Sales.

As Josie changes the plastic sac containing his intravenous saline solution, an orderly pushes a cart into the room and asks Stephen if he wants a print for his wall.

"Would you like me to choose something for you?" Josie asks.

Stephen shakes his head and asks the orderly to show him all the prints. Most of them are familiar still lifes and pastorals, but one catches his attention. It is a painting of a wheat field. Although the sky looks ominously dark, the wheat is brightly rendered in great, broad strokes. A path cuts through the field and crows fly overhead.

"That one," Stephen says. "Put that one up."

After the orderly hangs the print and leaves, Josie asks Stephen why he chose that particular painting.

"I like Van Gogh," he says dreamily as he tries to detect a rhythm in the surges of abdominal pain. But he is not nauseated, just gaseous.

"Any particular reason why you like Van Gogh?" asks Josie. "He's my favorite artist too."

"I didn't say he was my favorite," Stephen says, and Josie pouts, an expression that does not fit her prematurely lined face. Stephen closes his eyes, glimpses the cold country, and says, "I like the painting because it's so bright that it's almost frightening. And the road going through the field"—he opens his eyes—"doesn't go anywhere. It just ends in the field. And the crows are flying around like vultures."

"Most people see it as just a pretty picture," Josie says.

"What's it called?"

"Wheat Field with Blackbirds."

"Sensible. My stomach hurts, Josie. Help me turn over on my side." Josie helps him onto his left side, plumps up his pillows, and inserts a short tube into his rectum to relieve the gas. "I also like the painting with the large stars that all look out of focus," Stephen says. "What's it called?"

"Starry Night."

"That's scary too," Stephen says. Josie takes his blood pressure, makes a notation on his chart, then sits down beside him and holds his hand. "I remember something," he says. "Something just—" He jumps as he remembers, and pain shoots through his distended stomach. Josie shushes him, checks the intravenous needle, and asks him what he remembers.

But the memory of the dream recedes as the pain grows sharper. "I hurt all the fucking time, Josie," he says, changing position. Josie removes the rectal tube before he is on his back.

"Don't use such language, I don't like to hear it. I know you have a lot of pain," she says, her voice softening.

"Time for a shot."

"No, honey, not for some time. You'll just have to bear it."

Stephen remembers his dream again. He is afraid of it. His breath is short and his heart feels as if it is beating in his throat, but he recounts the entire dream to Josie.

He does not notice that her face has lost its color.

"It is only a dream, Stephen. Probably something you studied in history."

"But it was so real, not like a dream at all."

"That's enough!" Josie says.

"I'm sorry I upset you. Don't be angry."

"I'm *not* angry."

"I'm sorry," he says, fighting the pain, squeezing Josie's hand tightly. "Didn't you tell me that you were in the Second World War?"

Josie is composed once again. "Yes, I did, but I'm surprised you remembered. You were very sick. I was a nurse overseas, spent most of the war in England. But I was one of the first women to go into any of the concentration camps."

Stephen drifts with the pain; he appears to be asleep.

"You must have studied very hard," Josie whispers to him. Her hand is shaking just a bit.

It is twelve o'clock and his room is death-quiet. The sharp shadows seem to be the hardest objects in the room. The fluorescents burn steadily in the hall outside.

Stephen looks out into the hallway, but he can see only the far white wall. He waits for his night nurse to appear: it is time for his injection. A young nurse passes by his doorway. Stephen imagines that she is a cardboard ship sailing through the corridors.

He presses his buzzer, which is attached by a clip to his pillow. The night nurse will take her time, he tells himself. He remembers arguing with her. Angrily, he presses the buzzer again.

Across the hall, a man begins to scream, and there is a shuffle of nurses into his room. The screaming turns into begging and whining. Although Stephen has never seen the man in the opposite room, he has come to hate him. Like Stephen, he has something wrong with his stomach; but he cannot suffer well. He can only beg and cry, try to make deals with the nurses, doctors, God, and angels. Stephen cannot muster any pity for this man.

The night nurse finally comes into the room, says, "You have to try to get along without this," and gives him an injection of Demerol.

"Why does the man across the hall scream so?" Stephen asks, but the nurse is already edging out of the room.

"Because he's in pain."

"So am I," Stephen says in a loud voice. "But I can keep it to myself."

"Then, stop buzzing me constantly for an injection. That man across the hall has had half of his stomach removed. He's got something to scream about."

So have I, Stephen thinks; but the nurse disappears before he can tell her. He tries to imagine what the man across the hall looks like. He thinks of him as being bald and small, an ancient baby. Stephen tries to feel sorry for the man, but his incessant whining disgusts him.

The drug takes effect; the screams recede as he hurtles through the dark corridors of a dream. The cold country is dark, for Stephen cannot persuade his night nurse to bring him some ice. Once again, he sees two entrances. As the world melts behind him, he steps into the coal-black doorway.

In the darkness he hears an alarm, a bone-jarring clangor.

He could smell the combined stink of men pressed closely together. They were all lying upon two badly constructed wooden shelves. The floor was dirt; the smell of urine never left the barrack.

"Wake up," said a man Stephen knew as Viktor. "If the guard finds you in bed, you'll be beaten again."

Stephen moaned, still wrapped in dreams. "Wake up, wake up," he mumbled to himself. He would have a few more minutes before the guard arrived with the dogs. At the very thought of dogs, Stephen felt revulsion. He had once been bitten in the face by a large dog.

He opened his eyes, yet he was still half asleep, exhausted. You are in a death camp, he said to himself. You must wake up. You must fight by waking up. Or you will die in your sleep. Shaking uncontrollably, he said, "Do you want to end up in the oven, perhaps you will be lucky today and live."

As he lowered his legs to the floor, he felt the sores open on the soles of his feet. He wondered who would die today and shrugged. It was his third week in the camp. Impossibly, against all odds, he had survived. Most of those he had known in the train had either died or become Musselmanner. If it were not for Viktor, he, too, would have become a Musselmann. He had a breakdown and wanted to die. He babbled in English. But Viktor talked him out of death, shared his portion of food with him, and taught him the new rules of life.

"Like everyone else who survives, I count myself first, second, and third—then I try to do what I can for someone else," Viktor had said.

"I will survive," Stephen repeated to himself as the guards opened the door, stepped into the room, and began to shout. Their dogs growled and snapped, but heeled beside them. The guards looked sleepy; one did not wear a cap, and his red hair was tousled.

Perhaps he spent the night with one of the whores, Stephen thought. Perhaps today would not be so bad. . . .

And so begins the morning ritual: Josie enters Stephen's room at a quarter to eight, fusses with the chart attached to the footboard of his bed, pads about aimlessly, and finally goes to the bathroom. She returns, her stiff uniform making swishing sounds. Stephen can feel her standing over the bed and staring at him. But he does not open his eyes. He waits a beat.

She turns away, then drops the bedpan. Yesterday it was the metal ashtray; day before that, she bumped into the bedstand.

"Good morning, darling, it's a beautiful day," she says, then walks across the room to the windows. She parts the faded orange drapes and opens the blinds. "How do you feel today?"

"Okay, I guess."

Josie takes his pulse and asks, "Did Mr. Gregory stop in to say hello last night?"

"Yes," Stephen says. "He's teaching me how to play gin rummy. What's wrong with him?"

"He's very sick."

"I can see that; has he got cancer?"

"I don't know," says Josie as she tidies up his night table.

"You're lying again," Stephen says, but she ignores him. After a time, he says, "His girlfriend was in to see me last night, I bet his wife will be in today."

"Shut your mouth about that," Josie says. "Let's get you out of that bed, so I can change the sheets."

Stephen sits in the chair all morning. He is getting well but is still very weak. Just before lunchtime, the orderly wheels his cart into the room and asks Stephen if he would like to replace the print hanging on the wall.

"I've seen them all," Stephen says. "I'll keep the one I have." Stephen does not grow tired of the Van Gogh painting; sometimes, the crows seem to have changed position.

"Maybe you'll like this one," the orderly says as he pulls out a cardboard print of Van Gogh's *Starry Night*. It is a study of a village nestled in the hills, dressed in shadows. But everything seems to be boiling and writhing as in a fever dream. A cypress tree in the foreground looks like a black flame, and the vertiginous sky is filled with great, blurry stars. It is a drunkard's dream. The orderly smiles.

"So you did have it," Stephen says.

"No, I traded some other pictures for it. They had a copy in the West Wing."

Stephen watches him hang it, thanks him, and waits for him to leave. Then he gets up and examines the painting carefully. He touches the raised facsimile brushstrokes, and turns toward Josie, feeling an odd sensation in his groin. He looks at her, as if seeing her for the first time. She has an overly full mouth, which curves downward at the corners when she smiles. She is not a pretty woman—too fat, he thinks.

"Dance with me," he says, as he waves his arms and takes a step forward, conscious of the pain in his stomach.

"You're too sick to be dancing just yet," but she laughs at him and bends her knees in a mock plié.

She has small breasts for such a large woman, Stephen thinks. Feeling suddenly dizzy, he takes a step toward the bed. He feels himself slip to the floor, feels Josie's hair brushing against his face, dreams that he's all wet from her tongue, feels her arms around him, squeezing, then feels the weight of body pressing down on him, crushing him. . . .

He wakes up in bed, catheterized. He has an intravenous needle in his left wrist, and it is difficult to swallow, for he has a tube down his throat.

He groans, tries to move.

"Quiet, Stephen," Josie says, stroking his hand.

"What happened?" he mumbles. He can only remember being dizzy.

"You've had a slight setback, so just rest. The doctor had to collapse your lung; you must lie very still."

"Josie, I love you," he whispers, but he is too far away to be heard. He wonders how many hours or days have passed. He looks toward the window. It is dark, and there is no one in the room.

He presses the buzzer attached to his pillow and remembers a dream. . . .

"You must fight," Viktor said.

It was dark, all the other men were asleep, and the barrack was filled with snoring and snorting. Stephen wished they could all die, choke on their own breath. It would be an act of mercy.

"Why fight?" Stephen asked, and he pointed toward the greasy window, beyond which were the ovens that smoked day and night. He made a fluttering gesture with his hand—smoke rising.

"You must fight, you must live; living is everything. It is the only thing that makes sense here."

"We're all going to die, anyway," Stephen whispered. "Just like your sister . . . and my wife."

"No, Sholom, we're going to live. The others may die, but we're going to live. You must believe that."

Stephen understood that Viktor was desperately trying to convince himself to live. He felt sorry for Viktor; there could be no sensible rationale for living in a place like this. Everything must die here.

Stephen grinned, tasted blood from the corner of his mouth, and said, "So we'll live through the night, maybe."

And maybe tomorrow, he thought. He would play the game of survival a little longer.

He wondered if Viktor would be alive tomorrow. He smiled and thought, If Viktor dies, then I will have to take his place and convince others to live. For an instant, he hoped Viktor would die so that he could take his place.

The alarm sounded. It was three o'clock in the morning, time to begin the day.

This morning, Stephen was on his feet before the guards could un-lock the door.

"Wake up," Josie says, gently tapping his arm. "Come on now, wake up."

Stephen hears her voice as an echo. He imagines that he has been flung into a long tunnel; he hears air whistling in his ears but cannot see anything.

"Whassimatter?" he asks. His mouth feels as if it is stuffed with cot-ton; his lips are dry and cracked. He is suddenly angry at Josie and the plastic tubes that hold him in his bed as if he were a latter-day Gulliver. He wants to pull out the tubes, smash the bags filled with saline, tear away his bandages.

"You were speaking German," Josie says. "Did you know that?"

"Can I have some ice?"

"No," Josie says impatiently. "You spilled again, you're all wet."

". . . for my mouth, dry. . . ."

"Do you remember speaking German, honey, I have to know."

"Don't remember, bring ice, I'll try to think about it."

As Josie leaves to get him some ice, he tries to remember his dream.

"Here now, just suck on the ice." She gives him a little hill of crushed ice on the end of a spoon.

"Why did you wake me up, Josie?" The layers of dream are beginning to slough off. As the Demerol works out of his system, he has to con-centrate on fighting the burning ache in his stomach.

"You were speaking German. Where did you learn to speak like that?"

Stephen tries to remember what he said. He cannot speak any Ger-man, only a bit of classroom French. He looks down at his legs (he has thrown off the sheet) and notices, for the first time, that his legs are as thin as his arms. "My God, Josie, how could I have lost so much weight?"

"You lost about forty pounds, but don't worry, you'll gain it all back. You're on the road to recovery now. Please, try to remember your dream."

"I can't, Josie! I just can't seem to get ahold of it."

"Try."

"Why is it so important to you?"

"You weren't speaking college German, darling, you were speaking slang. You spoke in a patois that I haven't heard since the forties."

Stephen feels a chill slowly creep up his spine. "What did I say?"

Josie waits a beat, then says, "You talked about dying."

"Josie?"

"Yes," she says, pulling at her fingernail.

"When is the pain going to stop?"

"It will be over soon." She gives him another spoonful of ice. "You kept repeating the name Viktor in your sleep. Can you remember anything about him?"

Viktor, Viktor, deep-set blue eyes, balding head and broken nose, called himself a Galitzianer. Saved my life. "I remember," Stephen says. "His name is Viktor Shmone. He is in all my dreams now."

Josie exhales sharply.

"Does that mean anything to you?" Stephen asks anxiously.

"I once knew a man from one of the camps." She speaks very slowly and precisely. "His name was Viktor Shmone. I took care of him. He was one of the few people left alive in the camp after the Germans fled." She reaches for her purse, which she keeps on Stephen's night table, and fumbles an old, torn photograph out of a plastic slipcase.

As Stephen examines the photograph, he begins to sob. A thinner and much younger Josie is standing beside Viktor and two other emaciated-looking men. "Then, I'm not dreaming," he says, "and I'm going to die. That's what it means." He begins to shake, just as he did in his dream, and, without thinking, he makes the gesture of rising smoke to Josie. He begins to laugh.

"Stop that," Josie says, raising her hand to slap him. Then she embraces him and says, "Don't cry, darling, it's only a dream. Somehow, you're dreaming the past."

"Why?" Stephen asks, still shaking.

"Maybe you're dreaming because of me, because we're so close. In some ways, I think you know me better than anyone else, better than any man, no doubt. You might be dreaming for a reason; maybe I can help you."

"I'm afraid, Josie."

She comforts him and says, "Now tell me everything you can remember about the dreams."

He is exhausted. As he recounts his dreams to her, he sees the bright doorway again. He feels himself being sucked into it. "Josie," he says, "I must stay awake, don't want to sleep, dream. . . ."

Josie's face is pulled tight as a mask; she is crying.

Stephen reaches out to her, slips into the bright doorway, into another dream.

It was a cold, cloudless morning. Hundreds of prisoners were working in the quarries; each work gang came from a different barrack. Most of the gangs were made up of Musselmanner, the faceless majority of the camp. They moved like automatons, lifting and carrying the great stones to the numbered carts, which would have to be pushed down the tracks.

Stephen was drenched with sweat. He had a fever and was afraid that he had contracted typhus. An epidemic had broken out in the camp last week. Every morning, several doctors arrived with the guards. Those who were too sick to stand up were taken away to be gassed or experimented upon in the hospital.

Although Stephen could barely stand, he forced himself to keep moving. He tried to focus all his attention on what he was doing. He made a ritual of bending over, choosing a stone of a certain size, lifting it, carrying it to the nearest cart, and then taking the same number of steps back to his dig.

A Musselmann fell to the ground, but Stephen made no effort to help him. When he could help someone in a little way, he would, but he would not stick his neck out for a Musselmann. Yet something niggled at Stephen. He remembered a photograph in which Viktor and this Musselmann were standing with a man and a woman he did not recognize. But Stephen could not remember where he had ever seen such a photograph.

"Hey, you," shouted a guard. "Take the one on the ground to the cart."

Stephen nodded to the guard and began to drag the Musselmann away.

"Who's the new patient down the hall?" Stephen asks as he eats a bit of cereal from the breakfast tray Josie has placed before him. He is feeling much better now; his fever is down and the tubes, catheter, and intravenous needle have been removed. He can even walk around a bit.

"How did you find out about that?" Josie asks.

"You were talking to Mr. Gregory's nurse. Do you think I'm dead already? I can still hear."

Josie laughs and takes a sip of Stephen's tea. "You're far from dead! In fact, today is a red-letter day, you're going to take your first shower. What do you think about that?"

"I'm not well enough yet," he says, worried that he will have to leave the hospital before he is ready.

"Well, Dr. Volk thinks differently, and his word is law."

"Tell me about the new patient."

"They brought in a man last night who drank two quarts of motor oil; he's on the dialysis machine."

"Will he make it?"

"No, I don't think so; there's too much poison in his system."

We should all die, Stephen thinks. It would be an act of mercy. He glimpses the camp.

"Stephen!"

He jumps, then awakens.

"You've had a good night's sleep, you don't need to nap. Let's get you into that shower and have it done with." Josie pushes the traytable away from the bed. "Come on, I have your bathrobe right here."

Stephen puts on his bathrobe, and they walk down the hall to the showers. There are three empty shower stalls, a bench, and a whirlpool bath. As Stephen takes off his bathrobe, Josie adjusts the water pressure and temperature in the corner stall.

"What's the matter?" Stephen asks after stepping into the shower. Josie stands in front of the shower stall and holds his towel, but she will not look at him. "Come on," he says, "you've seen me naked before."

"That was different."

"How?" He touches a hard, ugly scab that has formed over one of the wounds on his abdomen.

"When you were very sick, I washed you in bed as if you were a baby. Now it's different." She looks down at the wet tile floor as if she is lost in thought.

"Well, I think it's silly," he says. "Come on, it's hard to talk to someone who's looking the other way. I could break my neck in here and you'd be staring down at the fucking floor."

"I've asked you not to use that word," she says in a very low voice.

"Do my eyes still look yellowish?"

She looks directly at his face and says, "No, they look fine."

Stephen suddenly feels faint, then nauseated; he has been standing too long. As he leans against the cold shower wall, he remembers his last dream. He is back in the quarry. He can smell the perspiration of the men around him, feel the sun baking him, draining his strength. It is so bright. . . .

He finds himself sitting on the bench and staring at the light on the opposite wall. I've got typhus, he thinks, then realizes that he is in the hospital. Josie is beside him.

"I'm sorry," he says.

"I shouldn't have let you stand so long; it was my fault."

"I remembered another dream." He begins to shake, and Josie puts her arms around him.

"It's all right now; tell Josie about your dream."

She's an old, fat woman, Stephen thinks. As he describes the dream, his shaking subsides.

"Do you know the man's name?" Josie asks. "The one the guard ordered you to drag away."

"No," Stephen says. "He was a Musselmann, yet I thought there was something familiar about him. In my dream I remembered the photograph you showed me. He was in it."

"What will happen to him?"

"The guards will give him to the doctors for experimentation. If they don't want him, he'll be gassed "

"You must not let that happen," Josie says, holding him tightly.

"Why?" asks Stephen, afraid that he will fall into the dreams again.

"If he was one of the men you saw in the photograph, you must not let him die. Your dreams must fit the past."

"I'm afraid."

"It will be all right, baby," Josie says, clinging to him. She is shaking and breathing heavily.

Stephen feels himself getting an erection. He calms her, presses his face against hers, and touches her breasts. She tells him to stop but does not push him away.

"I love you," he says as he slips his hand under her starched skirt. He feels awkward and foolish and warm.

"This is wrong," she whispers.

As Stephen kisses her and feels her thick tongue in his mouth, he begins to dream. . . .

Stephen stopped to rest for a few seconds. The Musselmann was dead weight. I cannot go on, Stephen thought, but he bent down, grabbed the Musselmann by his coat, and dragged him toward the cart. He glimpsed the cart, which was filled with the sick and dead and exhausted; it looked no different than a cartload of corpses marked for a mass grave.

A long, gray cloud covered the sun, then passed, drawing shadows across gutted hills.

On impulse, Stephen dragged the Musselmann into a gully behind several chalky rocks. Why am I doing this? he asked himself. If I'm caught, I'll be ash in the ovens too. He remembered what Viktor had told him: "You must think of yourself all the time or you'll be no help to anyone else."

The Musselmann groaned, then raised his arm. His face was gray with dust and his eyes were glazed.

"You must lie still," Stephen whispered. "Do not make a sound. I've hidden you from the guards, but if they hear you, we'll all be punished. One sound from you and you're dead. You must fight to live; you're in a death camp; you must fight so you can tell of this later."

"I have no family, they're all—"

Stephen clapped his hand over the man's mouth and whispered, "Fight, don't talk. Wake up; you cannot survive the death camp by sleeping."

The man nodded, and Stephen climbed out of the gully. He helped two men carry a large stone to a nearby cart.

"What are you doing?" shouted a guard.

"I left my place to help these men with this stone; now I'll go back where I was."

"What the hell are you trying to do?" Viktor asked.

Stephen felt as if he was burning up with fever. He wiped the sweat from his eyes, but everything was still blurry.

"You're sick, too. You'll be lucky if you last the day."

"I'll last," Stephen said, "but I want you to help me get him back to the camp."

"I won't risk it, not for a Musselmann. He's already dead; leave him."

"Like you left me?"

Before the guards could take notice, they began to work. Although Viktor was older than Stephen, he was stronger. He worked hard every day and never caught the diseases that daily reduced the barrack's numbers. Stephen had a touch of death, as Viktor called it, and was often sick.

They worked until dusk, when the sun's oblique rays caught the dust from the quarries and turned it into veils and scrims. Even the guards sensed that this was a quiet time, for they would congregate together and talk in hushed voices.

"Come, now, help me," Stephen whispered to Viktor.

"I've been doing that all day," Viktor said. "I'll have enough trouble getting you back to the camp, much less carry this Musselmann."

"We can't leave him."

"Why are you so preoccupied with this Musselmann? Even if we can get him back to the camp, his chances are nothing. I know—I've seen enough—I know who has a chance to survive."

"You're wrong this time," Stephen said. He was dizzy and it was difficult to stand. The odds are I won't last the night, and Viktor knows it, he told himself. "I had a dream that if this man dies, I'll die too. I just feel it."

"Here we learn to trust our dreams," Viktor said. "They make as much sense as this. . . ." He made the gesture of rising smoke and gazed toward the ovens, which were spewing fire and black ash.

The western portion of the sky was yellow, but over the ovens it was red and purple and dark blue. Although it horrified Stephen to consider it, there was a macabre beauty here. If he survived, he would never forget these sense impressions, which were stronger than anything he had ever experienced before. Being so close to death, he was, perhaps for the first time, really living. In the camp, one did not even consider suicide. One grasped for every moment, sucked at life like an infant, lived as if there were no future.

The guards shouted at the prisoners to form a column; it was time to march back to the barracks.

While the others milled about, Stephen and Viktor lifted the Musselmann out of the gully. Everyone nearby tried to distract the guards. When the march began, Stephen and Viktor held the Musselmann between them, for he could barely stand.

"Come on, dead one, carry your weight," Viktor said. "Are you so dead that you cannot hear me? Are you as dead as the rest of your family?" The Musselmann groaned and dragged his legs. Viktor kicked him. "You'll walk or we'll leave you here for the guards to find."

"Let him be," Stephen said.

"Are you dead or do you have a name?" Viktor continued.

"Berek," croaked the Musselmann. "I am not dead."

"Then, we have a fine bunk for you," Viktor said. "You can smell the

stink of the sick for another night before the guards make a selection."
Viktor made the gesture of smoke rising.

Stephen stared at the barracks ahead. They seemed to waver as the
heat rose from the ground. He counted every step. He would drop
soon; he could not go on, could not carry the Musselmann.

He began to mumble in English.

"So you're speaking American again," Viktor said.

Stephen shook himself awake, placed one foot before the other.

"Dreaming of an American lover?"

"I don't know English and I have no American lover."

"Then, who is this Josie you keep talking about in your sleep . . . ?"

"Why were you screaming?" Josie asks as she washes his face with a
cold washcloth.

"I don't remember screaming," Stephen says. He discovers a fever
blister on his lip. Expecting to find an intravenous needle in his wrist,
he raises his arm.

"You don't need an I.V.," Josie says. "You just have a bit of a fever. Dr.
Volk has prescribed some new medication for it."

"What time is it?" Stephen stares at the whorls in the ceiling.

"Almost 3 P.M. I'll be going off soon."

"Then I've slept most of the day away," Stephen says, feeling something crawling inside him. He worries that his dreams still have a hold
on him. "Am I having another relapse?"

"You'll do fine," Josie says.

"I should be fine now; I don't want to dream anymore."

"Did you dream again, do you remember anything?"

"I dreamed that I saved the Musselmann," Stephen says.

"What was his name?" asks Josie.

"Berek, I think. Is that the man you knew?"

Josie nods and Stephen smiles at her. "Maybe that's the end of the
dreams," he says; but she does not respond. He asks to see the photograph again.

"Not just now," Josie says.

"But I have to see it. I want to see if I can recognize myself. . . ."

Stephen dreamed he was dead, but it was only the fever. Viktor sat
beside him on the floor and watched the others. The sick were moan-
ing and crying; they slept on the cramped platform, as if proximity to

one another could ensure a few more hours of life. Wan moonlight seemed to fill the barrack.

Stephen awakened, feverish. "I'm burning up," he whispered to Viktor.

"Well," Viktor said, "you've got your Musselmann. If he lives, you live. That's what you said, isn't it?"

"I don't remember; I just knew that I couldn't let him die."

"You'd better go back to sleep; you'll need your strength. Or we may have to carry *you*, tomorrow."

Stephen tried to sleep, but the fever was making lights and spots before his eyes. When he finally fell asleep, he dreamed of a dark country filled with gemstones and great quarries of ice and glass.

"What?" Stephen asked, as he sat up suddenly, awakened from dampblack dreams. He looked around and saw that everyone was watching Berek, who was sitting under the window at the far end of the room.

Berek was singing the Kol Nidre very softly. It was the Yom Kippur prayer, sung on the most holy of days. He repeated the prayer three times, and then once again in a louder voice. The others responded, intoned the prayer as a recitative. Viktor was crying quietly, and Stephen imagined that the holy spirit animated Berek. Surely, he told himself, that face and those pale, unseeing eyes were those of a dead man. He remembered the story of the golem, shuddered, found himself singing and pulsing with fever.

When the prayer was over, Berek fell back into his fever trance. The others became silent, then slept. But there was something new in the barrack with them tonight, a palpable exultation. Stephen looked around at the sleepers and thought, We're surviving, more dead than alive, but surviving. . . .

"You were right about that Musselmann," Viktor whispered. "It's good that we saved him."

"Perhaps we should sit with him," Stephen said. "He's alone." But Viktor was already asleep; and Stephen was suddenly afraid that if he sat beside Berek, he would be consumed by his holy fire.

As Stephen fell through sleep and dreams, his face burned with fever.

Again he wakes up screaming.

"Josie," he says, "I can remember the dream, but there's something else, something I can't see, something terrible. . . ."

"Not to worry," Josie says, "it's the fever." But she looks worried, and Stephen is sure that she knows something he does not.

"Tell me what happened to Viktor and Berek," Stephen says. He presses his hands together to stop them from shaking.

"They lived, just as you are going to live and have a good life."

Stephen calms down and tells her his dream.

"So you see," she says, "you're even dreaming about surviving."

"I'm burning up."

"Dr. Volk says you're doing very well." Josie sits beside him, and he watches the fever patterns shift behind his closed eyelids.

"Tell me what happens next, Josie."

"You're going to get well."

"There's something else. . . ."

"Shush, now, there's nothing else." She pauses, then says, "Mr. Gregory is supposed to visit you tonight. He's getting around a bit, he's been back and forth all day in his wheelchair. He tells me that you two have made some sort of a deal about dividing up all the nurses."

Stephen smiles, opens his eyes, and says, "It was Gregory's idea. Tell me what's wrong with him."

"All right, he has cancer, but he doesn't know it and you must keep it a secret. They cut the nerve in his leg because the pain was so bad. He's quite comfortable now, but remember, you can't repeat what I've told you."

"Is he going to live?" Stephen asks. "He's told me about all the new projects he's planning, so I guess he's expecting to get out of here."

"He's not going to live very long, and the doctor didn't want to break his spirit."

"I think he should be told."

"That's not your decision to make, nor mine."

"Am I going to die, Josie?"

"No!" she says, touching his arm to reassure him.

"How do I know that's the truth?"

"Because I say so, and I couldn't look you straight in the eye and tell you if it wasn't true. I should have known it would be a mistake to tell you about Mr. Gregory."

"You did right," Stephen says. "I won't mention it again. Now that I know, I feel better." He feels drowsy again.

"Do you think you're up to seeing him tonight?"

Stephen nods, although he is bone tired. As he falls asleep, the fever

patterns begin to dissolve, leaving a bright field. With a start, he opens
his eyes: he has touched the edge of another dream.

"What happened to the man across the hall, the one who was always
screaming?"

"He's left the ward," Josie says. "Mr. Gregory had better hurry if he
wants to play cards with you before dinner. They're going to bring the
trays up soon."

"You mean he died, don't you."

"Yes, if you must know, he died. But *you're* going to live."

There is a crashing noise in the hallway. Someone shouts, and Josie
runs to the door.

Stephen tries to stay awake, but he is being pulled back into the cold
country.

"Mr. Gregory fell trying to get into his wheelchair by himself," Josie
says. "He should have waited for his nurse, but she was out of the room
and he wanted to visit you."

But Stephen does not hear a word she says.

There were rumors that the camp was going to be liberated. It was
late, but no one was asleep. The shadows in the barrack seemed larger
tonight.

"It's better for us if the Allies don't come," Viktor said to Stephen.

"Why do you say that?"

"Haven't you noticed that the ovens are going day and night? The
Nazis are in a hurry."

"I'm going to try to sleep," Stephen said.

"Look around you; even the Musselmanner are agitated," Viktor said.
"Animals become nervous before the slaughter. I've worked with animals. People are not so different."

"Shut up and let me sleep," Stephen said, and he dreamed that he
could hear the crackling of distant gunfire.

"Attention," shouted the guards as they stepped into the barrack.
There were more guards than usual, and each one had two Alsatian
dogs. "Come on, form a line. Hurry."

"They're going to kill us," Viktor said; "then they'll evacuate the camp
and save themselves."

The guards marched the prisoners toward the northern section of the
camp. Although it was still dark, it was hot and humid, without a trace
of the usual morning chill. The ovens belched fire and turned the sky

aglow. Everyone was quiet, for there was nothing to be done. The guards were nervous and would cut down anyone who uttered a sound, as an example for the rest.

The booming of big guns could be heard in the distance.

If I'm going to die, Stephen thought, I might as well go now, and take a Nazi with me. Suddenly, all of his buried fear, aggression, and revulsion surfaced; his face became hot and his heart felt as if it were pumping in his throat. But Stephen argued with himself. There was always a chance. He had once heard of some women who were waiting in line for the ovens; for no apparent reason, the guards sent them back to their barracks. Anything could happen. There was always a chance. But to attack a guard would mean certain death.

The guns became louder. Stephen could not be sure, but he thought the noise was coming from the west. The thought passed through his mind that everyone would be better off dead. That would stop all the guns and screaming voices, the clenched fists and wildly beating hearts. The Nazis should kill everyone, and then themselves, as a favor to humanity.

The guards stopped the prisoners in an open field surrounded on three sides by forestland. Sunrise was moments away; purple-black clouds drifted across the sky touched by gray in the east. It promised to be a hot, gritty day.

Half-step Walter, a Judenrat sympathizer who worked for the guards, handed out shovel heads to everyone.

"He's worse than the Nazis," Viktor said to Stephen.

"The Judenrat thinks he will live," said Berek, "but he will die like a Jew with the rest of us."

"Now, when it's too late, the Musselmann regains consciousness," Viktor said.

"Hurry," shouted the guards, "or you'll die now. As long as you dig, you'll live."

Stephen hunkered down on his knees and began to dig with the shovel head.

"Do you think we might escape?" Berek whined.

"Shut up and dig," Stephen said. "There is no escape, just stay alive as long as you can. Stop whining, are you becoming a Musselmann again?" Stephen noticed that other prisoners were gathering up twigs and branches. So the Nazis plan to cover us up, he thought.

"That's enough," shouted a guard. "Put your shovels down in front of you and stand in a line."

The prisoners stood shoulder to shoulder along the edge of the mass grave. Stephen stood between Viktor and Berek. Someone screamed and ran and was shot immediately.

I don't want to see trees or guards or my friends, Stephen thought as he stared into the sun. I only want to see the sun, let it burn out my eyes, fill up my head with light. He was shaking uncontrollably, quaking with fear.

Guns were booming in the background.

Maybe the guards won't kill us, Stephen thought, even as he heard the crackcrack of their rifles. Men were screaming and begging for life. Stephen turned his head, only to see someone's face blown away.

Screaming, tasting vomit in his mouth, Stephen fell backward, pulling Viktor and Berek into the grave with him.

Darkness, Stephen thought. His eyes were open, yet it was dark. I must be dead, this must be death. . . .

He could barely move. Corpses can't move, he thought. Something brushed against his face, he stuck out his tongue, felt something spongy. It tasted bitter. Lifting first one arm and then the other, Stephen moved some branches away. Above, he could see a few dim stars; the clouds were lit like lanterns by a quarter moon.

He touched the body beside him; it moved. That must be Viktor, he thought. "Viktor, are you alive, say something if you're alive." Stephen whispered, as if in fear of disturbing the dead.

Viktor groaned and said, "Yes, I'm alive, and so is Berek."

"And the others?"

"All dead. Can't you smell the stink? You, at least, were unconscious all day."

"They can't *all* be dead," Stephen said; then he began to cry.

"Shut up," Viktor said, touching Stephen's face to comfort him. "We're alive, that's something. They could have fired a volley into the pit."

"I thought I was dead," Berek said. He was a shadow among shadows.

"Why are we still here?" Stephen asked.

"We stayed in here because it is safe," Viktor said.

"But they're all dead," Stephen whispered, amazed that there could be speech and reason inside a grave.

"Do you think it's safe to leave now?" Berek asked Viktor.

"Perhaps. I think the killing has stopped. By now the Americans or

English or whoever they are have taken over the camp. I heard gunfire and screaming; I think it's best to wait a while longer."

"Here?" asked Stephen. "Among the dead?"

"It's best to be safe."

It was late afternoon when they climbed out of the grave. The air was thick with flies. Stephen could see bodies sprawled in awkward positions beneath the covering of twigs and branches. "How can I live when all the others are dead?" he asked himself aloud.

"You live, that's all," answered Viktor.

They kept close to the forest and worked their way back toward the camp.

"Look there," Viktor said, motioning Stephen and Berek to take cover. Stephen could see trucks moving toward the camp compound.

"Americans," whispered Berek.

"No need to whisper now," Stephen said. "We're safe."

"Guards could be hiding anywhere," Viktor said. "I haven't slept in the grave to be shot now."

They walked into the camp through a large break in the barbed-wire fence, which had been bit by an artillery shell. When they reached the compound, they found nurses, doctors, and army personnel bustling about.

"You speak English," Viktor said to Stephen as they walked past several quonsets. "Maybe you can speak for us."

"I told you, I can't speak English."

"But I've heard you!"

"Wait," shouted an American army nurse. "You fellows are going the wrong way." She was stocky and spoke perfect German. "You must check in at the hospital; it's back that way."

"No," said Berek, shaking his head. "I won't go in there."

"There's no need to be afraid now," she said. "You're free. Come along, I'll take you to the hospital."

Something familiar about her, Stephen thought. He felt dizzy and everything turned gray.

"Josie," he murmured as he fell to the ground.

"What is it?" Josie asks. "Everything is all right, Josie is here."

"Josie," Stephen mumbles.

"You're all right."

"How can I live when they're all dead?" he asks.

"It was a dream," she says as she wipes the sweat from his forehead. "You see, your fever has broken, you're getting well."

"Did you know about the grave?"

"It's all over now, forget the dream."

"Did you know?"

"Yes," Josie says. "Viktor told me how he survived the grave, but that was so long ago, before you were even born. Dr. Volk tells me you'll be going home soon."

"I don't want to leave, I want to stay with you."

"Stop that talk, you've got a whole life ahead of you. Soon you'll forget all about this, and you'll forget me, too."

"Josie," Stephen asks, "let me see that old photograph again. Just one last time."

"Remember, this is the last time," she says as she hands him the faded photograph.

He recognizes Viktor and Berek, but the young man standing between them is not Stephen. "That's not me," he says, certain that he will never return to the camp.

Yet the shots still echo in his mind.

HARLAN ELLISON

Mom

If you have been blessed with a Jewish mother, then you know there are four things she wants for you: (1) You should be healthy; (2) you should be successful, a doctor, maybe, or if you have to choose second best, then a lawyer, but you must make enough money so you should have a good life and make the neighbors and relatives grind their capped teeth with envy; (3) and now we're getting to the heart of the matter, you should marry a nice girl who can make you a nice family, even if she can't cook as well as your mom; and (4) this is the most important, she must be Jewish.

Now it's up to a mother to give her son a little push here, a little push there, to make sure he's doing the right thing. Isn't that right? And a mother who loves her son would try to help him even if, with God's help, she passed away into the next world, for what kind of mother could rest in Heaven knowing that her son wasn't settled . . . ?

*

IN THE LIVING ROOM, the family was eating. The card tables had been set up and *tante* Elka had laid out her famous tiny meat knishes, the matzoh meal pancakes, the deli trays of corned beef, pastrami, chopped liver, and potato salad; the lox and cream cheese, cold kippers (boned, for God's sake, it must have taken an eternity to do it), and smoked whitefish; stacks of corn rye and a nice pumpernickel; cole slaw, chicken salad; and flotillas of cucumber pickles.

In the deserted kitchen, Lance Goldfein sat smoking a cigarette, legs crossed at the ankles, staring out the window at the back porch. He jumped suddenly as a voice spoke directly above him.

"I'm gone fifteen minutes only, and already the stink of cigarettes. Feh."

He looked around. He was alone in the kitchen.

"It wasn't altogether the most sensational service I've ever attended, if I can be frank with you. Sadie Fertel's, now *that* was a service."

He looked around again, more closely this time. He was still alone in the kitchen. There was no one on the back porch. He turned around completely, but the swinging door to the dining room, and the living room beyond, was firmly closed. He was alone in the kitchen. Lance Goldfein had just returned from the funeral of his mother, and he was alone, thinking, brooding, in the kitchen of the house he now owned.

He sighed; heaved a second sigh; he must have heard a snatch of conversation from one of the relatives in the other room. Clearly. Obviously. Maybe.

"You don't talk to your own mother when she speaks to you? Out of sight is out of mind, is that correct?"

Now the voice had drifted down and was coming from just in front of his face. He brushed at the air, as though cleaning away spiderwebs. Nothing there. He stared at emptiness and decided the loss of his mother had finally sent him over the brink. But what a tragic way to go bananas, he thought. I finally get free of her, may God bless her soul and keep her comfortable, and I still hear her voice *nuhdzing* me. I'm coming, Mom; at this rate I'll be planted very soon. You're gone three days and already I'm having guilt withdrawal symptoms.

"They're really *fressing* out there," the voice of his mother said, now from somewhere down around his shoe tops. "And, if you'll pardon my being impertinent, Lance my darling son, who the hell invited that *momser* Morris to my wake? In life I wouldn't have that *shtumie* in my home, I should watch him stuff his face when I'm dead?"

Lance stood, walked over to the sink, and ran water on the cigarette. He carried the filter butt to the garbage can and threw it in. Then he turned very slowly and said—to the empty room—"This is not fair. You are not being fair. Not even a little bit fair."

"What do I know from fair," said the disembodied voice of his mother. "I'm dead. I should know about fair? Tell me from fair; to die is a fair thing? A woman in her prime?"

"Mom, you were sixty-six years old."

"For a woman sound of mind and limb, that's prime."

He walked around the kitchen for a minute, whistled a few bars of "Eli Eli," just be on the safe side, drew himself a glass of water, and drank deeply. Then he turned around and addressed the empty room again. "I'm having a little trouble coming to grips with this, Mom. I don't want to sound too much like Alexander Portnoy, but why me?"

No answer.

"Where are you . . . hey, Mom?"

"I'm in the sink."

He turned around. "Why me? Was I a bad son, did I step on an insect, didn't I rebel against the Vietnam war soon enough? What was my crime, Mom, that I should be haunted by the ghost of a *yenta*?"

"You'll kindly watch your mouth. This is a mother you're speaking to."

"I'm sorry."

The door from the dining room swung open and Aunt Hannah was standing there in her galoshes. In the recorded history of humankind there had never been snow in Southern California, but Hannah had moved to Los Angeles twenty years earlier from Buffalo, New York, and there had been snow in Buffalo. Hannah took no chances. "Is there gefilte fish?" she asked.

Lance was nonplussed. "Uh, uh, uh," he said, esoterically.

"Gefilte fish," Hannah said, trying to help him with the difficult concept. "Is there any?"

"No, Aunt Hannah, I'm sorry. Elka didn't remember and I had other things to think about. Is everything else okay out there?"

"Sure, okay. Why shouldn't it be okay on the day your mother is buried?" It ran in the family.

"Listen, Aunt Hannah, I'd like to be alone for a while, if you don't mind."

She nodded and began to withdraw from the doorway. For a moment Lance thought he had gotten away clean, that she had not heard him speaking to whatever or whomever he had been speaking to. But she paused, looked around the kitchen, and said, "Who were you talking to?"

"I was talking to myself?" he suggested, hoping she'd go for it.

"Lance, you're a very ordinary person. You don't talk to yourself."

"I'm distraught. Maybe unhinged."

"Who were you speaking to?"

"The Sparkletts man. He delivered a bottle of mountain spring mineral water. He was passing his condolences."

"He certainly got out the door fast as I came in; I heard you talking before I came in."

"He's big, but he's fast. Covers the whole Van Nuys and Sherman Oaks area all by himself. Terrific person, you'd like him a lot. His name's Melville. Always makes me think of big fish when I talk to him."

He was babbling, hoping it would all go away. Hannah looked at him strangely. "I take it all back, Lance. You're not that ordinary. Talking to yourself I can believe."

She went back to the groaning board. Sans gefilte fish.

"What a pity," said the voice of Lance Goldfein's mother. "I love Hannah, but she ain't playing with a full deck, if you catch my drift."

"Mom, you've *got* to tell me what the hell is going on here. Could Hannah hear your voice?"

"I don't think so."

"What do you mean: you don't *think* so? You're the ghost, don't you know the rules?"

"I just got here. There are things I haven't picked up yet"

"Did you find a mah jongg group yet?"

"Don't be such a cutesy smartmouth. I can still give you a crack across the mouth."

"How? You're ectoplasm."

"Don't be disgusting."

"You know, I finally believe it's you. At first I thought I was going over the edge. But it's you. What I still want to know is *why?!?* And why you, and why me? Of all the people in the world, how did this happen to us?"

"We're not the first. It happens all the time."

"You mean Conan Doyle really *did* speak to spirits?"

"I don't know him."

"Nice man. Probably still eligible. Look around up there, you're bound to run into him. Hey, by the way: you *are* up *there,* aren't you?"

"What a dummy I raised. No, I'm not *up there,* I'm down here. Talking to you."

"Tell me about it," he murmured softly to himself.

"I heard that."

"I'm sorry."

The door from the dining room swung open again and half a dozen relatives were standing there. They were all staring at Lance as though he had just fallen off the moon. "Lance, darling," said Aunt Rachel, "would you like to come home tonight with Aaron and me? It's so gloomy here in the house all alone."

"What gloomy? It's the same sunny house it's always been."

"But you seem so . . . so . . . distressed. . . ."

From one of the kitchen cabinets Lance heard the distinct sound of a blatting raspberry. Mom was not happy with Rachel's remark. Mom had never been that happy with Rachel, to begin with. Aaron was Mom's brother, and she had always felt Rachel had married him because he had a thriving poultry business. Lance did not share the view; it had to've been true love. Uncle Aaron was a singularly unappetizing human being. He picked his nose in public. And always smelled of defunct chickens.

"I'm not distressed, Rachel. I'm just unhappy, and I'm trying to decide what I'm going to do next. Going home with you would only put it off for another day, and I want to get started as soon as I can. That's why I'm talking to myself."

They stared. And smiled a great deal.

"Why don't you all leave me alone for a while. I don't mean it to sound impertinent, but I think I'd like to be by myself. You know what I mean?"

Lew, who had more sense than all the rest of them put together, understood perfectly. "That's not a bad idea, Lance. Come on, everyone; let's get out of here and let Lance do some thinking. Anybody need a lift?"

They began moving out, and Lance went with them to the front room where Hannah asked if he minded if she put together a doggie bag of food, after all why should it go to waste such terrific deli goodies. Lance said he didn't mind, and Hannah and Rachel and Gert and Lilian and Benny (who was unmarried) all got their doggie bags, savaging the remains on the card tables until there was nothing left but one piece of pastrami (it wouldn't look nice to take the last piece), several pickles, and a dollop of potato salad. The *marabunta* army ants could not have carried out a better program of scorching the earth.

And when they were gone, Lance fell into the big easy chair by the television, sighed a sigh of release, and closed his eyes. "Good," said his mother from the ashtray on the side table. "Now we can have a long mother-son heart-to-heart."

Lance closed his eyes tighter. *Why me?* he thought.

He hoped Mom would never be sent to Hell, because he learned in the next few days that Hell was being a son whose mother has come back to haunt him, and if Mom were ever sent there, it would be a terrible existence in which she would no doubt be harassed by her own long-dead mother, her grandmothers on both sides, and God only knew how many random *nuhdzing* relatives from ages past.

Primary among the horrors of being haunted by a Jewish mother's ghost was the neatness. Lance's mother had been an extremely neat person. One could eat off the floor. Lance had never understood the efficacy of such an act, but his mother had always used it as a yardstick of worthiness for housekeeping.

Lance, on the other hand, was a slob. He liked it that way, and for most of his thirty years umbilically linked to his mother, he had suffered the pains of a running battle about clothes dropped on the floor, rings from coffee cups permanently staining the teak table, cigarette ashes dumped into the wastebaskets from overflowing ashtrays without benefit of a trash can liner. He could recite by heart the diatribe attendant on his mother's having to scour out the wastebasket with Dow Spray.

And now, when by all rights he should have been free to live as he chose, at long last, after thirty years, he had been forced to become a housemaid for himself.

No matter where he went in the house, Mom was there. Hanging from the ceiling, hiding in the nap of the rug, speaking up at him from the sink drain, calling him from the cabinet where the vacuum cleaner reposed in blissful disuse. "A pigsty," would come the voice, from empty air. "A certifiable pigsty. My son lives in filth."

"Mom," Lance would reply, pulling a pop-tab off a fresh can of beer or flipping a page in *Oui*, "this is not a pigsty. It's an average semiclean domicile in which a normal, growing American boy lives."

"There's *shmootz* all over the sink from the peanut butter and jelly. You'll draw ants."

"Ants have more sense than to venture in here and take their chances with you." He was finding it difficult to live. "Mom, why don't you get off my case?"

"I saw you playing with yourself last night."

Lance sat up straight. "You've been spying on me!"

"Spying? A mother is spying when she's concerned her son will go blind from doing personal abuse things to himself? That's the thanks I get after thirty years of raising. A son who's become a pervert."

"Mom, masturbation is not perversion."

"How about those filthy magazines you read with the girls in leather."

"You've been going through my drawers."

"Without opening them," she murmured.

"This's got to stop!" he shouted. "It's got to end. E-n-d. End! I'm going crazy with you hanging around!"

There was silence. A long silence. Lance wanted to go to the toilet, but he was afraid she'd check it out to make sure his stools were firm and hard. The silence went on and on.

Finally, he stood up and said, "Okay, I'm sorry."

Still silence.

"I *said* I was sorry, fer chrissakes! What more do you want from me?"

"A little respect."

"That's what I give you. A little respect."

More silence.

"Mom, you've got to face it, I'm not your little boy anymore. I'm an adult, with a job and a life and adult needs and . . . and . . ."

He wandered around the house but there was only more silence and more free-floating guilt, and finally he decided he would go for a walk, maybe go to a movie. In hopes Mom was housebound by the rules for ghost mothers.

The only movie he hadn't seen was a sequel to a Hong Kong kung fu film, *Return of the Street Fighter.* But he paid his money and went in. No sooner had Sonny Chiba ripped out a man's genitals, all moist and bloody, and displayed them to the audience in tight closeup, than

Lance heard the voice of his mother behind him. "This is revolting. How can a son of mine watch such awful?"

"Mom!" he screamed, and the manager came down and made him leave. His box of popcorn was still half full.

On the street, passersby continued to turn and look at him as he walked past conversing with empty air.

"You've got to leave me alone. I need to be left alone. This is cruel and inhuman torture. I was never *that* Jewish!"

He heard sobbing, from just beside his right ear. He threw up his hands. Now came the tears. "Mommmm, *please!*"

"I only wanted to do right for you. If I knew why I was sent back, what it was for, maybe I could make you happy, my son."

"Mom, you'll make me happy as a pig in slop if you'll just go away for a while and stop snooping on me."

"I'll do that."

And she was gone.

When it became obvious that she was gone, Lance went right out and picked up a girl in a bar.

And it was not until they were in bed that she came back.

"I turn my back a second and he's *shtupping* a bum from the streets. That I should live to see this!"

Lance had been way under the covers. The girl, whose name was Chrissy, had advised him she was using a new brand of macrobiotic personal hygiene spray, and he had been trying to decide if the taste was, in fact, as asserted, papaya and coconut, or bean sprout and avocado, as his taste buds insisted. Chrissy gasped and squealed. "We're not alone here!" she said. Lance struggled up from the depths; as his head emerged from beneath the sheet, he heard his mother ask, "She isn't even Jewish, is she?"

"Mom!"

Chrissy squealed again. *"Mom?"*

"It's just a ghost, don't worry about it," Lance said reassuringly. Then, to the air, "Mom, will you, fer chrissakes, get out of here? This is in very poor taste."

"Talk to me taste, Lance my darling. That I should live to see such a thing."

"Will you stop saying that?!?" He was getting hysterical.

"A *shiksa*, a Gentile yet. The shame of it."

"Mom, the *goyim* are for practice!"

"I'm getting the hell out of here," Chrissy said, leaping out of the bed, long brown hair flying.

"Put on your clothes, you *bummerkeh*," Lance's mother shrilled. "Oh, God, if I only had a wet towel, a coat hanger, a can of Mace, *some*thing, *anything!!*"

And there was such a howling and shrieking and jumping and yowling and shoving and slapping and screaming and cursing and pleading and bruising as had never been heard in that block in the San Fernando Valley. And when it was over and Chrissy had disappeared into the night, to no one knew where, Lance sat in the middle of the bedroom floor weeping—not over his being haunted, not over his mother's death, not over his predicament: over his lost erection.

And it was all downhill from there. Lance was sure of it. Mom trying to soothe him did not help in the least.

"Sweetheart, don't cry. I'm sorry. I lost my head, you'll excuse the expression. But it's all for the best."

"It's not for the best. I'm horny."

"She wasn't for you."

"She was for me, she was for me," he screamed.

"Not a *shiksa*. For you a nice, cute girl of a Semitic persuasion."

"I *hate* Jewish girls. Audrey was a Jewish girl; Bernice was a Jewish girl; that awful Darlene you fixed me up with from the laundromat, she was a Jewish girl; I hated them all. We have nothing in common."

"You just haven't found the right girl yet."

"I HATE JEWISH GIRLS! THEY'RE ALL LIKE YOU!"

"May God wash your mouth out with a bar of Fels-Naptha," his mother said in reverential tones. Then there was a meaningful pause and, as though she had had an epiphany, she said, "*That's* why I was sent back. To find you a nice girl, a partner to go with you on the road of life, a loving mate who also not incidentally could be a very terrific cook. That's what I can do to make you happy, Lance, my sweetness. I can find someone to carry on for me now that I'm no longer able to provide for you, and by the way, that *nafkeh* left a pair of underpants in the bathroom, I'd appreciate your burning them at your earliest opportunity."

Lance sat on the floor and hung his head, rocked back and forth and kept devising, then discarding, imaginative ways to take his own life.

The weeks that followed made World War II seem like an inept performance of Gilbert & Sullivan. Mom was everywhere. At his job.

(Lance was an instructor for a driving school, a job Mom had never considered worthy of Lance's talents. "Mom, I can't paint or sculpt or sing; my hands are too stubby for surgery; I have no power drive and I don't like movies very much so that eliminates my taking over 20th Century-Fox. I *like* being a driving teacher. I can leave the job at the office when I come home. Let be already.") And, of course, at the job she could not "let be." She made nothing but rude remarks to the inept men and women who were thrust into Lance's care. And so terrified were they already, just from the *idea* of driving in traffic, that when Lance's mother opened up on them, the results were horrendous:

"A driver you call this idiot? Such a driver should be driving a dirigible, the only thing she could hit would be a big ape on a building maybe."

Into the rear of an RTD bus.

"Will you look at this person! Blind like a *litvak!* A refugee from the outpatient clinic of the Menninger Foundation."

Up the sidewalk and into a front yard.

"Now I've seen it all! This one not only thinks she's Jayne Mansfield with the blonde wig and the skirt up around the *pupik*, hopefully she'll arouse my innocent son, but she drives backwards like a pig with the staggers."

Through a bus stop waiting bench, through a bus stop sign, through a car wash office, through a gas station and into a Fotomat.

But she was not only on the job, she was also at the club where Lance went to dance and possibly meet some women; she was at the dinner party a friend threw to celebrate the housewarming (the friend sold the house the following week, swearing it was haunted); she was at the dry cleaner's, the bank, the picture framers, the ballet, and inevitably in the toilet, examining Lance's stools to make sure they were firm and hard.

And every night there were phone calls from girls. Girls who had received impossible urges to call this number. "Are you Lance Goldfein? You're not going to believe this, but I, er, uh, now don't think I'm crazy, but I heard this *voice* when I was at my kid brother's bar mitzvah last Saturday. This voice kept telling me what a swell fellah you are, and how we'd get along so well. My name is Shirley and I'm single and . . ."

They appeared at his door, they came up to him at work, they stopped by on their lunch hour, they accosted him in the street, they called and called and called.

And they were *all* like Mom. Thick ankles, glasses, sweet beyond belief, Escoffier chefs every one of them, with tales of potato *latkes* as light as a dryad's breath. And he fled them, screaming.

But no matter where he hid, they found him.

He pleaded with his mother, but she was determined to find him a nice girl.

Not a woman, a girl. A nice girl. A nice *Jewish* girl. If there were easier ways of going crazy, Lance Goldfein could not conceive of them. At times he was *really* talking to himself.

He met Joanie in the Hughes Market. They bumped carts, he stepped backward into a display of Pringles, and she helped him clean up the mess. Her sense of humor was so black it lapsed over into the ultraviolet, and he loved her pixie haircut. He asked her for coffee. She accepted, and he silently prayed Mom would not interfere.

Two weeks later, in bed, with Mom nowhere in sight, he told her he loved her, they talked for a long time about her continuing her career in advocacy journalism with a small Los Angeles weekly, and decided they should get married.

Then he felt he should tell her about Mom.

"Yes, I know," she said, when he was finished.

"You know?"

"Yes. Your mother asked me to look you up."

"Oh, Christ."

"Amen," she said.

"What?"

"Well, I met your mother and we had a nice chat. She seems like a lovely woman. A bit too possessive, perhaps, but basically she means well."

"You *met* my mother . . . ?"

"Uh-huh."

"But . . . but . . . Joanie . . ."

"Don't worry about it, honey," she said, drawing him down to her small, but tidy, bosom. "I think we've seen the last of Mom. She won't be coming back. Some *do* come back, some even get recorporeated, but your mother has gone to a lovely place where she won't worry about you anymore."

"But you're so unlike the girls she tried to fix me up with." And then he stopped, stunned. "Wait a minute . . . you *met* her? Then that means . . ."

"Yes, dear, that's what it means. But don't let it bother you. I'm perfectly human in every other way. And what's best of all is I think we've outfoxed her."

"We have?"

"I think so. Do you love me?"

"Yes."

"Well, I love you, too."

"I never thought I'd fall in love with a Jewish girl my mother found for me, Joanie."

"Uh, that's what I mean about outfoxing her. I'm not Jewish."

"You're not?"

"No, I just had the right amount of soul for your mother and she assumed."

"But, Joanie . . ."

"You can call me Joan."

But he never called her the Maid of Orléans. And they lived happily ever after, in a castle not all that neat.

A MINI-GLOSSARY OF YIDDISH WORDS USED IN "MOM"

bummerkeh (buḿ-er-keh)   A female bum; generally, a "loose" lady.

"Eli Eli" (á-lee á-lee)   Well-known Hebrew-Yiddish folk song composed in 1896 by Jacob Koppel Sandler. Title means "My God, my God." Opens with a poignant cry of perplexity: "My God, my God, why hast thou forsaken me?" from Psalm 22:2 of the Old Testament. Owes its popularity to Cantor Joseph Rosenblatt, who recorded and sang it many times as an encore during concerts in early 1900s. Al Jolson also did rather well with it. Not the kind of song Perry Como or Bruce Springsteen would record.

fressing (fresś-ing)   To eat quickly, noisily; really stuffing one's face; synonymous with eating mashed potatoes with both hands.

latkes (lot́-kess)   Pancakes, usually potato pancakes but can also be made from matzoh meal. When made by my mother, not unlike millstones.

Litvak (lit́-vahk)   A Jew from Lithuania; variously erudite but pedantic, thin, dry, humorless, learned but skeptical, shrewd and clever; but used in this context as a derogatory by Lance's mom, who was a *Galitzianer,* or Austro-Polish Jew; the antipathy between them is said to go back to Cain and Abel, one of whom was a Litvak, the other a Galitzianer . . . but that's just foolish. I guess.

momser (muhḿ-zer)   An untrustworthy person; a stubborn, difficult person; a detestable, impudent person; not a nice person.

nafkeh (nahf́-keh)   A nonprofessional prostitute; a *bummerkeh* (see above); not quite a hooker, but clearly not the sort of woman a mother would call "mine darling daughter-in-law."

nuhdzing (noooood-jing)   To pester, to nag, to bore, to drive someone up a wall.

The core of the story: Practiced by mothers of all ethnic origins, be they Jewish, Italian, or WASP. To bore; to hassle; to be bugged into eating your asparagus, putting on your galoshes, getting up and taking her home, etc. Very painful.

pupik (pip̱-ik or puhp̱-ik)   Navel. Belly button.

shiksa (shik-suh)   A non-Jewish woman, especially a young one.

shmootz (shmootz)   Dirt.

shtumie (shtoom̄-ee)   Lesser insult-value than calling someone a *schlemiel* (shleh-meal´). A foolish person, a simpleton; a consistently unlucky or unfortunate person; a social misfit, a clumsy, gauche, butterfingered person; more offhand than *schlemiel*, less significant; the word you'd use when batting away someone like a gnat.

shtupping (shtooooop̄-ing)   Sexual intercourse.

tante (tahn̄-tuh)   Aunt.

yenta (yen̄-tuh)   A woman of low origins or vulgar manners; a shrew; a shallow, coarse termagant; tactless; a gossipy woman or scandal spreader; one unable to keep a secret or respect a confidence; much of the *nuhdz* in her. If it's a man, it's the same word, a blabbermouth.

GARDNER DOZOIS

Disciples

One of the basic tenets of Judaism is that after various signs and portents the Messiah will come to redeem the people of Israel. In the next story by Gardner Dozois a momentous event is seen through the nervous eyes of Nicky the Horse, a panhandler who earns his meager living by spreading the word of the Lord. Although Nicky stretches out his hand to every likely passer-by and announces that the Last Days are indeed coming, he can't quite believe that the Messiah could be Murray Kupferberg, a plumber from Pittsburgh.
The story reminds me of these lines from Isaiah:

> The people that walked in darkness
> Have seen a brilliant light;
> On those who dwelt in a land of gloom
> Light has dawned.

*

NICKY THE HORSE was a thin, weaselly-looking man with long dirty black hair that hung down either side of his face in greasy ropes, like inkmarks against the pallor of his skin. He was clean-shaven and hollow-cheeked, and had a thin but rubbery lower lip upon which his small yellowed teeth were forever biting, seizing the lip suddenly and worrying it, like a terrier seizing a rat. He wore a grimy purple sweater under a torn tan jacket enough sizes too small to look like something an organ-grinder's monkey might wear, one pocket torn nearly off and both elbows worn through. Thrift-store jeans and a ratty pair of sneakers he'd once found in a garbage can behind the YMCA completed his wardrobe. No underwear. A crucifix gleamed around his neck, stainless steel coated to look like silver. Track marks, fading now, ran down both his arms, across his stomach, down his thighs, but he'd been off the junk for months; he was down to an occasional Red Devil, supplemented by the nightly quart of cheap chianti he consumed as he lay in the dark on his bare mattress at the "Lordhouse," a third-floor loft in a converted industrial warehouse squeezed between a package store and a Rite-Aid.

He had just scavenged some two-day-old doughnuts from a pile of boxes behind a doughnut store on Broad Street, and bought a paper container of coffee from a Greek delicatessen where the counterman (another aging hippie, faded flower tattoos still visible under the bristly black hair on his arms) usually knocked a nickel or two off the price for old time's sake. Now he was sitting on the white marble steps of an old brownstone row house, eating his breakfast. His breath steamed in the chill morning air. Even sitting still, he was in constant motion—his fingers drumming, his feet shuffling, his eyes flicking nervously back and forth as one thing or another—a car, some wind-blown trash, pigeons taking to the air—arrested and briefly held his attention; at such times his shoulders would momentarily hunch, as if he expected something to leap out at him.

Across the street, a work crew was renovating another old brownstone, swarming over the building's partially stripped skeleton like carrion beetles; sometimes a cloud of plaster-powder and brick dust would puff from the building's broken doorway, like foul air from a dying mouth. Winos and pimps and whores congregated on the corner, outside a flophouse hotel, their voices coming to Nicky thin and shrill over the rumbling and farting of traffic. Occasionally a group of med students would go by, or a girl with a dog, or a couple of Society Hill faggots in bell-bottomed trousers and expensive turtlenecks, and Nicky would call out "Jesus loves you, man," usually to no more response than a nervous sideways glance. One faggot smirked knowingly at him, and a collegiate-jock type got a laugh out of his buddies by shouting back "You bet your ass he does, honey." A small, intense-looking woman with short-cropped hair gave him the finger. Another diesel dyke, Nicky thought resignedly. "Jesus loves *you*, man," he called after her, but she didn't look back.

When his butt began to feel as if it had turned to stone, he got up from the cold stoop and started walking again, pausing only long enough to put a flyer for the Lordhouse on a lamp pole, next to a sticker that said EAT THE RICH. He walked on, past a disco, a gay bookstore, a go-go bar, a boarded-up storefront with a sign that read LIVE NUDE MODELS, a pizza stand, slanting south and east now through a trash-littered concrete park full of sleeping derelicts and herds of arrogantly strutting pigeons, stopping now and then to panhandle and pass out leaflets, drifting on again.

He'd been up to Reading Terminal early that morning, hoping to catch the shoppers who came in from the suburbs on commuter trains, but the Hairy Krishnaites had been there already, out in force in front of the station, and he didn't like to compete with other panhandlers, particularly fucking *groups* of them with fucking *bongos*. The Krishnaites made him nervous anyway—with their razor-shaved pates and their air of panting, puppyish eagerness, they always reminded him of ROTC second-lieutenants, fresh out of basic training. Once, in front of the Bellevue-Stratford, he'd seen a fight between a Krishnaite and a Moonie, the two of them arguing louder and louder, toe to toe, until suddenly they were beating each other over the head with thick rackets of devotional literature, the leaflets swirling loose around them like flocks of startled birds. He'd had to grin at that one, but some of the panhandling groups were *mean*, particularly the political groups, particularly the niggers. They'd kick your ass up between your shoulder blades if they caught you poaching on their turf, they'd have your balls for garters.

No, you scored better if you worked alone. Always alone.

He ended up on South Street, down toward the Two-Street end, taking up a position between the laundromat and the plant store. It was much too early for the trendy people to be out, the "artists," the night people, but they weren't such hot prospects anyway. It was Saturday, and that meant that there were tourists out, in spite of the early hour, in spite of the fact that it had been threatening to snow all day—it was cold, yes, but not as cold as it had been the rest of the week, the sun was peeking sporadically out from behind banks of dirty gray clouds, and maybe this would be the only halfway decent day left before winter really set in. No, they were here alright, the tourists, strolling up and down through this hick Greenwich Village, peering into the quaint little stores, the boutiques, the head-shops full of tourist-trap junk, the artsy bookstores, staring at the resident freaks as though they were on display at the zoo, relishing the occasional dangerous whiff of illicit smoke in the air, the loud blare of music that they wouldn't have tolerated for a moment at home.

Of course, he wasn't the only one feeding on this rich stream of marks: there was a juggler outside of the steak-sandwich shop in the next block, a small jazz band—a xylophone, a bass, and an electric piano—in front of the communist coffeehouse across the street, and, next to the upholsterer's, a fat man in a fur-lined parka who was tonelessly chanting "incense sticks check it out one dollar incense sticks check it out one dollar" without break or intonation. Such competition Nicky could deal with—in fact, he was contemptuous of it.

"Do you have your house in *order?*" he said in a conversational but carrying voice, starting his own spiel, pushing leaflets at a businessman, who ignored him, at a strolling young married couple, who smiled but shook their heads, at a middle-aged housewife in clogs and a polka-dot kerchief, who took a flyer reflexively and then, a few paces away, stopped to peek at it surreptitiously. "Did you know the Lord is coming, man? The Lord is *coming.* Spare some change for the Lord's work?" This last remark shot at the housewife, who looked uneasily around and then suddenly thrust a quarter at him. She hurried away, clutching her Lordhouse flyer to her chest as if it were a baby the gypsies were after.

Panhandling was an art, man, an *art*—and so, of course, of *course,* was the more important task of spreading the Lord's word. That was what *really* counted. Of course. Nevertheless, he brought more fucking change into the Lordhouse than any of the other converts who were out pounding the pavement every day, fucking-A, you better believe it. He'd always been a good panhandler, even before he'd seen the light, and what did it was making maximum use of your time. Knowing who to ask and who not to waste time on was the secret. College students, professional people, and young white male businessmen made the best marks—later, when the businessmen had aged into senior executives, the chances of their coming across went way down. Touristy types were good, straight suburbanites in the 25–50 age bracket, particularly a man out strolling with his wife. A man walking by himself was much more likely to give you something than a man walking in company with another man—faggots were sometimes an exception here. Conversely, women in pairs—especially prosperous hausfraus, although groups of teenage girls were pretty good too—were much more likely to give you change than were women walking by themselves; the housewife of a moment before had been an exception, but she had all the earmarks of someone who was just religious enough to feel guilty about not being more so. Brisk woman-executive types almost never gave you anything, or even took a leaflet. Servicemen in uniform were easy touches. Old people never gave you diddley-shit, except sometimes a well-heeled little old white lady would, especially a W.H.L.O.W.L. who had religion herself, although they could also be more trouble than their money was worth. There were a lot of punkers in this neighborhood, with their '50s crewcuts and greasy motorcycle jackets, but Nicky usually left them alone; the punks were more violent and less gullible than the hippies had been back in the late '60s, the Golden Age of Panhandling. The few remaining hippies—and the college kids who passed for hippies these days—came across often enough that Nicky made a point of hitting on them, although he gritted his teeth each time he did; they were by far the most likely to be wiseasses—once he'd told one "Jesus is coming to our town," and the kid had replied, "I hope he's got a reservation, then—the hotels are booked *solid*." Wiseasses. Those were also the types who would occasionally quote Scripture to him, coming up with some goddamn verse or other to refute anything he said; that made him uneasy—Nicky had never really actually *read* the Bible that much, although he'd meant to: he had the knowledge *intuitively*, because the Spirit was in him. At that, the hippie wiseasses were easier to take than the Puerto Ricans, who would pretend they didn't understand what he wanted and give him only tight bursts of superfast Spanish. The Vietnamese, now, being seen on the street with increasing frequency these days, the Vietnamese quite often *did* give something, perhaps because they felt that they were required to. Nicky wasn't terribly fond of Jews, either, but it was amazing how often they'd come across, even for a pitch about *Jesus*—all that guilt they imbibed with their mother's milk, he guessed. On the other hand, he mostly stayed clear of niggers—sometimes you could score off of a middle-aged tom in a business suit or some graying workman, but the young street dudes were impossible, and there was always the chance that some coked-up young stud would turn mean on you and maybe pull a knife. Occasionally you could get money out of a member of that endless, seemingly cloned legion of short, fat, cone-shaped black women, but that had its special dangers too, particularly if they turned out to be devout Baptists, or snakehandlers, or whatever the fuck they *were:* one woman had screamed at him, "Don't talk to me about Jesus! Don't talk to *me* about Jesus! Don't talk to me about *Jesus!*" Then she'd hit him with her purse.

"The Last Days are at hand!" Nicky called. "The Last Days are *coming,* man. The Lord is coming to our town, and the wicked will be left *behind,* man. The *Lord* is coming." Nicky shoved a leaflet into someone's hand and the someone shoved it right back. Nicky shrugged. "Come to the Lordhouse tonight, brothers and sisters! Come and get your soul *together.*" Someone paused, hesitated, took a leaflet. "Spare change? Spare change for the Lord's work? Every *penny* does the Lord's work . . ."

The morning passed, and it grew colder. About half of Nicky's leaflets were gone, although many of them littered the sidewalk a few paces away, where people had discarded them once they thought that they were far enough from Nicky not to be noticed doing so. The sun had been swallowed by clouds, and once again it looked like it was going to snow, although once again it did not. Nicky's coat was too small to button, but he turned his collar up, and put his hands in his pockets. The stream of tourists had pretty much run dry for the moment, and he was just thinking about getting some lunch, about going down to the hot dog stand on the corner where the black dudes stood jiving and hand-slapping, their giant radios blaring on their shoulders, he was just *thinking* about it when, at that very moment, as though conjured up by the thought, Saul Edelmann stepped out of the stand and walked briskly toward him.

"Shit in my hat," Nicky muttered to himself. He'd collected more than enough to buy lunch, but, because of the cold, not that *much* more. And Father Delardi, the unfrocked priest—the *unfairly*

unfrocked priest—who had founded their order and who ran it with
both love and, yessir, an iron hand—Father Delardi didn't like it when
they came in off the streets at the end of the day with less than a certain amount of dough. Nicky had been hoping that he could con Saul
into giving him a free hot dog, as he sometimes could, as Saul sometimes *had,* and now here was Saul himself, off on some dumb-shit er-
rand, bopping down the street as fat and happy as a clam (although
how happy *were* clams anyway? come to think about it), which meant
that he, Nicky, was fucked.

"Nicky! My main man!" said Saul, who prided himself on an ability to
speak jivey street patois that he definitely did not possess. He was a
plump-cheeked man with modish-length gray-streaked hair, cheap
black plastic-framed glasses, and a neatly trimmed mustache. Jews
were supposed to have big noses, or so Nicky had always heard, but
Saul's nose was small and upturned, as if there were an Irishman in the
woodpile somewhere.

"Hey, man," Nicky mumbled listlessly. Bad *enough* that he wasn't
going to get his free hot dog—now he'd have to make friendly small
talk with this dipshit in order to protect his investment in free hot dogs
yet to come. Nicky sighed, and unlimbered his shit-eating grin. "Hey,
man! How you been, Saul? What's *happenin'*, man?"

"What's happening?" Saul said jovially, responding to Nicky as if he
was really asking a question instead of emitting ritual noise. "Now how
can I even begin to tell you what's happening, Nicky?" He was radiant
today, Saul was, full of bouncy energy, rocking back and forth as he
talked, unable to stand still, smiling a smile that revealed teeth some
Yiddish momma had sunk a lot of dough into over the years. "I'm glad
you came by today, though. I wanted to be sure to say good-bye if I
could."

"Good-bye?"

Saul's smile became broader and broader. "Yes, good-bye! This is it,
boychick. I'm off! You won't see me again after today."

Nicky peered at him suspiciously. "You goin' away?"

"You bet your ass I am, kid," Saul said, and then laughed. "Today I
turned my half of the business over to Carlos, signed all the papers,
took care of everything nice and legal. And now I'm free and clear, free
as a damn bird, kid."

"You sold your half of the stand to *Carlos?*"

"Not sold, *boychick*—gave. I *gave* it to him. Not one red cent did I
take."

Nicky gaped at him. "You *gave your business away,* man?"

Saul beamed. "Kid—I gave *everything* away. The car: I gave that to old Ben Miller who washes dishes at the Green Onion. I gave up the lease on my apartment, gave away my furniture, gave away my savings—if you'd've been here yesterday, Nicky, I would've given you something too."

"Shit!" Nicky said harshly, "you go crazy, man, or what?" He choked back an outburst of bitter profanity. Missed out again! Screwed out of getting *his* yet *again!*

"I don't *need* any of that stuff anymore, Nicky," Saul said. He tapped the side of his nose, smiled. "Nicky—He's come."

"Who?"

"The *Messiah.* He's come! He's finally come! Today's the day the Messiah comes, after all those thousands of years—think of it, Nicky!"

Nicky's eyes narrowed. "What the fuck you talkin' about, man?"

"Don't you *ever* read the paper, Nicky, or listen to the radio? The Messiah has come. His name is Murray Kupferberg, He was born in Pittsburgh—"

"*Pittsburgh?*" Nicky gasped.

"—and He used to be a plumber there. But He *is* the Messiah. Most of the scholars and the rabbis deny Him, but He really *is.* The Messiah has really come, at last!"

Nicky gave that snorting bray of laughter, blowing out his rubbery lips, that was one reason—but *only* one reason—why he was sometimes called Nicky the Horse. "*Jesus* is the Messiah, man," he said scornfully.

Saul smiled good-naturedly, shrugged, spread his hands. "For you, maybe he *is.* For you people, the *goyim,* maybe he *is.* But *we've* been waiting for almost three thousand years—and at last He's come."

"Murray Kupferberg? From *Pittsburgh?*"

"Murray Kupferberg," Saul repeated firmly, calmly. "From Pittsburgh. He's coming *here, today.* Jews are gathering here today from all over the country, from all over the world, and *today*—right *here*—He's going to gather His people to Him—"

"You stupid fucking kike!" Nicky screamed, his anger breaking free at last. "You're crazy in the head, man. You've been *conned.* Some fucking con man has taken you for *everything,* and you're too fucking dumb to see it! All that *stuff,* man, all that good stuff *gone*—" He ran out of steam, at a loss for words. All that good stuff gone, and he hadn't gotten *any* of it. After kissing up to this dipshit for all those years . . . "Oh, you dumb kike," he whispered.

Saul seemed unoffended. "You're wrong, Nicky—but I haven't got time to argue with you. Good-bye." He stuck out his hand, but Nicky refused to shake it. Saul shrugged, smiled again, and then walked briskly away, turning the corner onto Sixth Street.

Nicky sullenly watched him go, still shaking with rage. Screwed again! There went his free hot dogs, flying away into the blue on fucking gossamer wings. Carlos was a hard dude, a street-wise dude—Carlos wasn't going to *give* him anything, Carlos wouldn't stop to piss on Nicky's head if Nicky's *hair* was on fire. Nicky stared at the tattered and overlapping posters on the laundromat wall, and the faces of long-dead politicians stared back at him from among the notices for lost cats and the ads for Czech films and karate classes. Suddenly he was cold, and he shivered.

The rest of the day was a total loss. Nicky's sullen mood threw his judgment and his timing off, and the tourists were thinning out again anyway. The free-form jazz of the communist coffeehouse band was getting on his nerves—the fucking xylophone player was chopping away as if he were making sukiyaki at Benihana of Tokyo's—and the smell of sauerkraut would float over from the hot dog stand every now and then to torment him. And it kept getting colder and colder. Still, some obscure, self-punishing instinct kept him from moving on.

Later in the afternoon, what amounted to a little unofficial parade went by—a few hundred people walking in the street, heading west against the traffic, many of them barefoot in spite of the bitter cold. If they were all Jews on their way to the Big Meeting, as Nicky suspected, then some of them must have been black Jews, East Indian Jews, even *Chinese* Jews.

Smaller groups of people straggled by for the next hour or so, all headed uptown. The traffic seemed to have stopped completely, even the crosstown buses; this rally must be *big*, for the city to've done that.

The last of the pilgrims to go by was a stout, fiftyish Society Hill matron with bleached blue hair, walking calmly in the very center of the street. She was wearing an expensive ermine stole, although she was barefoot and her feet were bleeding. As she passed Nicky, she suddenly laughed, unwrapped the stole from around her neck, and threw it into the air, walking on without looking back. The stole landed across the shoulders of the communist xylophone player, who goggled blankly for a moment, then stared wildly around him—his eyes widening comically—and then bolted, clutching the stole tightly in his hands; he disappeared down an alleyway.

"You bitch!" Nicky screamed. "Why not *me?* Why didn't you give it to *me?*"

But she was gone, the street was empty, and the gray afternoon sky was darkening toward evening.

"The Last Days are coming," Nicky told the last few strolling tourists and window-shoppers. "The strait gate is narrow, sayeth the Lord, and few will fit *in,* man." But his heart wasn't in it anymore. Nicky waited, freezing, his breath puffing out in steaming clouds, stamping his feet to restore circulation, slapping his arms, doing a kind of shuffling jig that—along with his too-small jacket—made him look more than ever like an organ-grinder's monkey performing for some unlikely kind of alms. He didn't understand why he didn't just give up and go back to the Lordhouse. He was beginning to think yearningly of the hot stew they would be served there after they had turned the day's take in to Father Delardi, the hymn singing later, and after that the bottle of strong raw wine, and his mattress in the rustling, fart-smelling communal darkness, oblivion . . .

There was—a sound, a note, a chord, an upswelling of something that the mind interpreted as music, as blaring iron trumpets, only because it had no other referents with which to understand it. The noise, the music, the *something*—it swelled until it shook the empty street, the buildings, the world, shook the bones in the flesh, and the very marrow in the bones, until it filled every inch of the universe like hot wax being poured into a mold.

Nicky looked up.

As he watched, a crack appeared in the dull gray sky. The sky split open, and behind the sky was nothingness, a wedge of darkness so terrible and absolute that it hurt the eyes to look at it. The crack widened, the wedge of darkness grew. Light began to pour through the crack in the sky, blinding white light more intense and frightening than the darkness had been. Squinting against that terrible radiance, his eyes watering, Nicky saw tiny figures rising into the air far away, thousands upon thousands of human figures floating up into the sky, falling *up* while the iron music shook the firmament around them, people falling up and into and through the crack in the sky, merging into that wondrous and awful river of light, fading, disappearing, until the last one was gone.

The crack in the sky closed. The music grumbled and rumbled away into silence.

Everything was still.

Snowflakes began to squeeze like slow tears from the slate gray sky.

Nicky stayed there for hours, staring upward until his neck was aching and the last of the light was gone, but after that nothing else happened at all.

Acknowledgment is made for permission to print the following material:

"Camps" by Jack Dann. Copyright © 1979 by Mercury Press, Inc. From *The Magazine of Fantasy and Science Fiction*. Copyright reassigned to the author. Reprinted by permission of the author.

"The Celestial Orchestra" by Howard Schwartz. Copyright © 1980 by Howard Schwartz. Reprinted by permission of the author.

"Disciples" by Gardner Dozois. Copyright © 1981 by Penthouse International Ltd. Reprinted by permission of the author and his agent, Virginia Kidd.

"Dress Rehearsal" by Harvey Jacobs. Copyright © 1974 by Mercury Press, Inc. From *The Magazine of Fantasy and Science Fiction*, by permission of the author.

"Forcing the End" by Hugh Nissenson. Copyright © 1969 by Hugh Nissenson. From *In the Reign of Peace* by Hugh Nissenson, reprinted by permission of the author.

"The Hebrew Source" by Isaac Asimov. Copyright © 1981 by Nightfall, Inc. Published by permission of the Estate of Isaac Asimov c/o Ralph Vicinanza, Ltd.

"Isaiah" by Barry N. Malzberg. Copyright © 1973 by Ultimate Publications, Inc. From *Fantastic*, reprinted by permission of the author.

"A Lamed Wufnik" by Mel Gilden. Copyright © 1975 by Mercury Press, Inc. From *The Magazine of Fantasy and Science Fiction*, by permission of the author.

"The Last Demon" by Isaac Bashevis Singer. Copyright © 1961, 1962, 1963, 1964 by Isaac Bashevis Singer. From *Short Friday* by Isaac Bashevis Singer, reprinted with permission of Farrar, Straus & Giroux, Inc.

"Leviticus: In the Ark" by Barry N. Malzberg. Copyright © 1975 by Mercury Press, Inc. From *The Magazine of Fantasy and Science Fiction*, by permission of the author.

"The Mazel Tov Revolution" by Joe W. Haldeman. Copyright © 1974 by The Condé Nast Corporation. From *Analog*, by permission of the author.

"Mom" by Harlan Ellison appeared in the author's collection *Strange Wine*. Copyright © 1976 by Harlan Ellison. Reprinted by arrangement with and permission of the author. All rights reserved.

"The Scrolls" by Woody Allen. Copyright © 1974 by Woody Allen. From *Without Feathers* by Woody Allen. Reprinted by permission of Random House, Inc.

"Tauf Aleph" by Phyllis Gotlieb. Copyright © 1981 by Phyllis Gotlieb.

"Warm, Dark Places" by Horace L. Gold. Copyright © 1939 by Street & Smith for *Unknown Worlds;* copyright renewed 1967 by Condé Nast.

About JEWISH LIGHTS Publishing

People of all faiths and backgrounds yearn for books that attract, engage, educate and spiritually inspire.

Our principal goal is to stimulate thought and help all people learn about who the Jewish People are, where they come from, and what the future can be made to hold. While people of our diverse Jewish heritage are the primary audience, our books speak to people in the Christian world as well and will broaden their understanding of Judaism and the roots of their own faith.

We bring to you authors who are at the forefront of spiritual thought and experience. While each has something different to say, they all say it in a voice that you can hear.

Our books are designed to welcome you and then to engage, stimulate and inspire. We judge our success not only by whether or not our books are beautiful and commercially successful, but by whether or not they make a difference in your life.

We at Jewish Lights take great care to produce beautiful books that present meaningful spiritual content in a form that reflects the art of making high quality books. Therefore, we want to acknowledge those who contributed to the production of this book.

PRODUCTION
Marian B. Wallace & Bridgett Taylor

EDITORIAL & PROOFREADING
Sandra Korinchak & Martha McKinney

COVER DESIGN
Bronwen Battaglia & Bridgett Taylor

TEXT DESIGN
Sans Serif, Inc., Saline, Michigan

COVER & TEXT PRINTING AND BINDING
Versa Press, East Peoria, Illinois

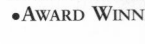

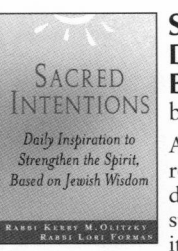

Spirituality

"WHO IS A JEW?"
Conversations, Not Conclusions
by *Meryl Hyman*

Who is "Jewish enough" to be considered a Jew? And by whom?

Meryl Hyman courageously takes on **this timely and controversial question to give readers the perspective necessary to draw their own conclusions.** Profound personal questions of identity are explored in conversations with Jews and non-Jews in the U.S., Israel and England.

6" x 9", 272 pp. Quality Paperback, ISBN 1-58023-052-0 **$16.95**
HC, ISBN 1-879045-76-1 **$23.95**

THE JEWISH GARDENING COOKBOOK
Growing Plants and Cooking for Holidays & Festivals
by *Michael Brown*

Wherever you garden—a city apartment windowsill or on an acre—with the fruits and vegetables of your own labors, the traditional repasts of Jewish holidays and celebrations can be understood in many new ways!

Gives easy-to-follow instructions for raising foods that have been harvested since ancient times. Provides carefully selected, tasty and easy-to-prepare recipes using these traditional foodstuffs for holidays, festivals, and life cycle events. Clearly illustrated with more than 30 fine botanical illustrations. For beginner and professional alike.

6" x 9", 224 pp. HC, ISBN 1-58023-004-0 **$21.95**

WANDERING STARS
An Anthology of Jewish Fantasy & Science Fiction
Edited by *Jack Dann*; with an Introduction by *Isaac Asimov*

Jewish science fiction and fantasy? *Yes!* Here are the **distinguished contributors:** Bernard Malamud, Isaac Bashevis Singer, Isaac Asimov, Robert Silverberg, Harlan Ellison, Pamela Sargent, Avram Davidson, Geo. Alec Effinger, Horace L. Gold, Robert Sheckley, William Tenn and Carol Carr. **Pure enjoyment. We laughed out loud reading it. A 25th Anniversary Classic Reprint.**

6" x 9", 272 pp. Quality Paperback, ISBN 1-58023-005-9 **$16.95**

THE ENNEAGRAM AND KABBALAH
Reading Your Soul
by *Rabbi Howard A. Addison*

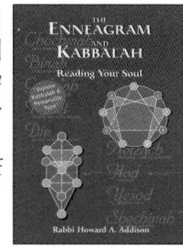

What do the Enneagram and *Kabbalah* have in common? Together, can they provide a powerful tool for self-knowledge, critique, and transformation?

How can we distinguish between acquired personality traits and the essential self hidden underneath?

6" x 9", 176 pp. Quality Paperback Original, ISBN 1-58023-001-6 **$15.95**

Spirituality

MEDITATION FROM THE HEART OF JUDAISM
Today's Teachers Share Their Practices, Techniques, and Faith
Edited by *Avram Davis*

A "how-to" guide for both beginning and experienced meditators, it will help you start meditating or help you enhance your practice.

Twenty-two masters of meditation explain why and how they meditate. *A detailed compendium of the experts' "Best Practices"* offers practical advice and starting points.

6" x 9", 256 pp. Quality Paperback, ISBN 1-58023-049-0 **$16.95**; HC, ISBN 1-879045-77-X **$21.95**

DISCOVERING JEWISH MEDITATION
Instruction & Guidance for Learning an Ancient Spiritual Practice
by *Nan Fink Gefen*

Helps readers of any level of understanding learn the practice of Jewish meditation on their own, starting you on the path to a deep spiritual and personal connection to God and to greater insight about your own life. An accessible, comprehensive introduction to a time-honored spiritual practice.

6" x 9", 208 pp. Quality PB Original, ISBN 1-58023-067-9 **$16.95**

SELF, STRUGGLE & CHANGE
Family Conflict Stories in Genesis and Their Healing Insights for Our Lives
by *Norman J. Cohen*

How do I find greater wholeness in my life and in my family's life?

The people described by the biblical writers of Genesis were in situations and relationships very much like our own. We identify with them. Their stories still speak to us because they are about the same problems we deal with every day. Here a modern master of biblical interpretation brings us greater understanding of the ancient text and of ourselves in this intriguing re-telling of conflict between husband and wife, father and son, brothers, and sisters.

6" x 9", 224 pp. Quality Paperback, ISBN 1-879045-66-4 **$16.95**; HC, ISBN 1-879045-19-2 **$21.95**

VOICES FROM GENESIS
Guiding Us through the Stages of Life
by *Norman J. Cohen*

A brilliant blending of modern *midrash* and the life stages of Erik Erikson's developmental psychology. Shows how the pathways of our lives are quite similar to those of the leading figures of Genesis who speak directly to us, telling of their spiritual and emotional journeys.

6" x 9", 192 pp. HC, ISBN 1-879045-75-3 **$21.95**

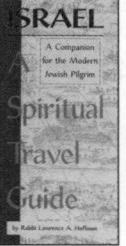

ISRAEL—A SPIRITUAL TRAVEL GUIDE
A Companion for the Modern Jewish Pilgrim
by *Rabbi Lawrence A. Hoffman*

Be spiritually prepared for your journey to Israel.

A Jewish spiritual travel guide to Israel, helping today's pilgrim tap into the deep spiritual meaning of the ancient—and modern—sites of the Holy Land. Combines in quick reference format ancient blessings, medieval prayers, biblical and historical references, and modern poetry. The only guidebook that helps readers to prepare spiritually for the occasion. More than a guide book: It is a spiritual map.

• AWARD WINNER • 4¾" x 10", 256 pp. Quality Paperback Original, ISBN 1-879045-56-7 **$18.95**

Spirituality—The Kushner Series

EYES REMADE FOR WONDER
A Lawrence Kushner Reader
Introduction by *Thomas Moore*

A treasury of insight from one of the most creative spiritual thinkers in America. Whether you are new to Kushner or a devoted fan, you'll find inspiration here. With samplings from each of Kushner's works, and a generous amount of new material, this is a book to be savored, to be read and reread, each time discovering deeper layers of meaning in our lives. Offers something unique to both the spiritual seeker and the committed person of faith.

6" x 9", 240 pp. Quality PB, ISBN 1-58023-042-3 **$16.95**; HC, ISBN 1-58023-014-8 **$23.95**

INVISIBLE LINES OF CONNECTION
Sacred Stories of the Ordinary
by *Lawrence Kushner*

Through his everyday encounters with family, friends, colleagues and strangers, Kushner takes us deeply into our lives, finding flashes of spiritual insight in the process.

5½" x 8½", 160 pp. Quality Paperback, ISBN 1-879045-98-2 **$15.95**
HC, ISBN 1-879045-52-4 **$21.95**

Award Winner•

HONEY FROM THE ROCK
An Easy Introduction to Jewish Mysticism
by *Lawrence Kushner*

"Quite simply the easiest introduction to Jewish mysticism you can read."

An introduction to the ten gates of Jewish mysticism and how it applies to daily life.

6" x 9", 176 pp. Quality Paperback, ISBN 1-879045-02-8 **$14.95**

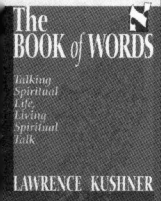

THE BOOK OF WORDS
Talking Spiritual Life, Living Spiritual Talk
by *Lawrence Kushner*

In the incomparable manner of his extraordinary *The Book of Letters*, Kushner now lifts up and shakes the dust off primary religious words we use to describe the spiritual dimension of life. For each word Kushner offers us a startling, moving and insightful explication. He concludes with a short exercise that helps unite the spirit of the word with our actions in the world.

" x 9", 160 pp., 2-color text, Quality PB, ISBN 1-58023-020-2 **$16.95**; HC, ISBN 1-879045-35-4 **$21.95**

THE BOOK OF LETTERS
A Mystical Hebrew Alphabet
by *Rabbi Lawrence Kushner*

n calligraphy by the author. Folktales about and exploration of the mystical meanings of the Hebrew Alphabet. Draws from ancient Judaic sources, weaving Talmudic commentary, Hasidic folktales, and kabbalistic mysteries around the letters.

Popular Hardcover Edition 6" x 9", 80 pp. HC, two colors, inspiring new Foreword. ISBN 1-879045-00-1 **$24.95**

Deluxe Gift Edition 9" x 12", 80 pp. HC, four-color text, ornamentation, in a beautiful slipcase. **$79.95**

•Award Winner•

Collector's Limited Edition 9" x 12", 80 pp. HC, gold-embossed pages, hand-assembled slipcase. With silkscreened print. **Limited to 500 signed and numbered copies.** ISBN 1-879045-04-4 **$349.00**

Spirituality

HOW TO BE A PERFECT STRANGER, In 2 Volumes
A Guide to Etiquette in Other People's Religious Ceremonies
Edited by *Stuart M. Matlins & Arthur J. Magida*

"A book that belongs in every living room, library and office!"

BEST REFERENCE BOOK OF THE YEAR

Explains the rituals and celebrations of America's major religions/denominations, helping an interested guest to feel comfortable, participat to the fullest extent possible, and avoid violating anyone's religious principles.

Answers practical questions from the perspective of *any* other faith.

VOL. 1: America's Largest Faiths
VOL. 1 COVERS: Assemblies of God • Baptist • Buddhist • Christian Science • Churches of Christ Disciples of Christ • Episcopalian • Greek Orthodox • Hindu • Islam • Jehovah's Witnesses • Jewis • Lutheran • Methodist • Mormon • Presbyterian • Quaker • Roman Catholic • Seventh-da Adventist • United Church of Christ

6" x 9", 432 pp. Hardcover, ISBN 1-879045-39-7 **$24.95**

VOL. 2: Other Faiths in America
VOL. 2 COVERS: African American Methodist Churches • Baha'i • Christian and Missionary Alliance • Christian Congregation • Church of the Brethren • Church of the Nazarene • Evangelical Free Church of America • International Church of the Foursquare Gospel • International Pentecostal Holiness Church • Mennonite/Amish • Native American • Orthodox Churches • Pentecostal Church of God • Reformed Church of America • Sikh • Unitarian Universalist • Wesleyan

6" x 9", 416 pp. Hardcover, ISBN 1-879045-63-X **$24.95**

GOD & THE BIG BANG
Discovering Harmony Between Science & Spirituality
by *Daniel C. Matt*

Mysticism and science: What do they have in common? How can one enlighte the other? By drawing on modern cosmology and ancient Kabbalah, Matt show how science and religion can together enrich our spiritual awareness and help recover a sense of wonder and find our place in the universe.

"This poetic new book...helps us to understand the human meaning of creation."
—*Joel Primack, leading cosmologist, Professor of Physics, University of California, Santa Cruz*

6" x 9", 216 pp. Quality Paperback, ISBN 1-879045-89-3 **$16.95**; HC, ISBN 1-879045-48-6 **$21.95**

MINDING THE TEMPLE OF THE SOUL
Balancing Body, Mind, & Spirit through Traditional Jewish Prayer, Movement, & Meditation
by *Tamar Frankiel* and *Judy Greenfeld*

This new spiritual approach to physical health introduces readers to a spiritual tradition that affirms the body and enables them to reconceive their bodies in a more positive light. Relying on Kabbalistic teachings and other Jewish traditions, it shows us how to be more responsible for our own psychological and physical health. Focuses on the discipline of prayer, simple Tai Chi–like exercises and body positions, and guides the reader throughout, step-by-step, with diagrams, sketches and meditations.

7" x 10", 184 pp. Quality Paperback Original, illus., ISBN 1-879045-64-8 **$16.95**

Audiotape of the Blessings, Movements & Meditations (60-min. cassette) **$9.95**
Videotape of the Movements & Meditations (46-min. VHS) **$20.00**

Spirituality

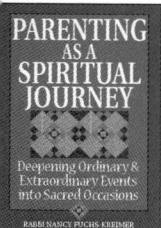

PARENTING AS A SPIRITUAL JOURNEY
Deepening Ordinary & Extraordinary Events into Sacred Occasions
by *Rabbi Nancy Fuchs-Kreimer*

A perfect gift for the new parent, and a helpful guidebook for those seeking to re-envision family life. Draws on experiences of the author and over 100 parents of many faiths. Rituals, prayers, and passages from sacred Jewish texts—as well as from other religious traditions—are woven throughout the book.

6" x 9", 224 pp. Quality Paperback, ISBN 1-58023-016-4 **$16.95**

STEPPING STONES TO JEWISH SPIRITUAL LIVING
Walking the Path Morning, Noon, and Night
by *Rabbi James L. Mirel & Karen Bonnell Werth*

How can we bring the sacred into our busy lives?

transforms our daily routine into sacred acts of mindfulness. Chapters are arranged according to the cycle of each day—and the cycle of our lives—providing spiritual activities, creative new rituals, meditations, acts of *kavannah* (spiritual intention) and prayers for any lifestyle.

6" x 9", 240 pp. HC, ISBN 1-58023-003-2 **$21.95**

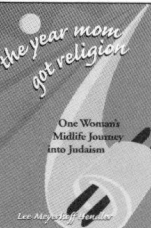

THE YEAR MOM GOT RELIGION
One Woman's Midlife Journey into Judaism
by *Lee Meyerhoff Hendler*

A frank, thoughtful, and humorous "spiritual autobiography" that will speak to anyone in search of deeper meaning in their religious life. The author shares with the reader the hard lessons and realizations she confronted as a result of her awakening to Judaism, including how her transformation deeply affected her lifestyle and relationships. Shows that anyone, at any time, can deeply embrace faith—and face the challenges that occur.

6" x 9", 208 pp. Quality Paperback, ISBN 1-58023-070-9 **$15.95**
HC, ISBN 1-58023-000-8 **$19.95**

MOSES—THE PRINCE, THE PROPHET
His Life, Legend & Message for Our Lives
by *Rabbi Levi Meier, Ph.D.*

How can the struggles of a great biblical figure teach us to cope with our own lives today? A fascinating portrait of the struggles, failures and triumphs of Moses, a central figure in Jewish, Christian and Islamic tradition. Draws from Exodus, *midrash*, the teachings of Jewish mystics, modern texts and psychotherapy. Offers new ways to create our own path to self-knowledge and self-fulfillment—and face life's difficulties.

6" x 9", 224 pp. Quality Paperback, ISBN 1-58023-069-5 **$16.95**
HC, ISBN 1-58023-013-X **$23.95**

ANCIENT SECRETS
Using the Stories of the Bible to Improve Our Everyday Lives
by *Rabbi Levi Meier, Ph.D.*

Drawing on a broad range of Jewish wisdom writings, distinguished rabbi and psychologist Levi Meier takes **a thoughtful, wise and fresh approach to showing us how to apply the stories of the Bible to our everyday lives.** The courage of Abraham, who left his early life behind and chose a new, more difficult and more rewarding path; the ability of Joseph to forgive his brothers; Moses' overpowering grief over the loss of his sister—the quests and conflicts of the Bible are still relevant, and still have the power to inform and change our lives.

5½" x 8¼", 288 pp. Quality Paperback, ISBN 1-58023-064-4 **$16.95**

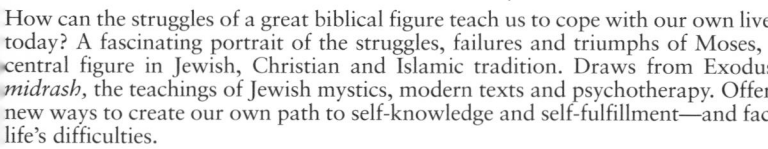

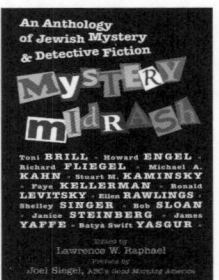